STANDING ALONE

STEPHEN LEATHER

STANDING ALONE

HODDER &
STOUGHTON

First published in Great Britain in 2022 by Hodder & Stoughton
An Hachette UK company

1

Copyright © Stephen Leather 2022

The right of Stephen Leather to be identified as the
Author of the Work has been asserted by him in accordance
with the Copyright, Designs and Patents Act 1988.

A CIP catalogue record for this title
is available from the British Library

Hardback ISBN 978 1 529 36746 1
Trade Paperback ISBN 978 1 529 36747 8
eBook ISBN 978 1 529 36748 5

Typeset in Plantin Light by
Palimpsest Book Production Limited, Falkirk, Stirlingshire

Printed and bound in Great Britain by
Clays Ltd, Elcograf S.p.A.

Hodder & Stoughton policy is to use papers that are natural, renewable and
recyclable products and made from wood grown in sustainable forests.
The logging and manufacturing processes are expected to conform
to the environmental regulations of the country of origin.

Hodder & Stoughton Ltd
Carmelite House
50 Victoria Embankment
London EC4Y 0DZ

www.hodder.co.uk

For Jack

CHAPTER 1

The sniper had been in position for two days and two nights, lying on plastic sheeting, covered by a camouflage net. He had eaten nothing but protein bars and nuts, and drunk sparingly from a plastic bottle. He was dug into a slope next to a lake. On the far side of the clear blue water was a line of five cabins, luxury waterside homes that rarely came on the market and when they did it was with a seven-figure price tag. The Colorado sky was cloudless and as blue as the lake, and behind the cabins was a steep hillside covered with towering pines. The sniper was focusing on the cabin in the middle. The target had arrived the previous evening, just as the sun dipped down behind the hill. He had come with his mistress and her Chihuahua in a two-door Mercedes, and a team of four bodyguards had accompanied them in a black SUV with tinted windows.

Next to the sniper was the rifle that he would use to kill the target. When he had been in the military, he had been issued with a Knight's Armament M110 Semi-Automatic Sniper System, which had a quick-change twenty-round magazine. It had been a superb weapon for taking out multiple targets at long range in a combat situation, but for the job in hand the Smith & Wesson M&P10 was a better bet. The magazine held ten rounds, which was more than enough, and it was chambered for the 6.5 Creedmoor round, which had originally been designed for target shooting but had quickly found favour with hunters – and professional assassins. The round was narrow and light and left the barrel at such a high velocity that, on a good day, the sniper could do a quick double-tap to the chest from 1,000 yards away. The M&P10 weighed just over nine pounds and was forty inches long, and the fact that it cost less than $2,000 meant it was pretty much disposable.

Once the job was done he planned to dig a hole and bury it in the woods, along with any cartridge cases expended. He'd keep the telescopic sight, though. That was too good – and expensive – to throw away. It was a Nightforce ATACR – Advanced Tactical Riflescope – and cost $1,000 more than the rifle. The US Marine Corps used it as part of their sniper system. It gave a crystal-clear view and was virtually inde-structible. This would be the fourth time that the sniper had used it on a paying job and it had never let him down.

The security team had been professional. Two had remained with the Mercedes while the others had done a sweep of the house and the grounds down to the lake. The sniper had tracked them with his rifle, regulating his breathing as if he was preparing for a shot. Once they were satisfied that the house and grounds were clear, all four bodyguards went inside with the target. There was a terrace at the rear of the house but the target had remained inside all night. He had briefly appeared at the bedroom window at night, but the sniper wasn't prepared to risk a shot through glass.

The target was a prospective congressman, but the sniper didn't know – or care – which party he represented. He knew the man's name and that he would be at the cabin, but that was all he knew. It was all he needed to know.

The rear door of the cabin opened and the target appeared. He was wearing an orange lifejacket over a grey sweatshirt and baggy shorts. Two of the bodyguards were with him, still wearing black suits and ties. The target pointed at a wooden shed and the bodyguards went inside and returned a minute later with a bright red kayak and a paddle.

The bodyguards carried the kayak to the water's edge and held it steady as the prospective congressman climbed in. The girlfriend appeared on the terrace, the Chihuahua clutched to her chest.

The sniper sighted on the target's chest, the stock of the rifle resting on the gunman's shoulder. He had calibrated the sights three days earlier in the Flat Tops Wilderness area, 235,000 acres of land between the Routt and White River national forests. He had used Google Maps to calculate the distance between his hide and the cabin, and had paced it out in the wilderness, before aiming at two large watermelons. By the time he had finished, both watermelons were a pulpy mess and the sights were perfect.

One of the bodyguards handed the paddle to the prospective congressman and then stood back. The target opened his mouth to say something and the sniper squeezed the trigger. The stock kicked against his shoulder but he was already braced for the recoil and he easily absorbed the impact. The target's chest turned red and the sniper pulled the trigger a second time. He'd aimed higher on the second shot and the man's head exploded, spraying blood and brain matter across the legs of one of the bodyguards.

The sniper crawled out of his hide. He rolled up his camouflage net and plastic sheeting and thrust them into his backpack with his water bottle. He picked up the two cartridge cases and put them in his pocket, moving quickly but methodically. There was no way they could drive around to his side of the lake, so if they did come after him it would have to be on foot. It would take at least two hours to reach his position that way, by which time he would be long gone. The two other bodyguards had run out of the cabin and all four men had drawn their handguns. 'Idiots,' muttered the sniper. Did they think they could pick off a sniper a thousand yards away using their Glocks? The woman dropped her dog and began to scream.

The sniper slung his backpack over his shoulder and picked up his rifle, then began threading his way through the trees. He had parked his car close to a motel about five miles away. He had switched off his phone before he headed to the lake, and he wouldn't be switching it on again until he was back at the motel. When he did get back, he'd check that the second payment had been made. He had been paid $50,000 as a deposit and he would receive the remaining $150,000 on completion. The money would be paid in bitcoin. He didn't really trust cryptocurrency, but it was the best way of making anonymous transactions. As soon as the bitcoins were in his digital wallet he would cash them in and move the money to a bank account in the Cayman Islands.

He heard a twig snap off to his right and he froze. There was a second, quieter crack. The sniper peered around a tree and saw a white-tailed deer standing a hundred yards away. It was a female, two years old at most, her head up and her nose twitching. The sniper smiled. 'Don't worry, honey,' he said. 'I don't shoot animals.'

CHAPTER 2

A gun was just a tool of Matt Standing's trade, but it always felt strange to be walking among hundreds of people knowing that tucked under his armpit was a weapon capable of ending dozens of lives. The Glock 19 held seventeen rounds in the extended clip and one in the chamber and he had two full clips in the pockets of his pea coat. He looked around as he walked through the crowds of shoppers. The Trafford Centre was five miles west of Manchester. Ten per cent of the UK's population lived within a forty-five minute drive of the centre, and more than thirty-five million people visited every year. It had the largest food court in Europe and the biggest cinema in the United Kingdom. If you were setting out to kill a large number of people in the shortest possible time, the Trafford Centre was a good bet.

Standing wasn't prowling the shopping centre for victims. He was an SAS trooper on the hunt for members of an Islamic cell, planning what the authorities referred to as an 'MTA', a marauding terrorist attack. An MTA could be with bladed weapons or firearms and there could be any number of assailants involved. But the end result of a successful MTA was always the same – a lot of dead and injured civilians.

MI5 had flagged the forthcoming MTA as a more-than-likely risk, based on an increase in chatter. Chatter was basically electronic gossip – emails, blog posts, texts and phone calls – that suggested an attack was coming. Unfortunately that was all MI5 had: chatter. There was no hard evidence or intelligence, and they had no idea who was involved or where they would attack. It was the equivalent of cows lying down before a thunderstorm. Sometimes the storm came, sometimes it didn't. But more often than not the cows got it right.

The chatter picked up by the spooks had been vague, but shopping centres had been mentioned, so the decision had been taken to put men on the ground in the country's main venues. The Joint Terrorism Analysis Centre had changed the UK terrorism threat level from 'critical' to 'severe', which meant that an attack was highly likely.

There were ten troopers covering two London shopping centres – Westfield London and Westfield Stratford – and another four based in the Bluewater centre in Kent. Three more had been posted to the Birmingham Bullring. For some reason the second biggest shopping centre in the UK, the Metrocentre in Gateshead, wasn't being protected, a fact that had been raised by one of the Geordie troopers during the briefing on the operation. The captain running the briefing had smiled and said that according to MI5, there were very few potential jihadists in Geordie-land, probably because the weather was so awful.

The captain had said that according to the chatter, knives were going to be used, but that the troopers should expect the worst. Again Standing had his misgivings – if they seriously thought that jihadists were going to be attacking shoppers with machetes, or guns, then why not put metal detectors at all the entrances? He decided against asking the question. The captain wasn't the mastermind behind the operation; like the troopers, he was only following orders.

Standing stopped and looked into the window of a Ted Baker shop. He caught sight of his reflection. He was wearing a black pea jacket with the collar turned up, Diesel jeans and Timberland boots. Around his neck was a black bandana that could be pulled up to cover his face if necessary.

He alternated his attention between a display of shirts and the reflections of people walking behind him. It was Saturday afternoon and the centre was packed. Families walking together, mums and dads out with the grandparents and the kids. Teenagers hanging out. Boyfriends and girlfriends on the way to catch a movie.

A woman screamed behind him and Standing whirled around. His hand reached towards the gun under his arm, but then he saw a young woman in a headscarf running after her toddler, who was waddling at full speed towards the escalator. Standing relaxed as the mother scooped up the child. He turned back to the shirts.

The centre and all the individual shops and restaurants were covered by CCTV cameras, which were monitored in a control room on the second floor. It would have made things easier for the SAS to have a man in the control room monitoring the CCTV feeds, but the decision had been taken to keep the Regiment's presence under wraps. If word were to get out that the SAS were working undercover in the Trafford Centre, then any jihadists planning to attack would switch to a different target.

Standing was all too aware of the difficulty they faced in protecting the tens of thousands of men, women and children thronging into the centre. There were two levels, with a total of two million square feet of shops and restaurants. The centre had almost 12,000 parking spaces, most of which were filled, and Standing's best guess was that there were close to 25,000 people walking around. There were three undercover SAS troopers covering the whole place – two on the ground floor, with Standing alone on the upper floor. The chances of them picking out the jihadists from the thousands of regular shoppers was next to nil. That meant they were waiting for the attack, and would then have to react to it. Dozens could die within seconds, hundreds within minutes; a fact that Standing had made clear during their early morning briefing. It had been over Zoom, because the officer who was organising the patrols was in Wellington Barracks, a few hundred yards from Buckingham Palace. The captain said he understood Standing's reservations, but that some cover was better than none. Standing hadn't pressed the point, but in his mind it would have made more sense to put dozens of armed police in the malls, in uniform and with their guns on display. The jihadists wanted to attack unarmed civilians, so there was every likelihood they would pack up and go home if they knew they would be facing lethal force.

'You should get the red one, it'll go with your eyes,' said Terry 'Paddy' Ireland in his right ear. Paddy had a rich Norfolk accent – the nickname had come from his surname rather than his country of birth. Standing looked over his shoulder and saw Ireland looking up at him from the ground floor, a big grin on his face. Ireland was tall and broad-shouldered, wearing a leather bomber jacket and impenetrable sunglasses. He was standing by a towering palm tree, one of many dotted around.

'What's he buying?' asked Ricky 'Mustard' Coleman.

Coleman was also on the ground floor but Standing couldn't see him.

'A Ted Baker shirt,' said Ireland.

'Only nonces wear Ted Baker,' said Coleman. He joined Ireland and gave Standing the finger. He was in his mid-thirties but had only been in the Regiment for five years. His receding hair was covered with a Manchester United baseball cap. They both had multicoloured bandanas around their necks, ready to be pulled up if and when it kicked off. The last thing they wanted was to be filmed and put on Instagram or Facebook.

'See now, that's wrong on so many levels,' said Standing. The earpiece picked up his voice and transmitted it through the radio tucked into the small of his back. Anyone who heard him talking would assume he was talking hands-free on his phone.

Coleman moved away from Ireland, heading towards the department store at the far end of the centre.

An Asian family walked past Standing, talking loudly in Pashto. There were two men, probably father and son, both dressed in the kameez-shalwar, the long tunic and baggy pants often worn by Muslims. With them was an old woman covered from head to foot in a black niqab, a woman in her twenties wearing a dark blue hijab and two little girls, who couldn't have been more than six, with headscarves and long coats. They wouldn't have looked out of place in an Afghan border town. Standing noticed that almost half the shoppers around him were Asian or black. As well as Pashto, he heard Arabic, Kurdish and Turkish, along with several African languages that he couldn't identify.

Standing started strolling again, heading towards the main

department store, which spanned both floors. He scanned left
and right as he walked. Two youths with beards and skullcaps
walked towards him, carrying backpacks – one Nike, the other
North Face. There was no way of telling what the backpacks
contained. They could have been filled with clothes, food or
gym gear – or hunting knives, or explosives wired up to triggers. One of the youths realised that Standing was looking at
him and he grinned. 'All right, Bruv?'

Standing nodded. 'Yeah, mate. All good.'

The youths walked by, arguing about who could bench press
the most. Standing turned to watch them go. It was racial
profiling, he knew. Two Asians carrying backpacks, so he was
immediately on alert. But they were just a couple of regular
guys, out shopping or on their way to the gym. That was what
terrorism did; it made people suspect everyone. It made
everything and everyone a threat. And it gave the government
the excuse to mount more surveillance and restrict the freedoms that people once took for granted. Two guys, no threat
to anyone, and Standing had been ready to pull his gun out
within a split second. The youths stopped to greet a young
girl in a headscarf, then the three of them continued to walk
away.

Standing carried on walking alongside the shops, his hands
in his pockets. He was constantly scanning the people around
him, but avoiding eye contact as much as possible. It was
tiring, physically and mentally, and he was on his fifth day.
They started when the shopping centre opened and were there
until it closed. They ate in the centre, used the bathrooms, and
were on their feet pretty much all the time. The operation was
open-ended, and the captain had said they would be in place
until either something happened or the chatter died down.

'You up for the pub tonight, Matt?' asked Coleman in his ear.

'Yeah, I don't see why not,' said Standing.

'Definitely,' said Ireland. 'And can we have a steak tonight? I'm fed up with curry.'

'Mate, Manchester has the best curries in the country,' said Standing. The centre was just six miles from the Curry Mile, a stretch of Wilmslow Road in the south of the city, famous for its seventy-odd curry and kebab houses. They had been there the last three nights, and Standing would be happy to eat there every night they were in town.

'Yeah, well I was on the toilet shitting fireballs this morning,' said Ireland.

'That's the sign of a good curry,' said Standing.

'It's a sign of salmonella, that's what it is,' said Coleman. 'I'm with Paddy, let's have steak tonight.'

'I'll go with the flow,' said Standing.

A group of four Asian girls were walking towards him, so close together that he had to move to the side to walk around them.

'Steak it is then,' said Ireland.

'Guys, I think I have a possible contact,' said Coleman. 'Two Asian males outside Boots. Oh shit.'

Almost immediately Standing heard shouts of 'Allahu Akbar' from down below.

'On way,' said Ireland in Standing's ear.

There were more shouts from the ground floor, followed almost immediately by screams. Standing was already running full pelt. Boots was at the far end of the shopping centre, spread across both floors. It was opposite Marks and Spencer, which was also on both floors.

He heard two shots. A Glock. More screams. Then two more shots. Standing hoped that the rounds had hit their targets and there were two dead jihadists on the ground. People were turning to look at him as he ran, while others were looking over the guardrail trying to see what was happening on the ground floor.

The screams were louder now, and people were running towards the exits downstairs. There were more shots, further away this time.

'Sitrep guys,' said Standing as he ran.

'Two tangoes down,' said Coleman.

There were two more shots, again in the distance. 'Two down here, I see two more just gone into a shop,' said Ireland. 'I'm following them in.'

There were more shots from down below.

Shoppers ahead of Standing were pushing towards the guardrail and peering down to the ground floor. He wanted to shout and warn them to stand back, but he knew it would be pointless. People always liked to look at violence, so long as it wasn't happening to them.

Boots was ahead of him, to the left. Marks and Spencer to the right. Standing was still running, his feet slapping on the floor. More people were turning to look at him. Some were pointing their phones his way so he pulled his bandana up over his mouth and nose. Two women shrieked and backed away as he ran by.

The two guys with backpacks he'd looked at earlier had turned to look at him, and he saw the fear in their eyes.

As he ran by them he saw three Asian men ahead of him, gathered outside Marks and Spencer. They were standing around a red tennis bag. One of the men knelt down and unzipped the bag as the other two pulled off their jackets to reveal black sweatshirts with white Arabic writing on them. The kneeling man pulled out a machete and handed it to one of his companions. Then he pulled out two more machetes and they screamed 'Allahu Akbar!' in unison.

Standing slowed and pulled out his Glock. The three men fanned out, their machetes held high. Shoppers were screaming in panic, running in all directions. Some rushed inside Boots and Marks and Spencer, others ran by Standing. To his amazement, some teenagers were standing with their phones held up, filming what was happening.

An old man in a tweed jacket and flat cap was hobbling away with a walking stick. One of the attackers slashed at him with his blade, slicing between the man's shoulder blades. 'Allahu Akbar!' the attacker screamed.

Standing fired twice in quick succession and both shots hit the jihadist in the chest. He staggered back, still holding his weapon, then slipped down against the Marks and Spencer window. The old man slumped to the floor, blood soaking into his jacket.

The other two attackers were running towards a group of girls in school uniform, shouting at the tops of their voices. They were side-on to Standing. He pulled the trigger and hit the first one in the head, so didn't bother with a double-tap. He fired twice at the other man, one round hitting him in the shoulder and spinning him around, and the second hitting him in the throat. Bloody foam frothed around his neck and the machete clattered to the floor.

Dozens of people were screaming and running away from the bodies. Standing heard another two shots from the ground floor and headed into Boots. There was an escalator heading down. There were several people on the escalator coming up but the one going the other way was empty. Standing held his gun high as he took the stairs three at a time.

As he reached the bottom of the stairs a man in a grey suit staggered towards him, blood streaming from two slashes in his right arm. His mouth was working soundlessly and his eyes were blank. Standing moved around him and saw a teenager with a black-and-white scarf tied around his mouth, brandishing a samurai sword. Standing shot him twice in the chest.

He heard two shots off to his right and turned to see Coleman standing with his gun in both hands as a jihadist staggered back into a toothpaste display.

'Where's Paddy?' asked Coleman.

Before Coleman could answer they heard two shots from outside. They sprinted out of the shop just as two masked men ran out of H&M waving blood-splattered machetes. Coleman took down the one on the right with a chest shot followed by a head shot, and Standing caught the one on the left with two shots to the heart.

Ireland emerged from the clothing store. He had his bandana pulled over his face. 'All clear inside,' he said. 'What's the story upstairs?'

'Three tangoes down,' said Standing. 'Two civilians hurt.'

All three men were looking around, their guns at the ready. Shoppers were streaming away towards the far end of the centre, but there were still people filming on their phones.

'What happened in H&M?' asked Standing.

'I took down two, plus the two you got,' said Ireland.

'You went in there after four of them?' said Standing. 'You after a medal?'

'I followed two in, the other two came in after me. The two

I got killed three people in there and injured another ten or so.'

'Shit,' said Standing. He looked around. There were no signs of the police or paramedics. He turned to a group of teenagers filming on their phones. 'Will you stop filming and phone 999!' he shouted. 'Tell them we need ambulances now!' He raised his free hand above his head and shouted at the shoppers still in the vicinity. 'Are any of you nurses or doctors? We have people who need first aid, now! If you can help, please step forward.'

He looked around. Two middle-aged Asian women wearing headscarves approached him nervously. 'We're nurses,' said one.

'Brilliant,' said Standing. He pointed at Ireland. 'My friend here can take you to the injured.' Ireland went with them inside the H&M store. A black man in a blazer came over to Standing, smiling apprehensively. 'I'm a GP,' he said. 'It's been a while since I've done any emergency work.'

'Thanks, Doctor,' said Standing. He pointed at the Boots store. 'There's a chap upstairs with a nasty wound to his back. Just outside the store on the next level.'

'I'll see to him,' said the doctor, hurrying away.

Coleman joined Standing, still looking around, his gun at the ready. 'You think we're done?'

Standing nodded. 'I think so.'

CHAPTER 3

S tanding, Coleman and Ireland had grabbed a corner table in the Castle in the Air pub. It was a Wetherspoons and Standing wasn't a fan of the chain, but Ireland was and he was hungry. He and Coleman had demolished rump steaks and all the trimmings and put away five pints of lager each. Standing hadn't felt like drinking but had managed two pints and a plate of fish and chips. They had left their guns in their hotel room safes.

There was a TV mounted on the wall opposite them showing CCTV footage from the Shepherd's Bush Westfield shopping centre. It had been attacked by twelve young jihadists at the same time as the attackers had pulled out their machetes in the Trafford Centre. The jihadists all had black-and-white scarves covering their faces and were waving a variety of weapons, including a samurai sword and a cleaver. They were running down the middle of the mall slashing anyone who wasn't quick enough to get out of the way. The TV people had blurred out the victims so it was all very confusing, but a headline across the bottom declared that twenty people had died – including the twelve jihadists – and another fifty-two were injured.

Two men in leather jackets appeared at the top of the screen, holding Glocks. They stood with their legs shoulder-width apart and began to fire as if they were on a range. 'Anyone recognise them?' asked Standing, waving his glass at the screen.

'They're not with the Regiment,' said Ireland.

'I can tell that from the way they're rooted to the spot,' said Standing. The SAS were trained to fire on the move and spent hour after hour in the Killing House, a high-tech facility that allowed them to run through scenarios in real time, firing live ammunition. The police's specialist firearms officers spent most of their time practising indoors, firing at static targets. Occasionally police officers were sent to Hereford to train with the SAS, but usually the damage was done by then and it was difficult to correct bad habits. Another problem was that the police firearms officers were trained to fire only as a last resort. And if they did shoot and kill a suspect they were immediately relieved of duty and treated as a potential murderer until cleared by an inquiry. The main tactic was to outgun and overwhelm the opposition so that they surrendered without a shot being fired. Generally it worked and most armed police officers went through their entire careers without firing a shot in anger – but the 'talk first and fire as a last resort' technique tended not to be successful when faced with a mob of machete-waving jihadists.

The blurred figures of the jihadists fell to the floor, but not before they managed to slash several shoppers.

There was more footage from another part of the shopping centre. So many figures had been blurred that it was hard to see specifics, but there appeared to be three jihadists stabbing at least a dozen shoppers as hundreds more ran for the exits. The footage changed again showing the attack from a different viewpoint. This time a man in a North Face fleece with a red bandána pulled over the lower part of his face ran into view.

He was holding a Glock, and as one of the jihadists ran towards him, he double-tapped the man in the chest then took two quick steps to the side and dropped another attacker. A jihadist came running up behind the gunman. The upper part of his body was blurred so Standing couldn't see what weapon the man was wielding, but whatever it was he was holding it high above his head. The man in the bandana whirled around in a crouch and fired upward into the man's chest. The jihadist staggered back and the man fired twice more. Unlike the armed cops, the SAS didn't face suspension when they fired their guns.

'That's Jack Ellis,' said Coleman.

'How can you know it's not Joe?' asked Ireland. Joe and Jack Ellis were twins. They had both distinguished themselves as paratroopers with the 4th Battalion before moving to the SAS.

Standing laughed. 'Because Joe's in Syria on a takedown mission,' he said.

The CCTV footage ended. A cute blonde newsreader with an appropriately worried frown began to speak, but the sound had been muted so there was no way of knowing what she was saying. Not that anyone in the pub was paying any attention to the screen.

Ireland was looking at his iPhone. 'Now they're saying ten civilians dead at Westfield,' he said. 'And another sixty injured.'

'Bastards,' said Standing. The Westfield in London's Shepherd's Bush was the biggest shopping centre in the United Kingdom. As far as Standing knew, there had only been five SAS troopers on duty, though they had been backed up by firearms officers from the Met and two additional counter-terrorism specialist firearms officers. The CTSFOs were the crème de la crème of the armed cops. They were given extra training, including handling descents from helicopters and use of live rounds in close-quarter combat. Much of the additional training was handled by the SAS, and Standing had been impressed with the level of ability of the CTSFOs. Their fitness levels were well below those of the SAS, though. They tried hard when they came to Hereford, but they clearly weren't up to forty-mile marches with seventy-pound bergens on their backs.

Standards among the Manchester cops were much lower and the decision had been taken not to use them at the Trafford Centre. With hindsight, Standing figured it had been the right decision. The Manchester cops were more used to the shock and awe technique of armed policing, and in a close-quarter combat situation there was no telling where their rounds would end up if they did pull the trigger. Standing, Coleman and Ireland had been able to move quickly and efficiently without worrying who else was going to be letting off rounds. Luck had played a part, too. The fact that the three jihadists on Standing's floor had started their attack just a few hundred feet away meant that he had been able to take them out before they killed anyone. And Ireland had been fast on his feet, too. In a perfect world no civilians would have died, but it had been many years since Standing had thought the world was even close to perfect. The world was a cold, hard, unforgiving place where bad things happened to good people and all you could do was face that fact and live with it.

'So where do you think we go from here?' asked Ireland, putting down his phone.

'Back to the sandpit, I'm guessing,' said Coleman.

'I'm thinking Iraq or Syria,' said Standing. 'Providing there's no more chatter about something kicking off here in the UK.'

'So we're reliant on the bloody spooks,' said Ireland. 'That never works out well.'

'They were on the money this time,' said Standing.

'Well, sort of,' said Coleman. 'They didn't know which shopping centre was going to be attacked, or when. We've been here for a week, remember.'

'It's not an exact science at the best of times,' said Standing. 'Mostly it's just a half-heard whisper or an ambiguous text or email. If they're lucky they'll have a snitch in place but it's not like the old IRA days when the organisation leaked like a sieve. These bastards are tight. Not much gets out. One thing's for sure, usually after something like this it goes quiet for a while. So that's good news.'

'Unless a copycat decides to have a go,' said Coleman.

'After what we did today?' said Standing. He grinned. 'They'd have to be barking.'

'Mate, they think they're going to heaven with seventy-two black-eyed virgins,' said Coleman. 'The guys we shot today weren't scared. They had knives and we had guns but that didn't stop them charging towards us.'

Standing shook his head. 'No, mate, they were drugged up. They usually are. They take amphetamines or coke, anything to get them fired up.' He finished the last of his lager and looked at his watch. 'I'm going to call it a night,' he said.

Ireland looked around. 'Yeah, there's no talent around, is there?' He emptied his glass and waved for the bill. They split it three ways and walked out of the pub. 'Which way's the hotel?' asked Coleman.

Ireland laughed. 'Fuck me, your navigation skills leave a lot to be desired,' he said, clapping him on the back.

'This way,' said Standing. He strode off to the left and

Coleman and Ireland hurried after him. They headed down the road and turned left, almost bumping into two constables in fluorescent jackets. The bigger of the two was a woman in her thirties, her colleague was almost half her size and ten years younger.

'Where are you heading, lads?' asked the woman. She flashed her colleague a quick look to check that he was paying attention.

The three troopers moved to walk around the police officers but they held out their arms to block their way.

'Just hang on a minute,' said the woman. 'Where are you headed?'

'What's it to you?' asked Standing.

'Watch your lip, we had a terrorist attack here today, mate,' said the male cop. He put his hands on his hips as if that would give him more gravitas. Standing was pretty sure he could knock him to the ground by just blowing at him.

'Did you really?' said Standing, faking surprise. 'Were you there then?'

'No, but the security level has been raised so we're asking who people are and where they're going.' He had a high-pitched voice and his eyes were darting nervously between the men.

'That's a bit like closing the stable door after the horse has bolted, isn't it?' said Standing.

The female cop frowned. 'What do you mean?'

'Well, the damage is done, isn't it? Bothering people now doesn't change that. The time to be asking people where they were going was before the shit hit the fan.'

'There's no need for language like that, sir,' said the woman.

'Leave it out, Matt,' said Coleman. 'They're only doing their job.'

'She's saying we look like terrorists,' said Standing. 'If they were doing their jobs properly they'd be out looking for terrorists before they get up to mischief instead of hassling the likes of you and me. And now she's taking offence at a good old English word like "shit", for fuck's sake.'

'Sir, I'm going to have to ask you to moderate your language or you'll be charged with a breach of the peace,' said the woman.

Coleman put his arm around Standing's shoulders and grinned at the constables. 'We're booked into the Premier Inn,' he said. 'We were in town on a contract but we're leaving tomorrow. Celebrating our final night, had a bit too much to drink.'

'Contract?' asked the female cop. 'What sort of contract?'

'Security,' said Coleman. 'We were looking after a building site but the job's done.' He flashed her a disarming smile. 'We're all in the security business, aren't we? Keeping the public safe.'

'Yeah, right,' she said. She jerked a thumb down the road. 'Off you go, and tell him to mind his mouth in future.'

'I will do officer,' said Coleman. 'And thank you for your service.'

Standing opened his mouth to say something but Coleman pulled him away and guided him towards the hotel. 'Leave it out, Matt. The last thing we need is a run-in with the plod.'

'We're fucking heroes, Mustard,' said Standing. 'And we still get treated like shit. By them.' He turned to glare at the two constables. 'They're great at hassling dogwalkers and hairdressers and kids who want to hug their grannies during a pandemic, not so great at confronting jihadists with machetes. Wankers!'

The two constables glared at the troopers but Ireland joined Coleman and took hold of Standing's arm. 'No point in getting upset with jobsworths,' said Ireland. He looked at his watch. 'What's the plan, guys?'

'We're not going anywhere tonight, but first thing we can drive to Hereford,' said Standing.

The three men walked to the hotel and into reception. 'One for the road?' asked Standing.

'I'm okay,' said Ireland.

'Yeah, me too,' said Coleman.

'Fucking wimps,' said Standing.

Coleman put his hands on Standing's shoulders and looked at him. 'You okay, mate?'

'Of course I'm okay.'

'That temper of yours. You need to keep a grip, mate.'

'Because of those wanker cops? Give me a break.'

'You looked like you were going to punch their lights out.'

Standing shook his head. 'Nah, that was never going to happen. I just wanted to give them a piece of my mind, that's all.'

Coleman laughed and ruffled Standing's hair. 'You can be a right tosser sometimes, mate. But there's no one in the world I'd rather have watching my back in a firefight.'

Standing grinned. 'Watching your back? Mate, every time the bullets start flying you're tucked in behind me using me for cover.'

The two men laughed and hugged.

'Fuck me, are you guys going to share a room tonight, or what?' laughed Ireland.

They headed to the lifts and went up together. Coleman and Ireland had rooms on the third floor so they got off first and Standing went up to the fourth floor. He took out his keycard and opened the door. There was a woman sitting at the desk, the chair turned to the side so that she was facing him. She was wearing a black coat and there was a black Chanel handbag on the desk. Her right hand was next to the bag, her left was in her lap. So no gun, no weapon of any kind. She was in her forties, he thought, though he had never been good at guessing a woman's age. Her hair was chestnut, shoulder length, and it swung to the side as she tilted her head to look at him with an amused smile on her face.

He closed the door behind him and took off his pea coat. 'There's obviously been a mistake because I didn't order a hooker,' he said. 'Maybe you got the wrong room.'

She arched one eyebrow. 'They didn't tell me you were a comedian,' she said.

'What did they tell you?'

'That you were a first-class SAS trooper with anger management issues, who made sergeant twice and both times had the rank taken away from him.'

'Three times,' he said. 'And I've got the anger management situation under control.'

'You're sure about that?'

He grinned. 'If I hadn't, I'd probably have thrown you through the window by now.'

She shook her head. 'No, Matt. You'd never hurt a woman. That's not your style.'

'How would you know about my style?' he asked.

'Oh, you'd be surprised how much I know about you, Matt.'

Standing narrowed his eyes. 'Who are you?'

'The name's Charlotte Button. My friends call me Charlie.'

'Never heard of you.'

She smiled brightly. 'I do try to keep a low profile,' she said. 'I work with The Pool.'

'Ah. That I have heard of.'

'Of course you have. Several of your former colleagues are on our books.'

'Listen, Miss Button. Or Mrs. Or whatever. I've had a hell of a day and I'd like to get some sleep before I head back to Hereford.' He looked at his watch. 'Don't you have somewhere to be?'

'I'm right where I need to be, Matt. I have a job that needs doing. No, let me rephrase that: I have a job that I need *you* to do.'

'I wouldn't work for The Pool if you paid me.'

'Oh, we will pay you. Handsomely.'

'I don't want your money. Look, I don't want to sound ungentlemanly, but would you please get the fuck out of my room?' He opened the door and waved at the corridor. 'Please?'

'Shut the door, Matt,' said Button quietly. 'You need to listen to what I have to say.'

'You've got nothing that I need to hear,' he said.

'I know you killed Jeremy Willoughby-Brown. That you shot him dead in the garden of an MI5 safe house in Victoria. You had your reasons, I know. But dead's dead. And murder's murder.'

The colour faded from Standing's face. He closed the door slowly and stood with his back to it.

Button looked around the room. 'They don't have minibars, do they? I suppose that's why they're so cheap. I really could do with a drink.'

'What do you want, Charlotte?'

'A nice crisp Chardonnay would hit the spot,' she said. She stood up. 'Let's go and get a drink in the bar.'

Standing stayed where he was, his arms folded. 'Is it a drink you want, or the safety of a public place?'

She waved away the question. 'I just think we'd find it easier to chat over a drink, that's all. And I gather you've had a busy day.'

'You heard about that?'

'Of course, Matt. I hear about everything. I have my finger on the pulse.' She looked at her watch. 'We should get a move on, I've no idea what time they call last orders in a Premier Inn.'

CHAPTER 4

Standing and Button sat in silence as the waitress placed a glass of Chardonnay and a pint of lager on the table. She offered Button a menu but she refused with a smile and a shake of the head. 'We're just here for a chat and a drink,' said Button. She sipped her wine as the waitress walked away. 'Surprisingly good,' she said.

Standing left his lager untouched. He folded his arms and sat back.

'So, congratulations on taking out the bad guys at the Trafford Centre.'

'People died,' he said quietly. 'So I don't regard it as a triumph.'

'It would have been a lot worse if you hadn't been there,' she said. 'You know there were similar attacks in Westfield and Bluewater.'

'Of course.'

'So what sort of intel did you have? I don't understand why they didn't move in earlier.'

'There was only chatter that a shopping centre was going to be attacked,' said Standing. 'No one seemed to know where or when.'

'Which makes what you guys did all the more impressive,' she said. 'I did wonder how it would have turned out if they had been equipped with automatic weapons.'

'You and me both,' said Standing. He looked down at his pint. Whoever she was, Charlotte Button was certainly one cool customer. She had a quiet authority about her that suggested she was used to people obeying her. She wasn't former military, he was sure of that, and didn't have the stiffness that he'd seen in senior police officers. She was probably a spook, or a former spook, which would explain how she knew about what had happened to Jeremy Willoughby-Brown. Standing had shot the man twice in the garden of a safe house in Victoria – exactly as Button had said. He had assumed only one other person knew about the killing, but it was clear that he'd been wrong.

Button had said she worked for The Pool. Everyone at Stirling Lines knew about The Pool. It did the jobs that the government couldn't be seen to be doing. Break-ins, disinformation operations, abductions, all sorts of black ops, up to and including assassinations. Standing knew of several former SAS guys who had done jobs for The Pool. They had to sign confidentiality contracts but after a few pints in the Victory pub their tongues would loosen and like soldiers the world over they would tell war stories. Two Regiment veterans had been paid to beat up a Russian Foreign Intelligence Service agent based at the Russian embassy in London. The plan was to make it look like a mugging but to hurt the man so badly that he would be shipped home. They caught him at night leaving Queensway Tube station – they stole his watch and wallet, broke his right arm and his left leg, punctured his right lung and burst his spleen. The two men had each been paid more than they earnt in a year with the SAS. Another job that Standing had been told about involved an MI6 officer who had been passing information to a drug cartel in Mexico. The decision had been taken at the very top of the agency that, rather than have the embarrassment of a trial, it would be preferable if the officer committed suicide. The agent ended up in a wardrobe naked with a belt around his neck and a plastic bag over his head. The fee, Standing was assured, was £20,000 for each of the three men who had done the job. Standing had enjoyed the war stories and the beer, but he had zero interest in working for The Pool. But the fact that Charlotte Button knew about Jeremy Willoughby-Brown gave her leverage that she was clearly planning to use.

When he looked up from his pint he realised she'd been watching him with an amused smile on her face. 'You need to get to the point,' he said flatly.

'Then I will,' she said. She took another drink from her glass. 'I have a job that needs doing and as I said I will happily pay you.' He opened his mouth to speak but she silenced him with a wave of her hand. 'Yes, I know, you said you're not interested, which is why I had to bring up poor Jeremy's demise. This is a job that only you can do, Matt. So I literally have to make you an offer you can't refuse. You know what I know, so why don't I tell you what the job is and the fee that we're prepared to pay. You do the job, I get the money transferred to an account of yours anywhere in the world and we both move on.'

'I have a job,' said Standing.

'We use men who are still serving,' said Button. 'Often with the approval of their commanding officers.'

'Then find someone who wants to do it,' said Standing.

'As I said, this is a job that only you can do,' she said. 'You really don't have a choice in the matter, not unless you want to spend a big chunk of your life in a category A prison.'

Standing picked up his glass and drank. His mind was racing and he could feel his heart pounding, but he tried to appear calm. He put down his glass and folded his arms again.

'I take no pleasure in doing this, Matt. But needs must.'

'What do you think you know?' he asked.

'You want me to lay down my cards, is that it?'

'If you're going to blackmail me, you need to tell me what I've done.'

'You think I might be bluffing?'

Standing shrugged. 'I think if you don't talk specifics I'm going to go back to my room to get a good night's sleep.'

Button smiled. 'Fair enough,' she said. 'You were clever, of course you were. You had an alibi, the Glock you used and left behind was covered in the fingerprints and DNA of an agent that Willoughby-Brown had been using. Ali Hussain. He owned a minicab company. They found Hussain with a plastic bag duct-taped around his head. It was suicide, according to the coroner, but nobody seemed to notice that Hussain's finger-prints weren't on the duct tape. The police obviously saw it as an open and shut case, especially when they saw the text messages between Hussain and Willoughby-Brown and details of a phone call Willoughby-Brown made to Hussain.' She smiled and raised her glass in salute. 'Nice. Hussain fixes up a meet with his handler, kills him and goes home and kills himself.'

Standing shrugged but didn't say anything.

'I understand why you did what you did, Matt. Willoughby-Brown was protecting the man who killed your sister. If Lexi had been my sister, I'd probably have done the same. I under-stand revenge, I really do. An eye for an eye. I get it. In fact the reason I'm sitting here with you and not behind a desk in Thames House is that I took revenge on the men responsible for the death of my husband.' She smiled thinly. 'Did I worry that I'd get caught? Not really. I just wanted them dead. Not out of any sense of justice, or fairness. Nothing like that. It was an eye for an eye.'

Standing sighed. 'What is it you want, Charlotte?'

'First of all I want you to understand that we're birds of a feather. And I'm not proud about having to put pressure on you like this. Business is business and needs must.'

'Fine, I understand. Just spit it out so I can tell you to go fuck yourself.'

Button feigned surprise and she patted her chest with the flat of her hand. 'Oh my, is that any way to talk to a lady?' she asked.

'I'm serious, Charlotte,' said Standing.

She nodded. 'I know. This is a serious matter. And you need to know that if you do indeed tell me to go fuck myself, your life will change forever.'

'I'll take that chance,' he said.

She took a sip of wine and looked at him over the top of her glass. He stared back at her with unblinking eyes. 'You're assuming that you got away with murdering Jeremy Willoughby-Brown,' she said eventually.

'As you said, the police take the view that a jihadist shot him and then killed himself. Open and shut.'

'And MI5 have always assumed that the police were right. But we both know what really happened.' Standing frowned and Button wagged a finger at him. 'Now you're wondering who else knows the true story of what happened to Willoughby-Brown. You're wondering if someone might have betrayed you.'

Standing tried not to react but that was exactly what he had been thinking.

Button smiled. 'It wasn't Spider. I can assure you of that. He was there, I know, but he's a loyal friend and he's never told anyone.'

Standing could feel his jaw tense and he knew that Button had spotted the reaction. She would have made a terrific poker player.

'But at the end of the day it doesn't matter who knows what or who says what,' she said. 'Or what proof there may or may not be. What matters is that, at the moment, you've got away with murder. But that situation may change, depending on what assistance you offer me.'

Standing realised his mouth had gone dry, so he took a gulp of his beer. He was still trying to work out how Button knew so much. He had absolutely no guilt about killing Willoughby-Brown. The man had deserved it, no question. The agent he was protecting had drugged and raped Standing's sister as part of a vicious grooming gang that had operated across London. They'd killed her eventually, with a heroin overdose. Killed her and discarded her like a broken toy. Willoughby-Brown had been running Ali Hussain as an agent and informant, and Standing had held him accountable. But Button was right, Standing had covered his tracks and covered them well. And he was sure that Dan 'Spider' Shepherd, a former SAS trooper turned MI5 officer, would never have betrayed him. But clearly she knew everything.

Button continued to stare at him with watchful eyes and he had absolutely no idea what was going through her mind.

'What assistance do you need?' he asked eventually.

'Do you remember an American Navy SEAL by the name of Ryan French? You were embedded with his team in Syria.'

'Sure.' Frenchy was a SEAL veteran. By the time Standing

met him, he'd done tours in Syria, Iraq and Afghanistan. He had a bushy beard that reached halfway down his chest, which was usually spotted with crumbs of whatever he had eaten that day. Frenchy's weapon of choice had been a Knight's Armament M110 Semi-Automatic Sniper System. The rifle was generally accurate up to 1,000 yards, but Standing had seen Frenchy take out targets much further away than that.

Standing had been embedded with the SEALs at an operational command centre on the outskirts of a town called Ayn Dadad, which was being used as a springboard for US special forces to mount search and destroy missions in the north of the country.

'Was he a friend?'

'I was based with his unit for going on six months.'

'That's not what I asked. I know where you were. Were you friends?'

'Not best buddies, no. But we were in firefights and lay in hides together for several days at a time, so we talked. But I'm not on his Christmas card list.'

'When was the last time you saw him?'

'The day I left Syria. I linked up with an SAS team that were heading back to Hereford. Hugs all round and then I was off.'

'Did you stay in touch with any of the SEALs?'

Standing picked up his beer, wondering how much Button knew. She was looking at him, her head tilted on one side, a slight smile on her face. He realised that she was waiting for him to lie, so he sipped his beer while he got his thoughts in order. 'I didn't stay in touch with Frenchy,' he said as he put his glass back down on the table. 'Once I left Syria I never saw him again. I did meet up with another SEAL, Bobby-Ray

Barnes. He'd been a training buddy of mine at the SEAL base in Coronado before we shipped out to Syria.'

'Where did you see Bobby-Ray?'

She was holding her glass again and weighing him up.

'I went to see him in LA a few years back. He had a bit of a problem and needed help.'

'That's a long way to fly to help out a mate.'

Standing shrugged but didn't answer. Button sipped her wine and waited for him to continue.

'He'd gotten into some trouble, that's all.'

'And he called you?'

'His sister did. It's a long story but it ended okay.'

'And what if, say, Ryan French was to give you a call, would you do the same?'

'He hasn't called. I told you, I've not spoken to him since I left Syria.'

'I was talking hypothetically, Matt. If he called and asked you for help, would you go?'

Standing considered the question. 'I don't know. It would depend on what the problem was, I guess.'

Button nodded slowly. 'Okay. Ryan French is no longer with the SEALs. In fact they sacked him after he made a number of operational errors, one of which resulted in civilian deaths. That, coupled with a nasty case of PTSD, meant that the SEALs had to let him go. He didn't take it well and a gun was pulled. He was escorted from the base and told never to darken its doorstep again.'

Standing sipped his beer, trying to work out what it was that she wanted him to do. The fact that she worked for The Pool meant that, whatever it was, it probably wouldn't be legal.

'He had a few jobs after leaving the SEALs but they always

ended in tears,' Button continued. 'Fights, arguments, discharged weapons. Then he became a hitman for hire. Over the last twelve months he's been responsible for three high-profile killings and probably a fair few others that went under the radar. The three biggies were a Russian mafia leader in New York, a prospective congressman in Colorado, and a Colombian drugs lord. The gangster and the drugs lord were fair game, but the politician has got people worried. Basically, French is happy enough to shoot anybody.'

'A hired killer without morals,' said Standing. 'Who would ever have guessed?'

Button flashed him a tight smile but didn't react to his sarcasm. 'The feeling is that French would be willing to shoot the president himself if someone paid him enough. Or the head of state of any other country. What if someone comes up with a contract to kill Putin? He does the job and then it comes out that a former Navy SEAL has killed the Russian head of state. Can you imagine the repercussions? He's a literal loose cannon, so he has to be stopped.'

'Stopped how?' asked Standing.

'Live by the sword, die by the sword.'

'So he's to be stabbed, then?'

Button's eyes narrowed, but then she smiled. 'I was warned about your anger management issues, but not your sense of humour. The Americans want French out of the killing business and they want him out permanently. And they want it to happen without actually getting their own hands dirty. They can't be seen to be killing one of their own. Even one who has clearly gone rogue. So they've approached The Pool.'

'And the British government knows about this?'

'They've green-lit it, yes. Though again they don't want to

be involved. It's a private contract with the funds coming from the Cayman Islands.'

Standing was pretty sure what was coming next, but he figured he should at least put up a fight. 'The Pool has plenty of talent you could draw on for a job like this. From what I understand, it's not that unusual a task.'

Her eyes narrowed. 'I do hope none of my employees have been speaking out of school,' she said. 'That is not something we approve of.'

'Just idle gossip,' he said. 'You spooks call it chatter. The point I'm making is that The Pool has more than enough in-house talent. Why do you have to sneak into my hotel room and blackmail me?'

'That is a very good question, Matt,' she said. She sipped her wine and took a quick look around before lowering her voice. 'After shooting the prospective congressman, French went to ground. Dropped off the grid. But two days before that he called his mother from a payphone in Humboldt County, in northern California. It's the cannabis-growing capital of the US, an area that produces almost two-thirds of the country's black-market marijuana. It's the Wild West. Just over 4,000 square miles of redwood forest, hundreds of small – and big – cannabis farms with armed security, and minimal police presence. Even if you could get a decent-sized police or army patrol up there, they'd be searching forever. And he'd know they were coming.' She shook her head. 'It wouldn't work.'

'But if he saw a friendly face?'

'Exactly.'

'You don't think he'd find it suspicious that someone he knows bumps into him in the middle of nowhere?'

'Not if you play it right. You don't go charging in, obviously.'

Standing sat back in his chair. 'This is fucked up.'

'What is, exactly?'

'Frenchy and I were on the same side. Brothers in arms. And here you are, expecting me to put a bullet in his head.'

'He's gone rogue, Matt. He has to be stopped.'

'So hunt him down, put him on trial and lock him away in a supermax.'

'Have you not been listening to me? First of all, no one is going to find him, never mind get near him. And second of all, in the very unlikely event that they did catch him, there's no way the government would want to see him on trial. He was a Navy SEAL, he's privy to a lot of national security information. Plus questions start to be asked about why a former SEAL was shooting a rising-star politician. They'd rather he was just dead and buried out in the wilderness.'

Standing shook his head. 'This is like that *Apocalypse Now* movie. Charlie Sheen sent into the jungle to assassinate Mad Max.'

Button chuckled. 'It was Martin Sheen, and the guy he was hunting was Colonel Kurtz. But yes, I see the similarities. One man on his own can often achieve more than an armed unit.'

'Fuck you, Charlotte Button.'

'You're angry, I can see that. What did your therapist say you should do to control your temper?'

He glared at her. 'She suggested I count to ten.'

'Does that work?'

'Sometimes.'

She smiled. 'There's absolutely no point getting angry in situations over which you have no control,' she said. 'You either do as I ask, or you don't. The choice is yours.'

He stared at her for several seconds. 'And if I refuse, I get kicked out of the SAS and probably end up behind bars?'

'You murdered a man in cold blood, Matt. The Security Service will want its pound of flesh.'

'He deserved it. And how will MI5 feel about its dirty laundry being aired in public?'

'I'm assuming that much of the case will be in camera.' She smiled. 'Do you know why they say "in camera" when they talk about secret court hearings?'

Standing shook his head.

'*Camera* is the Latin word for an arched or vaulted room. So the expression means "in the room", as in privately.' She shrugged. 'Basically they're not going to allow anything that damages national security to be talked about in open court, and that will cover most of Jeremy Willoughby-Brown's life. So you won't get the chance to go public. But I don't think it'll get to court. They'll offer you a deal, manslaughter probably, and you'll be released in six years or so.' She leant towards him. 'Matt, if this was out in Iraq or Syria, and you were ordered to go out and kill a rogue sniper, you wouldn't think twice about it.'

'Except that you're not my commanding officer.'

'This has been cleared at a level way above your colonel,' said Button.

Standing folded his arms and sat back, fighting to quell the rage that was threatening to overwhelm him. There was no way he would ever hit a woman – at least one who wasn't pointing a loaded AK-47 at him – but he wanted to pick up his chair and smash it into the ground. He took long, slow breaths as he stared at Button.

Button sat and looked at him, weighing him up again. She

was right, of course. There was no point in getting angry over something that he couldn't control. It was a waste of energy.

He began to tap on the table with the middle finger of his right hand. One. Two. Three. Four. Five. His breathing slowed. Six. Seven. Eight. Nine. Ten.'

'Okay, Charlotte,' he said. 'You win.' He looked towards the door and stiffened. 'Fuck,' he said.

Button smiled when she saw the two men who had just walked into the restaurant. 'Your pals?' she said. 'Clearly SAS, they have a confident look about them, but at the same time there's nothing threatening. The archetypal grey men.'

The men looked at Button then turned to look at each other, and Coleman said something. Standing didn't need to be a lip-reader to know that he'd said Standing had pulled. The way they both laughed was confirmation. 'You can always tell an SAS guy by the way they walk,' said Button, picking up her glass as they headed towards their table. 'Light on their feet, their arms loose at their sides, and their eyes sweeping the room. MI5 officers are also trained to read a room, to identify all the exits, location of fire extinguishers, CCTV cameras, and to weigh up everyone who's in the vicinity. But with the SAS, it's always as if they're expecting someone to pull out a gun and start firing.'

She sipped her drink. 'Okay, my name is Diane, you met me on your way to the room, I sell double-glazing and I'm in town for a conference.' She kept her eyes on him as the two men walked up to the table, then turned to look at them, feigning surprise. 'Oh my,' she said. 'Three for the price of one.'

'They're my colleagues,' said Standing. 'Pinky and bloody Perky. They said they were off to bed.'

'As did you, mate,' said Coleman. 'Instead you're in here, pulling the local talent.'

'I'm not local,' said Button. 'But thank you for the compliment.'

'We wanted one for the road but there's no minibar,' said Ireland.

'That's how they keep their prices down,' said Button.

'We did knock on your door,' Coleman said to Standing. 'Thought you were in the land of nod.' Coleman and Ireland sat down. Ireland waved to get the attention of the waitress and mimed to bring two more lagers.

'This is Diane,' said Standing. 'I met her in the corridor and she asked me for a nightcap.'

'And how could you refuse?' laughed Coleman. He held out his hand and Button shook it. 'My name's Ricky but they call me Mustard.'

'Because you're hot stuff?'

'Because he's yellow,' said Ireland. He shook hands with her. 'My name's Terry but they call me Paddy.'

'You don't sound Irish,' she said.

'I'm not, I'm from Norfolk. But my family name is Ireland.'

Button laughed. 'So what about Matt here? Does he have a nickname?'

'They call him Lastman. Lastman Standing. Because he's the last man anyone should fuck with. He has a bit of a temper.'

'Good to know,' said Button. 'I never had a nickname at school.' She sipped her wine. 'So Matt here tells me he's in the SAS. Is that true or is he just trying to impress me?'

'SAS?' laughed Ireland. 'Nah, he's a security guard. Looks after building sites, mostly.'

Button raised her eyebrows. 'Matt, were you lying to me?'

Standing couldn't help but smile. He'd almost forgotten the ultimatum that she'd given him just a few minutes earlier.

'Guys are always claiming to be in the SAS,' said Ireland. 'It makes the girls go wet.' He looked over at Button. 'No offence, Diane.'

'None taken,' said Button, and she giggled girlishly.

'Fuck you, Paddy,' said Standing, with a grin.

Ireland grinned at Button. 'See what I mean about his temper?'

The waitress returned with their drinks and placed them on the table.

'So now I'm confused,' said Button. 'Are you in the SAS or not?'

Coleman wagged a finger at her. 'We could tell you, Diane, but then we'd have to kill you.'

'So you were involved in the shootings today?' she asked.

'Involved is one way of putting it,' said Ireland. 'Bit like the chicken and the pig and the breakfast.'

Button frowned. 'You've lost me there, Paddy.'

He grinned at her. 'Breakfast, right? Egg, bacon, sausage. The chicken, he's involved. But the pig, he's committed.'

'What about the mushrooms?' asked Coleman.

'I hate mushrooms,' said Ireland.

'Baked beans then.'

'You're missing the point,' said Ireland.

'So you guys were committed?' asked Button.

'Full on,' said Coleman.

Button turned to look at Standing. 'What was it like? Seeing those men charging towards you with machetes? Weren't you scared?'

Standing shrugged. 'You don't really have time to be scared,' he said. 'You're too busy doing what has to be done.'

'Train hard, fight easy – that's our motto,' said Ireland.

'I thought it was "Who Dares Wins"?' said Button.

'Nah, that was Del Boy,' said Coleman. '*Only Fools and Horses*.'

Button laughed. 'It's hard to tell whether you're serious or not,' she said.

'We're serious when we need to be,' said Coleman. He sipped his lager. 'What about you, Diane? What do you do?'

'I work for a double-glazing company,' she said.

'I bet that's a "pane",' said Ireland. He grinned. 'Get it? Pane?'

'Haven't heard that one before,' she said. She looked at her watch. 'Well, I have to love you and leave you, guys. It's been a pleasure.' She stood up and the three men got to their feet. She grinned. 'Wow, they certainly teach you manners in the SAS. I don't know when a man last stood up for me.' She moved away from the table. 'And thanks for the drink, Matt,' she said. 'I'll be in touch.'

Ireland and Coleman watched her walk out of the restaurant as Standing sat down. 'Didn't know you went for older women,' said Ireland.

'How old do you think she is?' asked Coleman.

'Forty-five. Fifty maybe.'

'Guys, we were just having a drink,' said Standing. The two men sat down and picked up their lagers. 'Speaking of which, weren't you going to hit the hay?'

'Look who's talking,' said Ireland. 'You said you were heading for bed and then you sneak down here for a bit of posh.'

'It was just a drink.'

'She said she was going to call you, so you must have given her your number.'

Standing's jaw tightened. He hadn't given Button his telephone number, but he had no doubt that she had it.

CHAPTER 5

S tanding's phone rang. He'd left it on the passenger seat and he could see that the caller was withholding their number. He was on the A49 heading south towards Hereford. The phone stopped ringing but then a few seconds later he received a text message. 'ANSWER YOUR PHONE'. It started ringing again and this time he took the call on hands-free. It was Charlotte Button. 'I'd hate to think you were ignoring me, Matt,' she said.

'I'm driving,' he said.

'I know that,' she said. 'That still doesn't mean you should ignore me. I might get the impression that you don't want to talk to me, and that could end badly. For you.'

Standing felt a surge of anger and he took a deep breath to calm himself. 'You're withholding your number, Charlotte,' he said once he had recovered his composure. 'I'm not psychic.'

She ignored his sarcasm. 'So Mustard and Paddy are off to London, are they?'

Standing frowned, wondering how she knew that. Coleman and Ireland had been called by the Regiment first thing to report for duty at Wellington Barracks, so he was heading to Hereford on his own. 'Yes, they're on the train as we speak.'

'You and I need to meet, Matt. I have something for you.'

'As I said, Charlotte, I'm on the road at the moment, driving to Hereford.'

'I know exactly where you are, Matt.'

Standing's frown deepened, then the headlights of the car behind him flashed twice. He squinted in his rear-view mirror. Charlotte Button was at the wheel of a white two-seater Mercedes. 'How the hell did you do that?' he muttered to himself. He hadn't been aware of her behind him when he'd left the hotel, or when he'd dropped Coleman and Ireland at Piccadilly Station.

'Take the next exit, Matt. There's a truck stop cafe we can use. Whitley Services.'

Standing saw the exit fast approaching so he indicated and moved over. The Mercedes followed him. Button ended the call. Standing drove into Whitley Services and parked. Button parked next to him and she climbed out. She had clipped her hair back and was wearing a cream-coloured coat with the collar turned up. She reached into her car and took out her Chanel handbag, then pointed at the entrance to the cafe. Standing locked his car and followed her inside.

There were half a dozen truck drivers tucking into massive breakfasts and mugs of tea. Button bought two coffees and sat down at a table by the window. 'Do you want to eat?' she asked.

Standing shook his head. He'd eaten a full English breakfast with Coleman and Ireland before driving them to the station. 'Coffee is fine,' he said. He wanted to ask her how she'd managed to follow him. Had she put a tracking device on his car? Or was she able to track his mobile phone? There was no way of knowing what The Pool was capable of. But he didn't want to give her the satisfaction of knowing how much it was worrying him, so he just smiled and said nothing.

Button opened her Chanel bag and took out a bulky envelope, which she handed to him. It was sealed and she shook her head when he started to open it. 'Not here,' she said. 'In the car.'

He put the envelope on the table. 'Fine,' he said.

'There are two photographs in there to show around if necessary. Head shot and full body. Plus a copy of his last passport and driving licence. Also a map of the area where he made the call from.'

'Right.'

'There's a ticket to San Francisco. You can hire a car at the airport and drive to Humboldt County. You can fly to SF on your own passport, but in the envelope are a driving licence and a credit card under an assumed name. You can use them to pay for the car and anything else you need. Plus there's five thousand dollars in cash. You can also make cash withdrawals on the credit cards, though I'm not sure how many ATMs there'll be out there.'

'When is the ticket for?'

'Day after tomorrow.'

'What? I haven't even cleared it with the Regiment.'

'It'll be fine. You're owed just over six weeks of leave. You can get it sorted this afternoon. Tie up any personal business tomorrow and then you're good to go.'

Standing frowned, wondering how she knew how much leave he had. 'And what do I say to my commanding officer?'

'That you need two weeks' leave. You don't need to give specifics.' She smiled. 'Don't over-think this, Matt. You ask for leave and it'll be granted. Trust me.'

'Will the Regiment know I'm doing a job for The Pool?'

'The Regiment, no. But the colonel will have received a phone call asking that he assists you with your application for leave.'

'From who?'

She smiled brightly. 'As your pals said last night – I could tell you but then I would have to kill you.' She reached over and patted the back of his hand. 'This isn't my first rodeo, Matt. I know what I'm doing.' She sat back in her chair and held her coffee mug. 'The Americans need something doing and they reached out to the UK government who in turn reached out to The Pool. Everyone will be at an arm's length to the deed itself, but no one is going to put obstacles in our way. You will ask for two weeks' leave today and you'll get it, no questions asked.'

'And you want me to do what?'

'You find Ryan French and you remove him from the equation.'

'I'm guessing there isn't a gun in that envelope.'

She flashed him a tight smile. 'It's America. It won't be difficult to get a gun if that's the way you want to go. You've got options, obviously.'

'And what about the body?'

'The place you're going is known locally as Murder Mountain, I kid you not. It's a lawless wilderness. There are hundreds of bodies buried out there. Maybe thousands.'

'Are you serious?'

'You'll understand when you see it for yourself. It supplies most of the cannabis used in the US. There are Vietnam vets out there, hippies who never moved on, Russian mafia, Mexican cartels, Bulgarian gangsters, plus assorted psychos and nutters. There are hundreds of square miles of what have become no-go areas, pretty much. The growers tend to handle disputes themselves rather than dialling 911. And there's a long tradition of killing workers rather than paying them.'

'What the hell have you gotten me into?' whispered Standing.

'It's fine,' said Button. 'The fact that it's such a lawless place makes it easier for you.'

Standing sighed. 'So I remove him from the equation, as you describe it, then I bury him on Murder Mountain, and then what?'

'What do you mean?'

'Then we're done, right?'

'Of course. And I'll put the funds in any bank account you want.'

Standing shook his head fiercely. 'I don't want your money,' he said. 'I just want to be left alone.'

'You will be.'

'I'm serious, Charlotte. This is a one-off. I don't want you calling me again in three months or three years and blackmailing me again.'

'Blackmail is such an ugly word, Matt.'

'It is what it is. If you ever do this to me again, you'll be the one out of the equation.'

Her eyes hardened and she leant towards him. 'You really don't want to be threatening me, Matt.' She stared at him for several seconds, then her face broke into a smile. 'But you have my word, this is a one-time job. The only reason I'm using you is because you know Ryan French and you can get close to him. Once the job's done, I will forget everything about Jeremy Willoughby-Brown. Everything. So are we good?'

He smiled thinly. 'No, we're not good,' he said. 'But I'll do what you want.'

CHAPTER 6

Standing arrived at San Francisco Airport on a Virgin
Atlantic jet. He'd been pleasantly surprised to discover
that he'd been given an Upper Class ticket, so he had a decent
meal, a few beers and a good nap.

Once through immigration, he headed to the car rental lot
where he rented a car using the credit card and driving licence
that Button had given him. He chose a white SUV, a Ford
Explorer, but by the time he'd loaded his bags into it the sky
had darkened and he figured he'd be better overnighting in an
airport hotel and driving up to Humboldt County first thing.

He checked into a hotel a mile from the airport, again using
the card and driving licence he'd been given. It was a California
licence under the name of 'Dale Headley', and the same name
was on the two credit cards. He was fairly sure that the photograph was the one on his UK licence. The date of birth on
the driving licence was his own, plus one day, one month and
one year. It was as if Button was trying to demonstrate how
much she knew about him.

He took his bags up to his room on the fifth floor. He would
have preferred to have travelled light, with just hand luggage,
but as all the signs were that he'd be living rough for a while,
it made sense to bring the basics with him. He'd packed clothes
and shoes into a large nylon bag with wheels and a retractable

handle, and he had a carry-on holdall with toiletries, an iPad and some snacks he'd picked up at Heathrow.

He ordered a club sandwich and coffee from room service, then lay on the bed and used Google Maps on his iPad to check out the area that Button had referred to as 'Murder Mountain'. The call Frenchy had made to his mother had been from a telephone booth outside a store in Alderpoint, a small town about 250 miles from San Francisco Airport. It was described as a town but there were fewer than 200 inhabitants, though it had a post office, a volunteer fire department and a general store. It didn't appear to have a hotel. He looked at a satellite view of the town, then did a walk-through using Street View. There were only a handful of roads and it didn't take him long to find the general store. He was even able to see the telephone booth that Frenchy had used.

The nearest town with hotels and motels was Garberville, population close to 1,000, which was 200 miles north of San Francisco and an 18-mile drive from Alderpoint. He figured he'd make Garberville his base until he'd gotten the lie of the land.

The two towns were in Humboldt County. To the west was 110 miles of coastline, including Humboldt Bay. Most of the county was rural, with more than 6,000 square kilometres of dense mountainous public and private forests which produced almost a third of the nation's timber. It was the perfect place to disappear in.

Standing's food arrived and he continued to gather intel on Humboldt as he ate his sandwich and drank his coffee. Finding Frenchy wasn't going to be easy. As a SEAL he would have had similar survival training to Standing, which meant that he'd have no trouble living off the land. If he really wanted to disappear he could just go into the woods and keep walking. If that's what Frenchy had done then the chances of Standing finding him would be next to zero. Standing lay back on the bed and stared up at the ceiling as he considered his options. He could visit the spot where Frenchy had last been heard from. He could ask around and see if anyone remembered seeing him, and he could go to the places where a former Navy SEAL might be tempted to hang out, but other than that he didn't appear to have many options. And what would Charlotte Button do if he tried but failed? If in two weeks' time he had to tell her that he couldn't find Frenchy? Would she still carry out her threat to have him arrested for murder? Or would she send someone else from The Pool to do to him what he was supposed to do to Frenchy? He wouldn't put it past her. Either way he was caught between a rock and a hard place. All he could do was keep moving forward. His heart began to race, he clenched his hands and realised he was breathing heavily, all signs of the stress he was under. He closed his eyes and began square breathing, one of the techniques his therapist had taught him in order to control his anger levels. He breathed in for four seconds, held the air in his lungs for four seconds, exhaled for four seconds, and then waited another four seconds before breathing again. The combination of focusing on the count and the increased oxygen levels in his blood always calmed him down.

He ended up falling asleep fully clothed with the curtains open. He woke at dawn when the rays of the morning sun lanced across the bed. He got up, showered and shaved and changed into clean clothes. The hotel served a basic breakfast of weak coffee in polystyrene cups and toast and croissants served on paper plates with little pats of pre-wrapped butter and jam. Like soldiers the world over, Standing stocked up on food and sleep whenever it was available, so he ate as much as he could before settling his bill and starting the drive to Humboldt. It was one road – 101 North – all the way, and it was going to take him a little over four hours. On the way out of San Francisco he bought a Samsung smartphone and two T-Mobile pre-paid SIM cards.

The scenery seemed less inspiring than he had expected. The south of the state was in the midst of a drought and the vegetation was lifeless and the ground bone dry. But the further north he drove, the more spectacular the scenery became, with hillsides covered in towering redwoods. Garberville was in a small forested valley and the 101 North cut right by it, as if it was in a hurry to pass the town by.

To the left was Eel River, and to the right was the Garberville turn-off that took him by the Humboldt Redwoods Inn, a hotel geared up for tourists using the town as a base for visiting the Humboldt Redwoods State Park and the 31-mile scenic route called the Avenue of the Giants. Standing had read that the town postmaster, Jacob C. Garber, had named the town after himself in 1879, but he doubted that the man would have been proud of the way it had turned out. There were homeless people on the streets and beggars in front of several of the shops. There was a general air of neglect about the town and the roads were uneven and cracking. The town was only about 300 yards wide and he drove south to north in less than thirty seconds. Most buildings were one or two storeys and the air overhead was criss-crossed with phone lines and power cables.

Standing had booked a room in a motel in the north of the town, a wooden-clad building facing the hills. He showed his Dale Headley driving licence and credit card to an elderly man with a hearing aid and was given the key to a ground-floor room. He carried his bags to the room and let himself in.

The room was grubby, the bedspread was stained and there were cigarette burns in the carpet despite the 'NO SMOKING' sign stuck to the door. There was a small television on a bracket in the corner and a buzzing fridge next to a teak veneer desk. Standing put his bags under the desk. He opened the fridge to get a bottle of water but it was empty.

He went back outside, climbed into his SUV, and used Google Maps on his phone to find Alderpoint. It was just under twenty miles away on a narrow, twisting road that was never straight for more than a hundred yards. If Garberville was small, Alderpoint was tiny, just a few dozen buildings nestled into a bend in the Eel River. The fact he'd done a walk-through on his iPad meant he knew exactly where to find the general store, a single-storey wooden building with a peaked gable. To the left of the double-door entrance was a wooden statue of a bear standing on its hind legs, and off to the right, at the edge of the building, was the phone box that Frenchy had used.

Standing parked at the corner of the car park furthest away from the store and turned off the engine. There were half a dozen vehicles parked in front of the store, most of them pick-up trucks. He used one of the pre-paid SIM cards to set up the Samsung phone, then copied Charlotte Button's number from his own phone. He sent her a text message. 'Am in Alderpoint. Not sure how good the signal will be.'

Less than a minute later, he received a reply. 'OK.'

'Chatty,' he muttered to himself, and he put the phone into his coat pocket. He climbed out and stretched. A woman with two young children came out of the store. She was holding two large brown paper bags and the children were munching on snacks. They all climbed into a black pick-up truck.

As Standing walked towards the entrance, a women appeared in front of him. He moved to the right but she stepped to the side and blocked his way. Standing assumed she was going to ask him for money so he avoided her gaze and tried to get around her. She moved to the side to block his way again.

'Excuse me, sir. Have you seen my daughter?'

Standing stopped and frowned. 'I'm sorry?' For the first time, he looked at her. She was in her early forties with pale skin and dark patches under her eyes as if she hadn't slept well. She had a black wool beanie with a few stray strands of dyed blonde hair peeping out.

She thrust a flyer towards him. 'My daughter. Her name's Emma. Emma Mackenzie. From Sacramento. She's missing.' She wasn't wearing any make-up but her nails were manicured and there was a Cartier watch on her wrist. She had a blue fleece over a thick pullover and her jeans were tucked into high-heeled boots.

Standing looked at the flyer. Across the top were the words 'HAVE YOU SEEN ME?' Underneath were two photographs of a girl in her early twenties. She had short blonde hair and a sprinkling of freckles across a snub nose. One picture was a head-and-shoulder shot and she was looking at the camera and laughing. In the other picture she was wearing a green pullover, jodhpurs and riding boots and holding the reins of a chestnut horse. 'I'm sorry, no,' he said. 'I've only just arrived.'

'Okay, you're a tourist. From England?'

'Yes. Just here on holiday. Vacation.' He tried to give her back the flyer but she held up her hand and shook her head.

'Please keep it. You never know.' She held up the flyers she was holding. 'I have a lot.'

'How long has she been missing?'

'Two weeks,' said the woman.

'That's not long, she might just be travelling around.'

The woman shook her head emphatically. 'No. Emma would phone me twice a day. Every day. First thing in the morning and last thing at night. And she would text me five or six times a day. Then two weeks ago she stopped. And whenever I call her it goes straight through to voicemail, so her phone is off.'

'Have you talked to the police?'

'They had me fill in a missing person report but they said she's an adult so they won't be actively looking for her. To be honest, they didn't seem to care.'

'Was she on holiday? Vacation, I mean.'

'No, she said she was going to be a trimmigrant and that she'd make enough money to pay for a trip to Europe. She wanted to visit Paris and Barcelona.' She took a deep breath and shuddered. 'She wants to visit Paris and Barcelona. That's what she wants to do.' She blinked away tears. 'I'm sorry.'

'No, I'm the one who's sorry,' said Standing. He looked at the flyer again. 'She's very pretty. And she looks confident, as if she can take care of herself.'

'Oh that's Emma,' said the woman. 'Fearless.'

'And you said she was a trimmigrant? What's that?'

'It was a new word for me, too. It's what the locals call the transient workers who come here to help with the cannabis harvest. They get paid to trim the plants. So trimmer immigrants. Trimmigrants.'

'Ah, I see,' he said.

'Her plan was to come here and work with her best friend,

Lizzie, but at the last minute Lizzie had to cancel. I begged her not to go alone but she was so insistent.'

Tears were welling up in her eyes. Standing held up the flyer. 'I'll keep an eye out for her,' he said.

'Please,' she said. 'My number's on there. You can call me any time, day or night.'

Two elderly men in hunting gear walked from a red pick-up truck and the woman forced a smile and headed towards them.

To the left of the carved wooden bear was a large notice-board. Even from where he was, Standing could see the word 'MISSING' on more than a dozen flyers. He went up to get a better look. He counted the flyers. There were twenty-six. Those that didn't have the word 'MISSING' had 'HAVE YOU SEEN ME' or variations of it. Most of the photographs on the flyers were of young people, teenagers or adults in their early twenties, but some of the missing were middle-aged and one was a grey-haired bearded man in his seventies. Some of the flyers had dates on them. The most recent was just three weeks earlier and several were more than ten years ago. Half the missing were Caucasian, the rest were Asian, black and Hispanic. The messages on the flyers all followed the same pattern – the person had arrived in the area hoping to work and had then vanished. The flyers had been posted by parents, siblings and friends, appealing for information and listing email addresses and phone numbers. The phone numbers were mainly American but some were from Europe and one was Taiwanese.

Standing pushed open the door and went inside. There was a counter and a cash register to his right, rows of shelves filled with food and supplies in front of him and a selection of clothing, mainly aimed at the hunter market. At the far end of the store were glass-fronted cabinets containing frozen food, beer and soft drinks.

He picked up a six-pack of local beer, some apples and oranges, and some chocolate bars and cookies. The woman behind the counter was selling tobacco to a bearded hunter. She smiled at Standing when the hunter left. She was in her thirties with permed hair and round glasses. 'Anything else?' she asked as she rang up his total.

'I'm good,' he said. He handed over a $20 bill and she gave him his change. Through the glass doors they could see the woman continuing to hand out her flyers.

'Does that happen a lot?' he asked.

'People going missing or people looking for them?' she said.

'Both.'

The woman nodded. 'Too often,' she said. 'There's a lot of coming and going anyways, and plenty of people who do come here are looking not to be found, if you know what I mean.'

'She's looking for her daughter. Says she was a trimmigrant.'

The woman chuckled. 'That'll be right. They come here in their hundreds to make their fortunes on the cannabis farms. Sometimes it goes wrong and we get another flyer in the window.'

'So it's a dangerous place?'

'It can be. You're here on vacation?'

'Yeah, just driving around. Might do a little hunting while I'm here. How easy would it be for me to get a gun?'

'Where are you from, England?'

Standing nodded. 'Yeah.'

'It'd be difficult. Probably impossible unless you had a green card. You could maybe find a hunter who'd take you out and lend you a gun. There are some brochures and leaflets and whatnot by the door.' She put his purchases in a brown bag and slid it across the counter. 'You have a nice day.'

Standing took the bag. 'You too,' he said. He carried his bag over to the door where there was a wooden shelf with several piles of leaflets for local attractions and services. He took one of each, figuring he'd read them later, then went outside where the woman had taken up position next to the wooden bear. 'Can I ask you something?' he said.

'Sure.'

'When Emma came out here, did she have a job to go to?'

'No. That's why I said she shouldn't come. We're from Ohio and she was looking online but the farms she spoke to weren't prepared to give her a job unless she was here. People were always asking for jobs and then not turning up, that's what they told her.' She shrugged. 'Emma said I wasn't to worry, that all the farms were hiring and that she wouldn't have any trouble finding a job.'

'And did she? Did she get a job?'

'She worked for a couple of weeks on a farm in the north of Humboldt. But she didn't like the owner, he only hired young girls and was always pestering them. So she quit and came here. She'd heard there were plenty of farms hiring near Alderpoint.'

'And how did she get the first job?'

'She took a bus to Eureka. That's the main city in Humboldt County. She'd read that farmers who needed help would wait at the bus station and that's what happened. This guy offered her work but she realised what he was like and so she quit and came here. She was running out of money because the Eureka guy didn't pay her but in her last call she said she was meeting a farmer and that she was sure she'd have a job before long.'

'Where was she meeting the farmer?'

The woman frowned. 'Why do you have so many questions?' she asked.

Standing flashed her a reassuring smile. 'I'm going to be here for a few days so I thought I would ask around about your daughter, that's all.'

'Well, she was supposed to be having a drink with him at a bar down the road. The Shack, it's called.' She pointed down the road. 'That way, about half a mile on the left. But I've been there already. I spoke to the owner and I went in a couple of times to talk to customers, but no one remembers her. They put a flyer up but no one had called.' Tears were welling up in her eyes again.

'I'm sorry,' said Standing. 'Like I said, I'm here for a few days and I'll keep my eyes and ears open.'

She blinked away tears and mouthed 'Thank you'.

CHAPTER 7

S tanding eased his foot off the accelerator. He was only travelling at thirty miles an hour but the road was narrow and as it twisted its way through the forest visibility was down to fifty or sixty feet at most. He was driving east and heading up. Every few miles he'd pass tracks leading off the road, usually guarded by a gate and signs reading 'NO TRESPASSING', 'TRESPASSERS WILL BE SHOT', 'WE DON'T CALL 911' and 'KEEP OUT'. Several had POW-MIA signs, showing solidarity with the Vietnam vets who had never made it back. Pretty much all the gates were chained and padlocked.

Ahead of him the road curved to the right and a small dirt road led off to the left. Standing went left, knowing that he wasn't going to see anything by sticking to the main road. He was trying to get a feel for the number of cannabis farms in the area, and so far he hadn't seen anything that looked like a farm.

The dirt track was narrower than the main road, just about wide enough for two cars. He reached over for a cookie. They were chocolate chip and he was halfway through one of the packs. When he looked up again he saw a man in camouflage gear sitting on a quad bike parked off to the left. The man had a camouflage bandana over his mouth and nose and was wearing tinted goggles. Standing slowed to get a better look.

There was a rifle strapped to the man's back and he was holding a transceiver to his mouth.

Standing checked his rear-view mirror. The man stayed where he was, still talking into the transceiver.

The dirt track twisted and turned through the forest. It levelled off, curved around to the left and started to climb again. As the road straightened out, he saw two more quad bikes ahead of him, driving side by side so that there was no way he could overtake. The drivers were wearing hunting gear and had pump-action shotguns slung over their shoulders. The one on the right was driving one-handed and holding a transceiver to his ear. Standing cursed under his breath. He had a pretty good idea what was coming next. He continued to check his rear-view mirror and sure enough, after a few minutes, the other quad bike appeared.

The two quad bikes in front began to slow and as they reached walking pace, the one behind came up so close that Standing could see the man's eyes above the camouflage bandana. The quad bikes in front stopped and the two drivers got off and unslung their shotguns. The one on the right was a bear of a man, well over six and a half feet tall, with a barrel-like chest. He had a ginger beard and his eyes were hidden behind Oakley sunglasses. The shotgun looked like a toy in his shovel-sized hands. His companion was close to six feet tall, thin with a spindly neck. He'd covered his face with a skull and crossbones bandana. Both men had their fingers on their triggers, which Standing took as a bad sign.

He saw movement in the rear-view mirror. The man behind was climbing off his quad bike.

Standing looked through the windscreen. The two men were walking towards him on either side of the track. They both had handguns in holsters and large knives strapped to their calves. He raised his hands slowly to show that he was unarmed.

The guy on the right stopped at the front wing, his shotgun pointing at Standing's face. The big bearded man walked to Standing's window and tapped on it with the barrel of his shotgun.

Standing slowly moved his left hand to open the window. 'What's up guys?' he said, figuring the sooner they heard his English accent, the better.

'Where are you headed?' growled the bearded man.

'Just driving around,' said Standing. 'Taking in the scenery.'

'What scenery?'

'The trees. The redwoods.'

'Why this road?'

'No reason. I was just driving around.'

'You a cop? FBI? DEA?'

'Mate, I'm English. How could I be in the FBI? I'm a tourist. This is a rental. Anyway, who are you guys and what's this all about? Am I on private property because I thought this was a public road.'

'You're driving around on your own?' growled the bearded man.

'Do you see anyone with me?'

'You've got a mouth on you, haven't you?'

'I just don't understand all the questions or why you're pointing guns at me.'

'Ask him if he's got a gun on him!' shouted the man at the rear of the SUV.

'You got a gun?'

'I'm English. So, no, I don't have a gun. And I'm on holiday with my wife and kids. They're back at the hotel.'

'Which hotel?'

'The Redwoods.'

'Ain't no Redwoods Hotel in Alderpoint.'

'The hotel is in Garberville.'

The man's eyes narrowed. 'You're twenty miles from Garberville. You drove twenty miles to look at some trees?'

Standing shrugged. 'Just wanted some alone time, you know? Wife and kids were getting on my nerves, to be honest.'

The man stepped back and gestured with his shotgun. 'Get out of the car,' he said. 'Slowly.'

'Guys, I'll just be on my way. I'll turn around and head back to Garberville and you'll never see me again. I'm taking the family to Sacramento tomorrow.'

'Out of the car,' said the man, his finger tightening on the trigger.

'Do as he says,' said the other man. 'We're not fucking around here.'

'Okay, okay,' said Standing. He put the car in park and switched off the engine.

'Come on, hurry up!' shouted the bearded man. He stepped back and aimed at Standing's face.

Standing opened the door and raised his hands before pushing the door open with his left foot and stepping out. He backed away towards the rear of the car where the third man was pointing his shotgun at Standing's chest. He was Hispanic, small and wiry. He had a large machete hanging from his belt, similar to the ones Standing had seen wielded by the jihadists in the shopping centre, a lifetime ago. He heard the door slam behind him and turned to see the bearded man looming over him. 'Show me some ID,' he growled.

'What do you mean, ID?'

'I want to know who you are and who you're working for. And keep your hands where I can see them.'

'Look guys, I don't know what's upset you but I'm just a tourist, I have zero interest in you or whatever it is you're doing.'

'Why do you think we're doing anything?' said the Hispanic man.

'Because you've pulled me over and are pointing guns at me,' said Standing. 'That's not generally how people say hello where I'm from.'

'Where are you from?' barked the bearded man.

'I told you, England.'

'Give me your wallet,' said the man, gesturing with his shotgun.

'So it's robbery, is that it?' said Standing. 'Dick Turpin, stand and deliver.'

'Who's Dick Turpin?'

'A robber. A highwayman.'

'We're not here to rob you. We just want to know who you are.'

'I told you, I'm a tourist.'

'Take out your fucking wallet,' said the Hispanic.

Standing turned and stared at the man. He still had his hands in the air, fingers splayed, and he was trying to keep a smile on his face. The problem was that his wallet contained two sets of ID. There was his UK driving licence and credit cards, and the US driving licence and the American credit cards that Charlotte Button had given him, in the name of Dale Headley. If they'd let him just hand over his UK licence, all well and good, but if they discovered two sets of ID then the shit would hit the fan. They were presumably on the lookout for FBI or DEA, and the two sets of ID would be a major red flag. They didn't look as if they would hesitate to put a bullet in him and bury him out among the trees. He kept his left hand in the air and reached for his wallet in the right hand pocket of his jeans.

When the wallet was out he transferred it to his left hand and flicked through it to pull out his UK driving licence. 'Stop fucking around and give me the wallet,' said the Hispanic man, holding out his right hand. He was holding the shotgun with his left hand. With his right hand off the trigger the weapon was pretty much useless. Standing was between the Hispanic and the bearded man. All the bearded man could see was his back. The other guy was still at the other side of the car and would only be able to shoot high. It was three against one but Standing was a professional when it came to close-quarter combat.

Standing gave it one last try. 'My driving licence will show who I am,' he said.

'Hand over your fucking wallet!' said the bearded man behind him. Standing heard the crunch of the man's boot on the track and tensed in anticipation of the blow that he knew was coming. 'Do it!' shouted the man, who then smacked the butt of the shotgun against the back of Standing's right shoulder.

Standing staggered forward but then used the momentum to push against the Hispanic man. He tried to get his right hand back on the weapon but Standing had already grabbed it. He ripped it from the man's grasp and then turned and drove the butt into his groin. The breath exploded from his lungs as he bent double. Standing's finger slid over the trigger. He had no way of knowing what ammunition was in the shotgun. It could be birdshot or a single massive slug or anything in between.

The bearded man's mouth had fallen open in shock. He was still holding the shotgun across his chest.

The other man had his gun aimed across the top of the car. Standing dropped down into a crouch. He aimed the shotgun at the bearded man's legs and pulled the trigger. The gun kicked in his hands. The man's jeans were ripped apart and his legs were turned to a bloody mess. Standing figured it was buckshot, six to ten small ball bearings, generally used to kill game like large deer.

The man screamed in pain and fell back, the shotgun falling from his grasp.

The Hispanic man was gasping for breath and starting to straighten up. Standing slammed the butt of his shotgun against the man's head. He went down without a sound. Standing ejected the spent cartridge and chambered a fresh round.

The man at the front of the car fired but the shot went high. Standing heard the click-clack of the man chambering a new round. He dropped to the ground and peered under the SUV. He could just see the man's right foot and shin. He swung the shotgun around and fired. The shot ripped through the man's leg and he screamed in pain.

Standing pushed himself up and aimed over the top of the car. The man was howling in agony, his shotgun down at his side. Standing was automatically aiming but he checked himself. A shot to the head would kill and that was a line he didn't want to cross unless it was absolutely necessary. Standing moved towards the man and slammed the butt of his shotgun into his chest. The man collapsed on to the track.

The bearded man was groaning and reaching out for his shotgun. Standing ran over and stamped on the man's hand. The man swore at Standing, his eyes burning with hatred. He tried to sit up but Standing smacked the butt of his shotgun against the side of his head and he fell back, his eyes rolling up into their sockets.

Standing stood up and looked around, listening intently. His ears were buzzing from the sound of the shotgun blasts but the woods were silent. There was no birdsong and even the insects seemed to have gone quiet. If there were three, there could easily be more. He moved his head from side to side but there was nothing. No shouts, no engines, not a sound.

He bent down and pulled the bearded man's handgun from its holster. It was a Glock 22, by far the most popular police service pistol in the United States, and a firm favourite among drug dealers and gangsters. He shoved it into his jacket pocket. The other man at the front of the car had a SIG Sauer P226. He patted down the man's jacket and found a couple of spare magazines.

The man with the machete didn't have a handgun, but he did have a dozen spare shotgun shells in his pockets so Standing took them. He also took the man's transceiver.

He put the guns and the transceiver into the back of his SUV and then pulled the unconscious men off the track. The one he'd shot in the foot seemed to be losing a lot of blood, so he pulled off the man's belt and used it as a tourniquet around his thigh.

The bearded man was starting to come around, groaning and moving his head from side to side. He'd be out for a few more minutes and then he'd be able to call for help. That wouldn't be enough time for Standing to get away – he'd still be on the mountain and he had no idea how many armed men on quad bikes there were.

He rolled the man on to his front and then took the laces from his boots and used them to tie his wrists and ankles.

The Hispanic man was out for the count, but there was no way of knowing how long he'd stay that way. Standing's initial thought had been to allow the men to recover consciousness and for them to call for help on their radios, but that was looking impractical. He needed at least half an hour to get back to Alderpoint and ideally he'd prefer to be even further away. Alderpoint was a tiny town, he wouldn't be difficult to find there.

He went back to the bearded man, took the transceiver from its holster and stamped on it, smashing it into more than a dozen pieces. Then he did the same with the other man's radio. Now when they woke up they'd have to tend to their wounds and then drive back to their base, wherever that was. Hopefully that would give him more than enough time to get away.

He climbed into the SUV, started the engine and pulled a quick three-point turn before heading down the hill.

CHAPTER 8

Standing considered his options as he drove through Alderpoint and headed for Garberville. If he was lucky, the men he'd attacked would retire to lick their wounds and leave him alone and he could get on with the job in hand. But Standing didn't believe in luck and the men who'd stopped his car didn't seem the type to live and let live. They – or any colleagues they had – would be on his tail first chance they got.

The first thing he had to do was check out of his motel. He'd lied about staying at the Redwoods but there weren't many hotels in Garberville and it wouldn't take them long to track him down. He needed to pick up his stuff and get out as quickly as possible. Then he had to ditch the SUV. The white Explorer was a common enough vehicle in the US but he hadn't seen any others as he drove around and his San Francisco plates were a dead giveaway. It looked as if the firm's nearest car rental office was in Eureka, an hour's drive away, so he'd have to go there to hand the car back.

He checked his rear-view mirror but there was no one coming after him. He doubted it would be more than a few miles to their base so everything depended on how long it took them to recover consciousness and tend to their wounds. Ten minutes? Twenty? Thirty? He had no way of knowing.

He reached the motel and parked outside his room. He stowed the shotgun under the rear seat and put the Glock in the glove compartment, before tucking the SIG into his belt and buttoning up his coat. It took him less than a minute to go into his room and collect his bags. He threw them in the back of the SUV, then shoved in the SIG and hurried along to reception to settle his bill with one of the Dale Headley credit cards. Less than five minutes after arriving at the motel he was back on the road, heading to Eureka.

He kept checking his rear-view mirror but he was driving so quickly that no vehicles came up behind him. He had the transceiver on the passenger seat but all he heard was static as he drove.

He arrived at the car rental outlet in Eureka where an earnest young man with a hipster beard and rectangular-framed glasses explained that he wouldn't get a refund for returning the vehicle early, and that in fact there would be an extra payment due because he wasn't handing it back at the original location. Standing handed over his credit card with a smile.

Once he'd paid he carried his bag outside. There was a second-hand car dealer 200 yards away on the other side of the road. He crossed over and headed towards it. Eureka was quiet and had a worn-out feel to it. There were few cars driving by and even fewer pedestrians, though he passed two homeless people sleeping in the doorways of shops that had closed down.

The car dealership had a dozen or so vehicles parked outside, mainly trucks and SUVs, with a handful of saloons, predominantly Toyotas, inside. Standing spotted what he wanted almost immediately, a black Ford Ranger pick-up, a few years old with two doors and a row of powerful lights stripped across the cab, presumably to help with night-time hunting. The tyres looked okay, the windows were free of cracks, but the truck had obviously had a hard life, which was reflected in the $7,999 price tag. A salesman came out as Standing walked around the truck. He was in his fifties with slicked-back grey hair, and was sucking on an e-cigarette. 'You have a good eye,' he said, before blowing out a plume of peach-scented smoke.

'Really?' said Standing. He hadn't chosen the truck for any reason other than that he needed something that wouldn't stick out.

'The only reason we've got the truck for sale is because the owner passed away two weeks ago.'

'A little old lady who just drove to the shops once a week?'

The man grinned. 'You took the words right out of my mouth,' he said. 'Will you be paying cash or do you need credit?'

'I'll put it on my card, if the engine turns over and we can agree a price.'

'Do you need a test drive?'

Standing grinned. 'I don't think so, I'm sure it was driven here two weeks ago after the little old lady passed away,' he said.

The salesman took a set of keys from the pocket of his coat. He tossed them to Standing. Standing put his bag on the floor and opened the driver's side door. He climbed in. The engine started first time. 'Mind if I open the bonnet?' he asked.

'Say what now?'

'Sorry. Do you mind if I pop the hood?'

'Go ahead. You Australian?'

'English.' Standing pulled the lever to open the hood. The salesman propped it open. Standing climbed out of the cab and walked around the truck to stand next to him. The engine had been well looked after and Standing didn't see anything amiss.

'She's not the prettiest but you'll get another hundred thousand miles out of her, no problem,' said the salesman. He took another pull on his e-cigarette.

'How does seven thousand five hundred sound?'

'Almost five hundred less than I'm looking for,' said the salesman. 'But we could split the difference. Seven thousand seven hundred and fifty?'

'And you'll give me a full tank of gas?'

'The tank's full. We always fill them up when we put them on the lot.'

'The gauge says half empty. Or half full. Depending on your point of view.'

The salesman closed the hood and pressed it into place. 'I'll get it filled.'

'Then let's run the card,' said Standing. 'Hopefully it hasn't been reported stolen yet.' He grinned at the look of surprise that flashed across the man's face. 'Joke,' he said, 'English humour.'

'And I'll need to see a driving licence.'

Standing took out his wallet. 'Not a problem,' he said.

CHAPTER 9

It took less than fifteen minutes to do the paperwork, after which Standing was the proud owner of a 2011 Ford Ranger. The salesman had asked a mechanic to put more fuel in the tank but the gauge still only read three quarters. He drove down the main street and parked outside a diner. He went inside and took a booth by the window so that he could keep an eye on the truck. It wasn't until the waitress put a menu down in front of him that he realised he hadn't eaten all day, so he ordered steak and chips with a side order of onion rings, and a coffee.

As he waited for his food he took out his phone and looked at Google Maps. He checked the route he'd taken earlier that day but the track wasn't visible. He scanned back and forth but couldn't see anything that looked like a base or a farm. The close-packed trees shielded pretty much everything on the ground.

As he worked his way through Google Maps, he received a message from a UK number. Probably a throwaway. And almost certainly Charlotte Button. 'SITREP?' He grimaced, then tapped out a reply. 'AM HERE. LOOKING.' Part of him wanted to add something rude but he knew that would be churlish. He sent the message as the waitress returned with his food.

As he ate his steak and drank his coffee, he tried to put together a game plan. Driving around Alderpoint looking for places where Frenchy might be holed up clearly wasn't going to work. The security detail, whoever they were, had picked him up within minutes and he doubted that they'd be any less vigilant if he tried again. The first man he'd seen had obviously been a lookout and he'd radioed for back-up. There could well be sentries all over the mountain. He hadn't seen a single police or sheriff's vehicle since he'd arrived in Humboldt so it looked as if there wasn't much in the way of law enforcement in the area, which is why the guards had been so free and easy with their shotguns. The more Standing thought about it, the more he realised how close he had come to being buried among the redwoods. He had guns of his own now, but he wouldn't get anywhere if he went looking for a shoot-out.

Frenchy had been in Alderpoint, the phone call from the telephone booth outside the general store proved that. The question was, where had he gone after making the call? There was nowhere for him to stay in Alderpoint, and it wasn't on the way to anywhere, other than the mountain and the cannabis farms. He could just as easily have phoned from Garberville or any of the other towns in the state, so it seemed logical to assume that Alderpoint – or the mountain – had been his destination. So was he there to work, or to hide? He was a Navy SEAL, or at least a former Navy SEAL – so he'd be more than capable of living rough in the wilderness for weeks or even months. The Americans gave their special forces the same survival training that Standing had received in the SAS. Put him in any survival situation with just a knife and he'd be able to find food and water and build a shelter. But assuming he'd had notice, he could have taken any supplies and provisions he needed with him. If he had gone to Alderpoint to work, then it was a whole different ball game. Work could mean joining one of the security groups on the mountain, or it could mean that Frenchy was on the trail of a target. Button hadn't known which was the case, or if she had known she hadn't let on.

Standing chewed his steak and washed it down with a gulp of coffee. So far he was looking for a needle in a haystack and he needed some way of narrowing that haystack down.

He could follow the example of the woman outside the store and start showing the photograph of Frenchy around, but he doubted that he'd have any success and people might start to ask why he was looking for him.

Frenchy had liked a drink, so maybe that was the way in. Standing had spent a month at the SEAL training base in Coronado before heading out to Syria with Frenchy and his unit. The plan had been for Standing to be embedded with the SEAL unit for three months but it was eventually extended to six as it had proved to be so successful. His place in the SAS had been taken by a Navy SEAL who had apparently enjoyed his time there so much that he had asked for the transfer to be permanent.

While in Coronado, the SEALs had a number of favourite bars close to the base and he'd been on several punishing nights out with the guys. Most handled their alcohol as professionally as they handled their weapons, but Frenchy was in a league of his own. He was usually the first into the bar and last out. His favourite drink was scotch on the rocks but Standing had seen him knock back vodka, tequila, rum and brandy with equal enthusiasm, washed down with whatever beer was available. He wasn't a bad drunk, though – he was as amiable at the end of a session as he had been at the start. If Frenchy was anywhere near a bar, Standing doubted that he'd be able to resist the temptation to drop by. He Googled 'The Shack Alderpoint', the bar that the woman outside the general store had told him about. It didn't appear to have its own website or Facebook page, but there were a dozen or so reviews on Tripadvisor, mostly unfavourable and complaining about the food, cleanliness and clientele. He found the bar on Google Maps and then checked it out on Street View. It was a single-storey flat-roofed building with metal bars over the windows and a wooden terrace with barstools, presumably for smokers. There were two neon signs, one that said 'COLD BEER' and another that said 'HOT FOOD'. There were a number of marks on the wall by the door and when he zoomed in he realised they were almost certainly bullet holes.

He Googled 'second hand clothing Eureka' and came up with the Rescue Mission Thrift Store, just half a mile away. He paid his bill and drove to the store, a small building next to a Texaco gas station. He parked and went inside.

There were rows upon rows of clothing, and household items and furniture. He went slowly along the racks pulling out plaid shirts, baggy jeans, a camouflage jacket, a fur hat with ear flaps and a pair of gloves – clothing that would allow him to blend in with the sort of men he'd seen in Alderpoint. He found a two-man tent in a camouflage pattern, a set of portable cooking utensils, a sleeping bag and a rucksack big enough to contain everything. He paid in cash and took his purchases out to the car. He packed everything in the back.

Robert's Barbershop was a couple of hundred yards north on Broadway so he left the truck where it was and walked. There were no other customers so a man in his sixties who might well have been Robert himself waved him to a chair and asked him what he wanted.

'I'll have a buzz cut,' said Standing.

'No problem,' said the barber, reaching for his clippers. 'Number one, two, three or four?'

'Might as well go the whole hog,' said Standing. 'Number one it is.' He wasn't sure yet if he'd be sleeping rough in the forest, but if he was, the shorter his hair the better. Long hair harboured insects and was just plain uncomfortable. Plus it would hopefully change his appearance enough so that if he came across the men he'd taken down in the forest they might not recognise him.

The buzz cut took less than five minutes, and once done he filled the tank of the pick-up truck and drove back to Garberville.

The sun was setting by the time he reached the town. He found a motel with a 'VACANCY' sign and a parking lot shielded from the road, so he parked and walked around to reception. There was a middle-aged woman with a neck brace reading a newspaper and drinking Diet Coke sitting at the counter, and she smiled and asked him what he needed. He told her that he wanted a room for a week, but that he planned to go trekking in the woods so she wasn't to worry if she didn't see him around.

'You're from Australia?' she asked as she swiped his credit card.

'England.'

'Oh I love England. I've watched every episode of *Downton Abbey*. And *The Crown*. I'd love to go someday.'

'You should, you'd love it,' said Standing. Though if her idea of what England was like had come from *Downton Abbey* and *The Crown* then she'd be in for something of a surprise.

'You need to be careful in the woods,' she said. 'Lots of dangerous animals in there. This is the heart of black bear country. And some of the people aren't to be trusted either.'

'Why do you say that?' he asked.

'About the bears, or the people?'

Standing laughed. 'The people.'

'You know this is a big cannabis-growing area?'

'Sure. I heard that.'

'Well some of those cannabis growers are hippies left over from the Woodstock era, and they're okay. They have some strange ideas about how a life should be lived, but they wouldn't say boo to a goose. But during the Vietnam War, a lot of guys came back and couldn't settle in the cities so they moved here and headed for the woods. A lot died along the way but there's still a fair few out there, and many of them aren't right in the head. But generally they keep to themselves.' She waved her hand at him. 'I talk too much, sorry.'

'Actually, I'm fascinated,' said Standing.

'Really?'

Standing nodded. 'Really.'

She leant towards him. 'The problem is the outsiders. The Mexicans, the Russians, the I-don't-know-what. Once the government said they were going to legalise cannabis growing they flooded into Humboldt and that's when the trouble started. You see them driving through here sometimes, convoys of black SUVs with tinted windows, like they were guarding the president or something. They've been buying farms, or if they're not for sale they've been taking them.'

'Don't the police do anything?'

'There's no police in Garberville. There's a sheriff's office but they shut up shop in the evening. You never see the sheriffs out here, unless there's been a shooting. You can call 911 and they'll come eventually but that's about it. They certainly don't go into the forests.'

'They're scared?'

'With good reason,' she said. 'Let's suppose you're out there and you're up to no good. If a sheriff rolls up on his own, what's he going to do? You think anyone cares what he has to say? The sheriffs know that so they stay well clear. If they do go in it's like a military operation with helicopters and SWAT teams and what have you, but that's only when they're going in to close down an illegal grow. And that doesn't happen much these days.'

'Well I'm not planning on going near any cannabis farms,' Standing said.

'They're everywhere,' she said. 'From small one-man operations to the really big farms with hundreds of workers.'

'Hundreds? Really?'

'It's a labour-intensive business,' she said. 'Looking after the plants and then doing all the trimming and packaging.'

'You obviously know a lot about it,' said Standing.

She grinned. 'Back in the day I put myself through college working on the trim,' she said. 'It was a friendlier business back then. I wouldn't do the job these days.' She held up her hands. 'You need nimble fingers and I'm not as nimble as I used to be.'

The door opened behind him and a young couple walked in. The woman handed him his key and turned her attention to the new arrivals.

Standing parked his pick-up outside the room. He leant into the rear of the SUV, broke down the shotgun and retrieved the SIG. He put the guns into his rucksack, then carried it inside along with his other bags. The room was clean and functional. He stripped off his clothes and showered, then changed into jeans and a shirt that he'd bought from the thrift store. He put the clothes he'd brought with him from England on hangers in the wardrobe and packed the rest into the rucksack, along with the tent and the sleeping bag and the two parts of the shotgun. He put the SIG into one of the side pockets.

He checked that the hand luggage and suitcase were empty and put them on top of the wardrobe, then looked at his watch. It was just after seven-thirty and starting to get dark outside. Evening would be the best time to visit The Shack, but he needed to get his story straight. He looked the part now, but he needed a reason why a Brit was in Humboldt County looking for work. He had never worked undercover before. He'd heard stories in Hereford about the days when the IRA was the enemy and the SAS would wear civilian clothes and try to blend into the backstreets of Belfast, but now that the enemy was generally dark-skinned and Muslim, there were few opportunities to work undercover. He lay on his back, stared up at the ceiling and tried to work out what to say.

CHAPTER 10

The sun was low in the darkening sky when he climbed into his truck and drove back to Alderpoint. The Shack was set back from the road with a hand-painted sign above the entrance, which was flanked by deer antlers. There were half a dozen vehicles parked by the side of the bar: four trucks, a saloon and a van with the name of a roofing company on the side.

There were two men wearing desert camouflage jackets standing on the wooden terrace, smoking cigars and drinking beer. They turned to watch as Standing drove his pick-up truck on to the parking lot. Standing climbed out and slammed the door. He had left the Glock in the glove compartment and the shotgun and the SIG Sauer were in the rucksack in the back of the truck.

As he walked up to the main door, the two men turned to look at him. Standing figured that strangers were a rarity and probably regarded with suspicion so he smiled. 'How are you doing?' he said, giving them the chance to hear his English accent.

The two men nodded but didn't reply. As he reached for the door handle, he heard the roar of motorcycle engines and he turned to see four rugged-looking men arrive on low-slung Harley-Davidsons. They were all in their thirties and forties with bulging forearms and wearing stained denims. Standing went inside. A country and western song was playing on a Wurlitzer jukebox at the far end of the bar, and in front of it was a pool table. The main bar area was to the right, with a dozen empty stools lined up in front of it. Directly ahead of him were three wooden booths, all of them occupied by couples, and to the left were six round tables. Two men in hunting gear were eating steaks at one of the tables.

Standing walked down the line of barstools and took the one nearest the wall. A glass-eyed deer's head stared down at him reproachfully. The bartender was a young man in a plaid shirt with the sleeves rolled up to reveal several crude tattoos of skulls, roses and semi-naked women. He had chrome piercings in his nose and lip and a large one in the middle of his tongue.

'What's the local beer?' asked Standing.

'The Redwood Curtain is good,' said the bartender.

'Then that's what I'll have,' said Standing. He took a photograph of Ryan French from his pocket and held it out. 'You haven't seen my friend, have you? He might have been here a couple of weeks ago.' The bartender took the picture, looked at it for a few seconds, then shook his head. 'I don't think so, but I'm not here every night.' He gave the picture back to Standing and went to get his beer.

There was an empty glass and a pack of Marlboro in front of the stool three along from where he was sitting, and as the bartender returned with Standing's pint, a grey-haired man in a denim jacket and faded jeans came out of the men's room. He smiled at Standing as he slid on to his stool, then waved at the bartender for a refill. The bartender unscrewed the top off a bottle of Jack Daniel's and poured a double measure into the man's glass.

The country and western song came to an end and was

replaced by Elvis singing 'It's Now Or Never'. The doors opened and the four bikers came in. Three of them went over to the pool table and the fourth came over to the bar and ordered four beers.

Standing sipped his beer and nodded his appreciation. It wasn't half bad. He smelled something sweet and earthy and he sniffed his glass, but then he realised the smell was coming from the grey-haired man. It was cannabis and he reeked of it.

A waitress appeared from a door that presumably led to the kitchen, carrying plates of food. She took them over to one of the booths and put them down. Standing waved at her as she headed back to the kitchen. 'Could I have a menu?' he asked.

'On the wall,' she said, pointing to a blackboard between two windows. Standing looked over at it. There were three choices: 'STEAK', 'PORK CHOP', 'MEATLOAF'.

'What if I was a vegetarian?' he asked. 'Or vegan?'

She laughed. 'Then I guess you'd eat somewhere else.'

'What's the meatloaf like?'

'Like meatloaf,' she said. She stood with her hands on her hips, an amused smile on her face. She was wearing a black T-shirt and black jeans, and a baseball cap the wrong way around. 'My mom's own recipe.'

'That's good.'

'Well, it would be if my mom was cooking it. But as it's my dad in the kitchen, you take your chances.'

The man sitting down from Standing grinned across at him. 'The pork chop's good,' he said. 'Scarlett's right, the meat loaf is variable.'

'Then I'll take the pork chop,' said Standing.

The waitress made a gun with her hand, pointed it at him and mimed shooting him. 'Good choice.'

As she headed into the kitchen, Standing held out his hand to the man. 'Dale,' he said.

'Brett,' said the man. He offered a gnarled hand with a firm grip. Standing figured he was in his late seventies, but he was in good condition with strong white teeth and a full head of steel-grey hair. 'You're not from around here?'

'England,' said Standing.

'Just passing through?'

'Trying to find work, actually,' said Standing. 'I heard there was good money to be made on the farms.'

The man shrugged. 'Good money, but hard work.'

'I'm not afraid of hard work,' he said. 'A friend of mine was out here a couple of weeks ago, said they paid two or three hundred dollars a day.'

Brett nodded. 'They do. Trimming. But it's boring work and best suited to women.'

Standing grinned. 'You serious? My pal's over six feet tall and definitely not a woman.'

'Guys do it, but it's monotonous and repetitive. Girls like to chat as they work.' He sipped his Jack Daniel's. 'Where's your friend working?'

'That's the problem, he didn't tell me exactly where. Just said he was fixed up on a farm. But then I haven't heard from him in two weeks. I'm starting to think he might have gone missing.' He pointed at the noticeboard by the pool table. 'Was wondering if I should put up a flyer.'

Brett chuckled. 'I wouldn't worry too much,' he said. 'Cell phone coverage is patchy at best in the mountains. It's fine in town but a few miles into the forest and you're back in the Dark Ages. And sometimes they take the cell phones off their workers.'

Standing frowned. 'Why would they do that?'

Brett sipped his drink. 'Security. There's a lot of thieves and robbers out there. I took on a girl a while back, pretty little thing from Guatemala or somewhere down south. She was standing in front of the general store, looking for work. That should have been a red flag because usually they hang out at the bus station in Eureka. But she seemed okay, she'd left her kid with her sister in LA and wanted to work for a month or so. She'd done it before, she said, she knew the ropes. I asked her a few questions and she seemed okay so I took her on.'

'Oh, you're a farmer?'

'I wouldn't say that. Just a few acres. But I had a harvest and she seemed to know what she was doing.' He chuckled. 'I was a lot more trusting back then. So, there was just her and me and she did a good job. Trimmed a couple of pounds most days, sometimes a pound and a half. Hard worker. Diligent. I saw her on her phone a few times when we went into Alderpoint for supplies but figured she was talking to her kid. Anyways, she'd been there a week and a truck appears in the middle of the night. I was asleep and they cold-cocked me in bed. She'd seen where I kept some of my money and they took that and all the weed she'd trimmed and pulled out most of my plants and took them.' He raised his glass. 'Lesson learnt. Never trust a pretty face.' He grinned. 'In fact, never trust anyone.' He drained his glass and waved for a refill from the bartender. 'Actually, I was lucky. These days they'd probably torture me to get all my cash and then kill me. It's a dog-eat-dog world, that's for sure.' The bartender poured more Jack Daniel's into his glass. 'So let me ask you a question, Dale.'

'Sure.'

Brett waved his glass at Standing's haircut. 'Military or convict?'

Standing laughed and ran his hand over his buzz cut. 'I had this done locally,' he said. 'But yeah, former military.'

'Can't always tell these days. See any action?'

'Some,' said Standing.

'Why former?'

Standing shrugged. 'Just wanted a change, I guess.'

'Change of career, change of country?'

'Both. I was fed up with being told what to do by morons who most of the time didn't have a clue what they were doing.'

'Yeah, nothing much changed there.' He sipped his drink.

'You were in the military?'

Brett nodded. 'Vietnam. Nineteen seventy.'

'That must have been rough.'

'It was an interesting time.' He took a gulp of whiskey. 'Being in country was bad enough, but coming back was worse. These days it's all "thank you for your service" but back then we were spat at and called babykillers.'

Standing drank his beer. Fifty years was a lifetime, but the man clearly hadn't gotten over his experience in Vietnam. It was understandable. Back then American kids – mainly black working class, like Brett – didn't have a choice about fighting for their country. They were given the minimum of basic training and then handed a gun and sent to the jungle to fight an enemy that looked exactly like every other civilian. In many ways the war in the Middle East was similar to what had happened in Vietnam. The enemy didn't wear a uniform or drive around in military vehicles, they fought when they wanted to fight and then they blended back into the civilian population. The constant stress of never knowing where the next attack was coming from wore down many a soldier out in Iraq, Afghanistan and Syria. Cases of post-traumatic stress disorder and suicides were the result, and back in England the streets were littered with homeless veterans who had never been able to get their heads straight after leaving the service. Even the SAS, which only took the best of the best, had more than its fair share of breakdowns and suicides.

Brett forced a smile, then clinked his glass against Standing's. 'Life is a waste of time, and time is a waste of life,' he said. 'So let's get wasted all of the time, and have the time of our life.' He banged his glass on the bar, then drank. Standing did the same.

'Are you local?' asked Standing. He gestured at the barman to refill Brett's glass and that it was to go on his bill.

'Sacramento,' said Brett. 'I was a mechanic when I got called up. Training to be one, anyway. They kept my job for me but when I got back I just couldn't stand being around people. Not the sort of people I was coming into contact with. They couldn't understand what I'd been through. Or what it was like walking through a jungle full of snakes and spiders never knowing when you were going to hit a booby trap or be shot in the face by an AK-47. I never slept more than a few hours in country and it didn't get better when I got home. So after a couple of months I quit the job and came here. Went into the woods and I never left.'

'Other than to pop in here for a drink.'

Brett laughed. 'I'm only here once a week. I come down to the general store and buy what I need, but I hunt for fresh meat and fish when I want so I don't need much. Then a few drinks here to remind myself what people sound like, then I'm back into the forest.'

'And you grow cannabis?'

'Enough to keep myself going,' he said. 'In the old days I used whatever land was available, but I made enough money in the eighties to buy a few acres for myself.' He sipped his Jack Daniel's. 'This friend of yours, is he military too?'

'Yeah, I met him out in Syria.'

'The sandbox.'

'We call it the sandpit. But yeah, the desert.' Standing had French's picture in his pocket, but he figured it best not to show it to Brett. Walking around with a photograph of a friend might have looked a bit strange.

'Because if he's military he might have been working security for one of the big farms. There's quite a few armed guys patrolling on the mountain these days.'

'Really?' Standing also figured it wouldn't be prudent to tell Brett about his run-in with the three armed men.

'Some of the bigger farms have thousands of plants and dozens if not hundreds of workers. There's a lot to protect.' He raised his glass. 'You might want to think about doing it yourself. Pays better than trimming.'

Standing nodded and took a drink of his beer. He wasn't sure what Frenchy was doing in the area but Standing hadn't considered the possibility that he was selling his services as an armed guard. But it made sense. He could lie low in the wilderness and earn money at the same time. 'Not sure that's possible, me being a Brit and all.'

Brett laughed. 'I just realised, I'm a Brett and you're a Brit. Brothers in arms.'

'I'll drink to that,' he said, and clinked his glass against Brett's. He put down his glass. 'I'm just going to check out the noticeboard over there,' he said, and slid off his stool. He walked over to the board. Two of the bikers who were playing pool looked at him and he smiled. They ignored him and continued to play. There were notices about a local pool tournament, several guns for sale and a flyer from a local taxi firm, but most were appeals for missing people. The one for Emma – whose mother he had spoken to outside the general store – was at the top. Some were copies of flyers he'd seen already, but several were new.

Something hard thudded into the small of his back. He turned to see one of the bikers holding a pool cue and glaring at him. 'Watch where you're standing, we're trying to play a game here,' said the biker. He was wearing a leather waistcoat over his denims and had an inverted crucifix hanging from his left ear.

'My bad,' said Standing, taking a step to the side.

'Just be careful where you stand,' said the biker. 'Next time this cue will be so far up your ass you'll be spitting out chalk.'

His three companions laughed. 'Spitting out chalk,' repeated one.

Standing held up his hands. 'All good, guys,' he said.

The four men glared at him as he backed away and then turned and went back to his seat.

'So you met our local meth dealers?' said Brett as Standing slid on to his stool.

The waitress returned with a massive pork chop, accompanied by mashed potato and corn and a bowl of apple sauce. 'Enjoy,' she said as she put the plate down in front of him, along with a knife and fork wrapped in a paper napkin.

Standing looked over his shoulder. The bikers were still playing, with a lot of barracking and swearing. They had 'OUTLAWS' on their jackets. One of them was standing with his back to the wall and he looked over at Standing, his eyes hard. Standing looked away. 'Seriously?' said Standing. 'Meth dealers?'

'They've got a place out in the woods somewhere,' said Brett. 'Every now and then you'll see a van go by with their supplies. No one's happy about it but there's not much anyone can do. They've as much right to be here as anyone else, but the stuff they make is evil.' He shuddered. 'Have you seen what meth does to a body?'

Standing nodded. 'Yeah. It's vile.'

'It's so different from weed, right? Weed relaxes you, calms you down, gets you mellow. Meth just hot-wires your brain and gets you into all sorts of trouble.'

Standing started on his chop, which was more than an inch thick and edged with crispy fat.

'Four beers,' said a man behind him. Standing knew without looking that it was one of the bikers. The bartender flashed him a thumbs up and walked away. A hand gripped Standing's shoulder. 'That looks good,' said the biker. Standing turned. The biker was big and bearded and had a steel chain around his neck. The hand on Standing's shoulder had a heavy steel ring on each finger. One of them was a swastika. 'Can I try some?' Before Standing could answer, the man reached for the plate with his other hand and grabbed the pork chop.

Standing reached for the hand on his shoulder, grabbed it and twisted it as he slid off his stool. The biker grunted in pain as Standing continued to put pressure on the wrist, then jerked the arm back. There was a satisfying crack from the man's elbow. Standing kept a grip on the biker's hand and twisted again, this time forcing him back. He used his left foot to sweep the biker's legs from under him and released his grip as he hit the ground like a sack of potatoes. The biker reached out to try to grab Standing's foot and Standing stamped down on his hand, then kicked him in the side of the head. He went still.

All Standing's movements had been instinctive and it had taken him less than two seconds to disable the man. His heart rate had barely changed and he was breathing slowly and evenly as he looked up at the three other bikers. Two of them were holding pool cues, swinging them side to side, gearing themselves up to fight.

'You boys need to take this outside,' said Brett calmly. 'There'll be hell to pay if you smash the place up.'

'Thanks for your support, Brett,' said Standing.

Brett grinned and raised his glass. 'I think you can handle this yourself, but if you feel you need a hand from a septuagenarian who has had a few drinks, you just holler.'

Standing gestured at the bikers and pointed at the door. 'You heard what the man said. Let's do this outside.'

The biker on the floor started to get up but Standing punched him hard at the base of the neck and he went down hard.

The three other men moved towards Standing, but stopped short when the bartender appeared and whacked a baseball bat down on the bar. 'Not in here!' he yelled, then waved the bat at the door. 'And leave the pool cues where they are!'

The two bikers with the cues threw them on to the pool table and then headed to the door, glaring sullenly at Standing. Standing stared at the remaining biker. He was in his forties with his grey hair pulled back in a ponytail. He had bulging forearms and a thick neck and was an inch or two taller than Standing, but Standing knew that size was pretty much irrelevant when it came to a fight. Standing gestured at the door with his thumb but the man shook his head and stood his ground.

'Whatever,' said Standing. He took off his coat and gave it to Brett, then walked by the biker to the door. He heard the man's boots crunch on the floor behind him and smiled to himself. The remaining biker was planning a sneak attack and was probably feeling very pleased with himself. That was about to change.

He grabbed the door handle and pulled. The two bikers outside were standing about ten feet apart facing the door, rolling their shoulders as they clenched and unclenched their fists. Standing stepped out on to the wooden terrace. He heard the man behind him take a breath and then the scrape of his boot against the floor. Standing twisted to the side just as the man thrust out with both hands. The right hand missed but the left caught Standing on the shoulder. The biker's momentum carried him forward. Standing put his hand behind the biker's neck and pulled him out on to the porch, then kicked him in the backside as he went by. The biker staggered with his arms flailing, then he fell off the porch and on to his knees. Standing took two quick steps and kicked the man in the back, and he slammed into the ground, face first.

The biker on the left had pulled out a large knife from a scabbard. The other had undone a chain from around his waist and began swinging it. The chain looked impressive but the knife was the deadlier weapon.

The biker on the floor tried to get up but Standing stamped on him between the shoulder blades to keep him down and then stamped on his left knee to immobilise him. The joint cracked and the biker began to sob.

The biker with the knife took a step towards Standing which suited him just fine. He took three quick steps to the left to put some distance between him and the man with the chain. He moved towards the knifer, staying up on the balls of his feet. Was the biker a stabber or a slasher? A stab was more likely to be a killing blow, but it was easier to deal with. Slashing tended to produce less damaging wounds but the weapon was harder to grab. Horses for courses.

The biker had his eyes hidden behind sunglasses and that was a problem because the eyes often gave warning of an attack. All Standing could see was his own reflection, which meant he would have to be guided by the man's body language. Most of the biker's considerable weight was on his back foot which meant he was planning to spring forward. That made a stab more likely.

Standing had his hands out, fingers curled, elbows bent. The other biker was grunting and swinging his chain around his head, but the man was a moron – his friend was in the way and he was expending all his energy on a show.

The knifer had the weapon close to his chest and was snarling at Standing. At first glance he looked big and dangerous, but close up it was clear that most of his bulk was fat, not muscle. He grunted and lunged with the knife but there was no chance of it doing any damage – the man was just too slow.

Standing knew all there was to know about the mechanics of a knife fight. He knew that three-quarters of all knife attacks were launched at a distance of three feet or less. But more importantly, the same percentage of knife attacks were initiated with the empty hand, the hand that wasn't holding the knife. Attackers tended to punch or claw with the free hand, and to grab if they could, only stabbing when they were in close. It was counter-intuitive; most people would assume that the knife was the thing to concentrate on, but in most fights it was the free hand that was the problem.

The biker was moving the knife now and Standing was fairly sure that he was doing it to distract him from his free hand. The man knew his limitations – he knew his only chance of stabbing Standing was to grab him first. Standing was fine with that scenario. He shuffled sideways so that the man now had his back to his chain-swinging colleague. Standing moved his hands to the side to make his chest a bigger target and dropped slightly to make himself look weaker. Then he moved his right hand forward, giving the biker the chance to grab it. The biker took the bait and lunged with his left hand but Standing blocked the arm with his right hand, then curled his fingers around the man's forearm. The biker began to thrust the knife but Standing had all the time in the world to pull the man's left arm across his body and at the same time grab the man's wrist with his left hand.

The biker cursed as he realised what had happened – Standing now had both hands on his left arm and was twisting him around. The knife flailed around in his right hand but there was no way he could get the blade near Standing's body.

Standing pulled the man to the side and down, then quickly twisted the arm down and back. He heard the meaty popping sound of the arm being twisted out of its socket. The biker screamed in pain and pitched forward on to his knees. Standing released his grip on the arm and punched him on the nose, a short, powerful jab that knocked the man clean out.

As the biker hit the ground, Standing picked up the knife and turned to face the remaining attacker. The chain was a ridiculous weapon, it was difficult to control and half the time it was heading in the wrong direction. Even if it did connect it wouldn't do any lasting damage unless Standing was unlucky enough to get hit in the face or the throat.

The biker was grunting with each swing, taking half-steps towards Standing. Standing drew back the knife and threw it at the biker's face. He didn't expect the knife to penetrate, but distracted the biker, who threw up his left hand to block the knife and lost all momentum with the chain. Standing moved quickly forward and punched the biker in the solar plexus, right, left and right again. The chain fell to the ground and the biker clutched his stomach, giving Standing all the time he needed to land a knock-out punch on the man's jaw. His eyes rolled up into the back of his head and he fell to the ground.

Standing straightened up, breathing slowly and evenly. The two hunters on the porch nodded their appreciation. 'That was nicely done, son,' said the older of the two. 'Was that what they call mixed martial arts?'

Standing grinned and shook his head. 'No, that's what they call me being angry,' he said. He looked at the knuckles of his right hand. He'd scraped the flesh but there'd be no lasting damage. He licked the blood off.

Standing realised that Brett was on the porch with his coat, an amused smile on his face. 'Looks like you didn't need any help,' said Brett. 'I figured as much. But you should go.' He gestured down the road. 'They've got friends and they'll come armed with more than knives and chains.'

Standing took his coat and pulled it on. 'How did you know I'd be okay?'

Brett patted him on the back. 'I've seen a few guys like you over the years,' he said. 'Where were you planning on sleeping tonight?'

'I've got a tent in my truck. Figured I could rough it for a while.'

'Man, you ain't sleeping in the woods. You can crash at my place. I've got a spare bed.'

'Are you sure?'

'Sure I'm sure. And we'd best be going. The guy in the bar is waking up and he'll be calling his posse. We need to be well gone by the time they get here.'

'I'll just get my check.'

'I took care of it,' said Brett. He pointed at a mud-splattered Jeep Wrangler. 'Follow me. The last few miles are a bit rough but you'll be okay if you take it slowly.'

CHAPTER 11

It took two hours to reach Brett's smallholding. The first thirty minutes was on a road that wound up the left side of the mountain. After that, there was a double-width dirt road that weaved its way through the redwoods, followed by a single track so rutted with potholes that they couldn't go much faster than walking pace.

There was no fence marking the boundary of Brett's land, but there were ropes linking the trees around three shipping containers, set into a U shape around an area of cleared ground. Doors and windows had been cut into the sides of the containers and they'd been covered with camouflage netting. In front of the container on the right were two brightly coloured deckchairs facing a fire pit ringed with stones. Brett climbed out of his Jeep. As Standing killed his engine and his headlights switched off, he realised just how dark it was. There were redwoods all around and their branches met high overhead, cutting out any starlight there might have been. He blinked, waiting for his night vision to kick in. The containers had disappeared into the blackness, as had Brett and his Jeep.

'Dark, right?' said Brett, off to his left. 'There's no dark like it. When there's a moon some light gets through, but on a night like this . . . it's as dark as the deepest deep cave.'

Standing heard a click and a flashlight beam cut through

the blackness, illuminating the container on the left. 'So this here is the sleeping area. It's in two, with separate doors. I've got two trimmigrants in the section on the left, you can have the right-hand section. There are six bunk beds, choose whichever you want.'

He ran the flashlight beam down the middle container. 'This is for storage. Food, meds, equipment.' Then he illuminated the container on the right. 'These are my quarters.'

'Bathroom?'

'Around the back. The toilet is a hole in the ground and every few weeks I fill it in and dig another.'

'Water?'

'I've run a pipe from a spring further up the mountain. It fills a tank and we draw from there. There's an outdoor shower.'

'It's quite a set-up you've got.'

'When it's light I'll show you the greenhouses and the processing areas.' He pointed the beam at Standing's truck. 'Grab your bag and I'll show you your room.'

Standing grabbed his rucksack from the back of the truck. Brett took him over to the container, pushed open the door and flicked a light switch. A small fluorescent tube fixed to the roof of the container flickered into life. 'So you've got electricity?'

'There's a couple of generators and I've got solar panels on the roofs of all the containers,' said Brett. 'They feed through to batteries and there's enough to run the basics.'

He stepped to the side so that Standing could go in. There were three sets of bunk beds and a cheap wooden wardrobe. 'Home sweet home,' said Brett.

'It's a lot more comfortable than the tent I'd been planning to use,' said Standing. He tossed the rucksack on to the lower bunk bed on the left. There were some paperbacks and sports magazines on a table, and two wooden chairs. And a very strong smell of cannabis.

Brett took him over to the container where he lived, opened the door and flicked on the light. There was a double bed at one end, a table with four chairs, and two plastic sofas facing each other across a low coffee table. 'Beer?' asked Brett, walking over to a small fridge under the window.

'Beer would be great,' said Standing. He flopped down on one of the sofas. There were half a dozen plastic bags containing cannabis buds on the coffee table, two small Tupperware containers filled with more buds, a large earthenware ashtray filled with cannabis ashes and a battered Zippo lighter.

Brett used a bottle opener chained to the handle of the fridge to flip the caps off the beers. He handed a bottle to Standing, dropped down on to the second sofa and swung his feet up on to the table. A black cat came in from outside and jumped on to the sofa next to Brett and he stroked its back. 'You'll need to be okay with cats,' he said. 'I've been adopted by a dozen strays.'

'Cats are good,' said Standing. He looked around. There was a bookcase filled with paperbacks by the window, most of them autobiographies and non-fiction, but with a sprinkling of James Patterson thrillers. There were two guitar cases and a saxophone leaning against the wall by the door. 'You live really well out here,' said Standing. 'I have to say I was expecting a lot worse.'

Brett waved his bottle in the air. 'I've been here a long time. A long, long time. You should have seen me when I first got here. I had a knife and a fire-starting kit and not much else. I built my own shelter and ate what I could find, which wasn't much. Then I started working on one of the farms nearby and saved enough money to buy a tent. I had the tent for going on ten years.' He grinned. 'I was young, I didn't need the creature comforts back then.'

'You own the land here?'

'Just a few acres, bought it back when they couldn't really give it away. Bought the first container when I got the land and then added to it over the years.'

'You've done well.'

Brett shrugged. 'I got the life I wanted. What about you? What sort of life are you looking for, Dale?'

Standing shrugged carelessly. 'A bit of peace and quiet,' he said. 'A chance to be myself and not what someone else wants me to be.'

'I hear that,' said Brett. 'Out here you're your own boss.' The cat curled up next to him and closed its eyes. 'Look, you're welcome to hang out here until you get your head straight,' said Brett. 'We're trimming right now, you can sit in with the girls.'

'The girls?'

'Angela and Amy. They're Taiwanese. They come and go. To be honest I'm not sure where they go to, but they work for a few months and then off they go. They say they're sisters but they don't look much alike. They're good workers. They each do two pounds a day, sometimes more.'

'They get paid by the pound?'

'Two hundred bucks a pound. These girls can earn close to twenty-five thousand bucks each in two months. They take their cash and off they go, and then a few months later they're back. Gambling, maybe. Or travelling. They never say.' He looked at Standing's hands. 'Big hands like yours, they're not great for trimming. But you should be okay for a pound a day.'

'I'll give it a go,' said Standing. 'Thanks.'

Brett sipped his beer. 'There's something that might be more in your line that I need help with tomorrow, if you're up for it.'

'Sure, what?'

'I've got an out-of-state buyer coming in to buy forty pounds of weed and I haven't done business with him before. Might be a good idea if you were around.'

'Not a problem. How much will they be paying?'

'It's good greenhouse weed, high potency, so they'll pay fifteen hundred dollars a pound. So sixty grand in total.'

'They pay more because it's grown in a greenhouse?'

Brett laughed. 'Yeah, I know it sounds crazy but the weed that's grown outside fetches the lowest price. At the moment, you can get it for as little as nine hundred bucks a pound. The greenhouse-grown weed is more expensive, but the most expensive is grown under artificial light and that can cost up to three times the outdoor crop. It's because the more control you have over the plants, the better the quality of the cannabis. Of course the costs of production go sky high because all the light is electric. You much of a smoker, Dale?'

Standing had been expecting the question. Drugs were a total no-no in the SAS, and in the UK military generally. All service personnel were subject to compulsory random drug testing and a positive result almost always ended in an administrative discharge. Standing had never heard of anyone in the Regiment being tested, but it was a theoretical possibility. Alcohol was the drug of choice in the SAS, to the extent that there was a high death rate from alcoholism among former troopers. Standing had smoked pot as a teenager and taken ecstasy when out with his mates in his younger days, but he had put all that behind him when he joined the army. The problem was that his story about looking for work on a cannabis farm wouldn't really hold up if he showed an aversion to the drug, so he smiled and said, 'Hell, yeah.'

'I'll show you the difference,' he said. He stood and went over to a bookcase, picked up two well-used bongs, one made of green glass, the other with a bluish hue, and carried them over to the coffee table.

He opened one of the Tupperware containers and held it out. 'This is the premium quality. Grown under lights, temperature controlled, all the right nutrients added. Pot doesn't come better than this.'

Standing sniffed. There was a heavy, earthy smell with a hint of fruit, but he had no idea whether it was good or bad.

Brett leant forward, grabbed the ziplock bag of cannabis buds and unzipped it. He smelled it and then gave it to Standing. 'This was grown outside. It's good, but it's not great.'

Standing sniffed it. There was less of a fruity fragrance and more of a soil-like smell, but while he could definitely tell them apart he had no way of telling which was superior. But he nodded enthusiastically anyway. 'I get it,' he said.

'The proof is in the pudding,' said Brett. He poured water from a plastic bottle into the bongs, then removed the bowls and used his fingers to crumble buds into them. He put the bowls back into the bongs. Brett pointed at the green one. 'This is regular weed,' he said. 'It's good, it's some of the best weed grown in the county, I can sell this for a grand a pound every day of the week.' He handed the bong to Standing. Standing took it, holding the smoke stem with his left hand.

Brett handed him the Zippo lighter. 'Knock yourself out,' he said, and slouched back on the sofa.

Standing had only ever smoked cannabis in roll-ups, but he had watched several YouTube videos about smoking bongs, in anticipation of a situation like this. He took a couple of slow, deep breaths, then put his mouth around the mouthpiece. He flicked the lighter open with his right hand, then span the wheel to spark the flint. The lighter flamed and he manipulated the flame to burn the cannabis in the bowl. As he lit the cannabis he inhaled, pulling the smoke into the smoke chamber. The smoke thickened and the chamber became opaque. Once the chamber was full of smoke he stopped inhaling and took away the lighter, flicking it closed. He put the lighter down on the coffee table and used his right hand to lift the bowl out of the stem. Then he finally sucked the smoke into his lungs. He did it slowly and didn't fill his lungs completely, because he wasn't sure what effect it would have on him. He grinned at Brett as he held the smoke in his lungs for two seconds, then he slowly exhaled.

He gave the bong to Brett, who took it and placed it on the table. Brett then picked up the blue bong. 'And this the premium,' he said. He took the lighter, lit the cannabis and took a deep lungful of smoke, which he held for a count of four before blowing a thick plume at the ceiling. 'Now that hits the spot,' he sighed, and put his feet up on the coffee table. 'Fuck, yeah.'

Brett handed the blue bong to Standing. He picked up the lighter and took a long pull on it. He could definitely tell the difference. The premium version was smoother and richer than the first bong, and whereas the first one had given him a slight high, the effects of the second bong hit him almost immediately.

A feeling of euphoria spread through his system and he had to fight the urge to giggle.

A grin spread across his face and Brett laughed and pointed at him. 'Yeah, man, you got it!' he said and slapped his own thigh. 'Hits the spot every time.'

Brett's comment felt like the funniest thing Standing had heard in years and he chuckled and then laughed out loud. He handed the bong over and Brett took a second hit. 'The downside to this one is that you're going to get the worst case of the munchies ever.'

Standing laughed again. 'Munchies,' he repeated. For some reason the sound of the word made him want to giggle.

'It's good shit, right?' asked Brett.

Standing nodded. He tried to speak but his tongue felt as if it was too big for his mouth.

Brett gave the bong back to Standing. Standing leant forward, ignited the cannabis again and took another hit. Once again the warmth spread across his chest and a wave of euphoria washed over him. He sat back in the sofa and stared up at the ceiling. 'Wow,' he said.

Brett laughed. 'That's what I'm selling tomorrow,' he said. 'The guys are coming in from Boise, Idaho. Weed is totally illegal there so they've no choice other than to buy out of state.'

'Boise?' repeated Standing. For some reason the name sounded hilarious.

'Boise is the state capital of Idaho,' said Brett. 'It's a twelve, thirteen-hour drive. I'm due to meet them at noon. They'll need to check the weed and we have to count the cash. Then we go our separate ways.'

Standing nodded. He knew that there were questions he should be asking but his brain felt as if it had been wrapped in cotton wool. He felt the bong being taken from his hands and looked over to see Brett preparing to take another hit. 'This is . . .' he began, but then trailed off as he couldn't find the right word. He tried to wave at Brett but his arm felt as if it was made of lead. That suddenly seemed very funny and he stared at his hands in his lap and chuckled.

CHAPTER 12

Standing groaned and opened his eyes. Light was coming in through the gap between the curtains over the container's single window. He was lying on the bottom bunk bed and he swung his legs over the side and sat up, rubbing his face. He was still wearing his clothes, though he had taken off his boots and socks. The floor was littered with wrappers from chocolate bars and there were three empty instant noodle containers at the end of the bed. There was a chemical taste in his mouth and his throat felt dry. He rubbed his eyes and looked around for something to drink. There was a plastic bottle of water on its side by the wall and he grabbed it and unscrewed the cap. He drank greedily, then wiped his mouth with the back of his hand. He put the empty bottle on the floor and stood up. His knees cracked and his neck was aching. He tried to lean down and touch his toes but his head swam and he realised he needed to take it slowly. He straightened up and did a few stretching exercises, then walked slowly to the door and pulled it open, blinking in the sunlight. Brett was sitting in a deckchair outside his container and he grinned when he saw Standing. 'The kraken awakes!' he shouted, raising his mug. 'Coffee's on!' There were two cats sitting at his feet, one sandy-coloured, the other with grey stripes.

'What is a kraken, anyway?'

'A legendary sea-monster,' said Brett. 'Lives off the coasts of Greenland and Norway and terrorises sailors. I think it's fictional.'

'Right,' said Standing. He went back inside and pulled on his socks and boots. When he emerged again, Brett was standing by the fire and picking up a metal coffee pot. He poured coffee into a mug and handed it to Standing. 'Milk and sugar are in my room,' he said.

'Black's fine,' said Standing. He sipped his coffee. 'I don't remember getting into bed,' he said.

'I helped you,' said Brett. 'And then you kept asking for food so I gave you some chocolate bars and liberated some of the girls' noodles.'

'I don't remember any of that.' He ran his hand through his hair and grinned. 'But no hangover. My head feels fine.'

'Because I grow a quality product,' said Brett. 'No impurities. There's a reason they use it for medicinal purposes. Alcohol is a poison, weed is a medicine. You hungry?'

Standing grinned. 'Hell, yeah.'

Brett put his mug down by the deckchair, then went inside his container, reappearing a few minutes later with a large skillet, plates, eggs and bacon.

'I'll cook,' said Standing.

'Damn right you will,' laughed Brett. 'I'm not your maid.' He gave everything to Standing and then flopped down on the deckchair.

Standing had done more than his fair share of cooking in the field, so egg and bacon al fresco was easy enough. He fried the bacon, slapped it on to plates and then scrambled the eggs. He handed one plate to Brett and sat on the ground with the other. Brett tucked in. 'You'll make someone a wonderful wife,' he said.

Standing laughed and wolfed down his breakfast. 'So you said the Idaho guys get here at noon?'

'Hell no, they're not coming anywhere near this place,' he said. 'We'll meet them on neutral territory, a motel on the way to Humboldt Redwoods State Park. About forty-five minutes' drive. I don't let anyone come here, not unless I know them or they're here to work.'

'You're scared someone will steal from you?'

Brett grinned. 'I'm not scared,' he said. 'Just cautious.'

'You've got guns, right?'

Brett winked at him. 'Yeah, I've got guns. Ain't no one coming here and taking what's mine.'

Standing finished his food and stood up. He went over to Brett and took his plate. 'I might as well earn my keep by doing the washing-up,' he said.

'Round the back,' said Brett.

Standing walked around the container. There was a wooden shelter with canvas sides over a table containing two washing-up bowls and a makeshift tap. There was a collection of pots and pans under the table. He turned on the tap and water gushed out. He washed the plates and cutlery and placed them on a dishcloth. When he went back to the fire, Brett was finishing the last of his coffee. 'We'd best be going,' he said. 'You can shower when you get back.'

Standing lifted his right arm and smelled his armpit. 'Bit ripe, yeah?'

'You smell like a tough guy, so it's no bad thing,' said Brett. He stood up and went over to the middle container. 'Let's get you kitted out,' he said. He opened the door and switched on the light. Standing followed him. To the right were shelves packed with tinned and dried food, including dozens of packs of noodles similar to the ones he'd eaten the previous night. To the left was a metal cage with two large padlocks. Brett unlocked them and pulled open the door to the cage. Standing whistled when he saw what it contained.

There were six handguns on one wall, including two Glock 19s and a .357 Smith & Wesson Magnum. On the wall facing the door were three assault rifles – an M16, a Heckler & Koch HK416 and a Heckler & Koch G3 – and a pump-action shotgun. On the right were shelves filled with boxes of ammunition.

'Are you expecting trouble, Brett?'

Brett laughed. 'Better safe than sorry,' he said. 'The guys we're seeing know that we'll be doing the swap at a motel so I doubt they'll be coming with big guns. Just take a handgun.'

Standing took one of the Glocks. He checked the action. The magazine was full. Brett took the Magnum. Standing grinned. 'Size isn't everything,' he said.

Brett chuckled. 'I beg to differ,' he said. He tucked the gun into his belt, then padlocked the door. 'We'll take my Wrangler,' he said. 'I've already loaded the weed.' He looked at his watch. 'Time to go.'

CHAPTER 13

Half an hour after they had left Brett's farm, his cell phone beeped to let him know he had a message. He looked at the screen as he drove. 'They're in their room,' he said.

'How do you normally play it when you meet with buyers you don't know?' asked Standing.

'There's an element of trust,' said Brett. 'It's not like the cocaine business where everyone is trying to fuck everyone else, and the DEA is breathing down your neck. The weed business is generally more relaxed. Partly because the money is that much less. Doesn't mean that there aren't bad apples out there, but most weed dealers aren't going to risk a gunfight in a public place for sixty grand. Be a whole different ball game if they were out in the woods, then there'd be no downside. But you never know, Dale. You never know. There might be local gangsters looking for an easy sixty grand so you have to be prepared for anything. But these guys come with a personal recommendation, so that's a good start.'

'The cannabis business is legal now, right?' asked Standing.

'Sure, legal for medicinal and recreational use. There are rules about where you can and can't smoke. So you can't smoke weed anywhere where smoking is banned, and that's pretty much everywhere these days. Plus it's illegal to smoke, vape or eat cannabis in public, and illegal to even open a package containing cannabis in public. But in your own home it's perfectly legal and you can carry up to an ounce on you. Crossing state lines is a no-no, though. And it can only be sold in licensed premises.'

'So what you're doing is legal?'

Brett laughed. 'Hell no,' he said, and slammed his palms against the steering wheel. 'Totally illegal. You can only grow cannabis for sale if you're licensed by the government and the state. Without a licence you're only allowed to have six plants, and they have to be grown indoors.'

'So why not go legal and get the licences you need?'

'Way too expensive,' said Brett. 'They bleed you dry. I know growers who've gone legit and they're not making any money at all. It's not just the cost of the licences, it's all the surveys you have to pay for. Wildlife, water, environment, it's never-ending. There are rules and regulations about road maintenance, fertiliser storage, generator noise. You have to pay for a bird-watcher to do a survey of the birds on your land in case you're disturbing a marbled murrelet or a spotted owl or whatever. I've heard of people paying more than three grand for that. Three grand for a birdwatcher. I'm not making this up! I get that the land needs protecting. Diverting water from streams to plants can mess up the ecosystem, no question, and most of the logging roads and tracks through the forest were never meant to be used every day. I get that, but guys like me have been here for decades and we've had next to no effect on the environment. Then there's all the paperwork you'd have to do if you went legal. There's the compliance inspections and audits. Odour control. Lab tests on all the weed you grow. And it all has to be filed and cross-referenced. These growers spend more time filling in spreadsheets than they do cultivating their plants.

So at the end of the day you'll be paying fifteen grand for the licence and another thirty grand for what they call discretionary costs plus all the time it takes to complete their records. On most small farms that would mean you're working for the government for half the year. And the legal work is so complicated the likes of me would have to employ a cannabis lawyer, and they charge you seven hundred and fifty bucks an hour.'

'What?'

'It's daylight robbery and there's no way around it,' said Brett. 'There are public notices that have to be written, community meetings, pre-licence inspections. You need legal representation at city council hearings, you need all your paperwork checked. That's a hundred hours easy, which means you have to find seventy-five grand up front. Then when you are up and running, you have to declare your earnings and pay state and federal taxes on that.' He shook his head. 'When they announced that recreational cannabis was going to be legalised, all the farmers were celebrating. But as time goes by, they're starting to realise that actually it's going to put them out of business.'

'So they're killing the golden goose?'

'For the small guys like me, sure. But for big pharma, it's a gold rush. It's all about economies of scale. You have a hundred farmers, each with a few acres, they can't turn a profit under the new regime. But a big drugs company can buy all the farms and lump them together, use their in-house legal team to do all the paperwork, and offset all their start-up costs against profits made elsewhere. They bring in their own workforce and security, they can get a grip of their costs and centralise their sales and distribution. They make money hand over fist.'

'So what's your plan?'

'My plan?' Brett laughed. 'To stay under the radar as long as possible. Save my money for the day they force me out of business. Providing I have enough hidden away I'll just cultivate my six plants for personal use and live off my savings. It's cool.'

'What do they do about the illegal farms?'

'At the moment, not much. They watch us with satellites and they fly choppers over but from the air my place doesn't look like much. It's hardly worth them sending in a clean-up squad. They'd need dozens of men but they know I'd see them coming so I'd be away and all they'd be able to do is to destroy the crops. Then when they've gone I'll be back. It's a pointless exercise so they just leave us alone, generally. But they don't need to destroy our plants to put us out of business. They'll just make it harder and harder for us to sell our product and one by one the small farmers will sell up or just quit.' He grinned. 'But that's long term. Short term I can still sell forty pounds for sixty grand, so all's right with the world.'

They turned on to route 101, heading south to the Humboldt Redwoods State Park, more than 50,000 acres of forest some thirty miles south of Eureka. The motel Brett was using was ten miles north of the forest, a two-storey building with fake redwood trees either side of the entrance and a swimming pool surrounded by potted plants. The car park was to the left and there were more than two dozen vehicles parked there, mainly pick-up trucks. There were twenty rooms facing the car park, ten on each floor. As Brett parked his truck, they saw two young men in denim shirts and jeans walking up the stairs at the side of the building, carrying bulging garbage bags. Brett laughed and gestured at the men. 'Amateurs,' he said. 'Could they make it more obvious that they're delivering weed?'

'Do you know them?'

'I know the type,' said Brett. The two men they were watching walked along the upper walkway and knocked on one of the doors. It opened and they slipped inside.

'So this is a well-known cannabis distribution point?' asked Standing.

'There's a few places like this,' said Brett. 'Probably half their customers are drug dealers. They do a half daily rate. A hundred bucks for four hours, no questions asked. And they save on housekeeping because the beds aren't used.' He grinned. 'Win-win.'

The two guys reappeared on the upper walkway. They no longer had the garbage bags and one of them was holding a padded envelope. 'Deal done,' said Brett. 'Small timers.' He looked at his phone. 'Room 104,' he said. 'Ground floor.'

'How do you want to play this?' asked Standing.

'We take the drugs in, we check the money, we leave. It's not rocket science.'

'Do I carry the drugs or do you? Do we go in with guns drawn?'

Brett chuckled. 'This isn't *Tombstone*.'

'Well there were outlaws at The Shack.'

'Yes there were. But these guys are dope dealers, not meth heads. Different class of outlaw. And this is a public space. Less likely for the shit to hit the fan here, no pun intended.'

'You're saying that deals here never go wrong?'

'I'm not saying that there aren't problems. Growers turn up light, buyers are short on the cash. But conflicts are generally resolved without guns being drawn. You just have to keep your wits about you.'

'Good to know,' he said. He looked over at the motel rooms. The room on the far left on the ground floor was 100. He counted off four rooms. There was a large pick-up truck parked in front of 104 that blocked his view of the door.

Brett reached for the door handle but Standing raised his hand to stop him. 'Just give me a few minutes to do a walk-around,' he said.

'Why?'

'The buyers are from Idaho, you said. Let me just check how many Idaho plates there are then we'll know if they came alone or not.'

'Good thinking,' said Brett.

Standing opened the passenger door and climbed out of the truck. Two men with a wheeled suitcase were heading towards the stairs. They were dressed in baggy jeans and heavy jackets and had mud-splattered boots. Both had long beards and were losing their hair. They could have been brothers.

Standing walked to the edge of the car park and checked the plates of the vehicles there. All were local. He walked towards the rooms, his hands in his pockets. Most of the trucks had California plates and pretty much all had stickers promoting marijuana and gun ownership. There was a white Lincoln Town Car with California plates in a Vegas plate-holder, presumably driven by a buyer.

The big pick-up truck in front of room 104 was the only vehicle near to the room with Idaho plates, which was a good sign. But there were several other vehicles parked outside the motel entrance, so Standing walked over to get a better look. They were all saloons or SUVs and three had out-of-state plates. One was from Nevada, one was from Oregon and the third – a white Honda CR-V – was from Idaho. There were two men sitting in the Honda, leaning back in their seats and smoking a joint. They were in their thirties, long-haired and wearing hoodies. They were laughing at something and paid him no attention as he walked by. Standing walked around the motel and back to Brett's truck. He went around to the driver's side and Brett wound down the window. 'Everything okay?' asked Brett.

'I'm not sure,' said Standing. 'There are two potheads in an Idaho car in front of reception. But they can't see 104 from there and they didn't look twice at me. It could just be a co-incidence.'

'A lot of buyers come from Idaho. We've got the best weed in the country. Hell, the whole world.' He opened his door. 'We'll just keep our eyes open.'

He climbed out and opened the passenger door behind him. He took out a black nylon holdall. 'I'll get that,' said Standing, hurrying around the front of the truck.

'What?' said Brett, slamming the door and swinging the holdall over his shoulder. 'You're saying the old guy can't carry forty pounds?'

Standing laughed. 'That's not what I was saying at all,' he said.

'I'm just busting your balls,' said Brett. 'Better if your arms are free, anyway.'

Standing nodded. 'That works,' he said. 'In fact you should stay here and I'll go and check the money. And check there are no surprises in the room.' He gestured over at the motel entrance. 'Keep your eyes peeled for two potheads in hoodies in a white CR-V.' He headed to the room, looking left and right. The curtains were drawn across the window and there was a 'DO NOT DISTURB' sign hanging from the doorknob. There was a scuffling sound to his left and he turned to see the two bearded men coming down the steps, this time without the wheeled suitcase. One of them was holding a bulging Walmart carrier bag.

Standing took a final look over his shoulder, looked left and right, then stood to the side and knocked on the door. It was force of habit never to stand at a door and knock, there was always the chance that a high-powered weapon could be fired through the wood. He heard muffled voices inside the room and the door opened on a security chain. Standing knew that the chain was more for psychological reassurance than a genuine barrier – one half-hearted kick would pull the chain from the wood. But he put on his most disarming smile and said 'special delivery' to whoever was standing on the other side of the door.

'You Brett?' said a voice.

'I'm with Brett.'

'Where's Brett?'

'With me.'

'Have you got the weed?'

'Forty pounds of Humboldt's finest,' said Standing.

The door closed and he heard the rattle of the chain, and then the door opened again. A man in his thirties with shoulder-length hair blinked in the sunlight. He had a broad chin and a boxer's nose, but the paunch and slightly bowed legs suggested he wasn't much of a fighter. He looked down at Standing's hands. 'Where's the weed?' he asked.

'I just need to check the room, make sure there's no nasty surprises,' said Standing.

'The room's fine. Just get the weed.'

'Open the door so that I can see who's inside.'

'There's just the two of us.'

'Mate, from where I'm standing you could have a marching band with all the instruments in there and I wouldn't know.'

'What, you think we're gonna hit you with a trombone?' asked the guy, which Standing had to admit was pretty funny.

'Just let me look inside and we're all good,' said Standing.

The man turned and said something to whoever else was in the room. He was clearly an amateur. If Standing had been up to no good he'd have drawn his gun, kicked open the door and shot everyone inside within two seconds. But he just smiled and waited. Eventually the man opened the door. Standing walked in, wrinkling his nose at the damp smell. There were stains on the ceiling and a large spider had set up its home in the corner above the double bed. There was a hard-shelled carry-on case on a stained bedspread. Another thirty-something man was sitting in an armchair in front of the window. He was balding and wearing steel-framed glasses. His hands were in his lap around a can of Diet Coke. Like the man who had opened the door, he didn't seem the type to be prone to violence. He smiled up at Standing. 'So you're happy now? No marching band.'

'Give me a second,' said Standing. He walked over to the bathroom and pushed open the door. There was mildew all over the bottom of the shower curtain and the washbasin was stained. He caught sight of his reflection in the mirror over the sink and saw that he had his hard face on. He grinned. 'You looking at me?' he said to his reflection.

'Can we get on with this?' said the man sitting in the armchair. 'We've got a long drive ahead of us.'

'No problem,' said Standing. He gestured at the case. 'Just open the case, I won't go near the cash, I just need to know it's there.'

The man who had opened the door went over to the bed. He unzipped the case and flipped it open. Standing could see a stack of a dozen plastic-wrapped packs of bills. He nodded and went over to the door. He walked out of the room and to the side of the truck to wave at Brett, who ambled across with the holdall over his shoulder. Standing stepped aside to let Brett go in, and then followed him and closed the door.

'So you're the legendary Brett,' said the man in the armchair.

'The man, the myth, the legend,' said Brett. He put the holdall on the bed.

The man got out of the armchair and held out his hand. 'I just want to shake your hand,' he said. 'Your weed is the best. The absolute best.'

'Well thank you for that,' said Brett. He shook the man's hand. 'I do try to please.'

The man who had opened the door went over to the holdall and opened it. He took out one of the plastic bags and unzipped it before pressing it to his face. He took a deep breath and then sighed. 'Oh that's good. That's so good.'

'Best weed in Humboldt County, which makes it the best weed in the US of A,' said Brett.

Brett took the packs of bills from the case. 'You can keep the case and we'll keep the holdall,' said the balding man. 'It'll make it easier.'

'No, we'll keep our own bags,' said Brett. 'That's my lucky bag, I've had it for years.' He counted out twelve packs and lined them up on the bed. 'Eenie, meenie, miney, mo,' he said, and picked up one of the packs. He ripped off the plastic and counted the bills.

The man who had opened the door took another of the bags of weed. He weighed it in his hand. 'So each bag is a pound?'

'That's the way we do it,' said Brett. 'Forty bags, forty pounds. Make sure you count them, I don't want you putting a shit review on Yelp.'

The man unzipped the bag and sniffed it. He grinned. 'Wow,' he said. He and his companion began taking the bags out of the holdall and putting them in the case.

Brett picked up a pack of bills and tossed it to Standing. Standing opened the pack and checked the bills. They seemed fine. He nodded at Brett. Brett scooped up the money and once the men had emptied the holdall of weed he took it from them and put the money into it. 'Right guys, it's been a pleasure doing business with you, and if you need more when that runs out, you've got my number,' said Brett.

Standing opened the door and looked both ways, then waved at Brett to leave. He let Brett walk to the Jeep first as he checked left and right for possible threats, then he stood guard as Brett put the holdall in the back of the Jeep, climbed into the driving seat and started the engine. Standing walked around to the passenger side, had another good look around, and climbed in.

As they pulled out of the car park, Standing looked over at the CR-V. The SUV was full of smoke and the two men hadn't moved. 'So is that really your lucky bag?' Standing asked as Brett put his foot down.

Brett chuckled. 'Nah,' he said. 'But I've heard of them putting GPS trackers in cases so that they can follow the case back to the farm. Mind you, those guys didn't seem the type. You see what I mean about weed deals not being like coke deals? Generally they're nice people we're selling to.' He checked his rear-view mirror. 'But that doesn't mean you can let your guard down. There's plenty of bad apples around.'

CHAPTER 14

As they drove back through Garberville, Standing saw a group of tents on a vacant lot and half a dozen men and women sitting in a circle smoking dope. Two large dogs were sitting in front of one of the tents. One had a peace symbol hanging from its collar, the other a metal marijuana leaf. 'So there's a big homeless population here?' he asked.

Brett's eyes flicked to his rear-view mirror. He'd taken a circuitous route through town to make sure that they weren't being followed. 'The official population of the town is just under a thousand,' said Brett. 'The last time they did a count of the homeless here, they found more than two hundred.'

'That's not good.'

'It's got worse since legalisation,' said Brett. 'I mean, there have always been transients and homeless here because of the nature of the work. Cannabis is a seasonal crop and so when there's no harvest there's no work. Some of the trimmigrants go home but some don't have anywhere to go, so they just live on the streets or camp in the forest. Back in the day if you saw someone down on their luck you'd sling them a few bucks. But it's a whole different ball game these days. The big companies bus in their own workers, and the underground farms are really careful about who they take on.'

'I thought anyone could just turn up here and find work?'

'Sure. New blood is fine. But the ones on the street, you don't know who they know or what they know. Plus a lot of them are serious drug addicts.' He saw the smile on Standing's face and chuckled. 'I know what you're thinking. Yes, I've smoked pot every day for the last fifty-odd years. But I'm not an addict. I have a bong in the morning to set me up for the day and a couple at night to keep the nightmares at bay, and the odd one or two hits if I'm not working. But these kids, when they come here it's like they've got the golden ticket and they take full advantage. And a lot move on to meth and crack, and before long they're no use to anyone. Garberville used to be a pleasant God-fearing town, but these days you wouldn't walk around at night.'

They drove out of the town and headed up the mountain. 'You said the big companies bus people in?' said Standing. 'How does that work?'

'Big pharma hire in the cities and then bus them into the farms. They live in dormitories, they get fed and they have access to phones and Wi-Fi so they can talk to their families. They have good security so they're not worried about being robbed. They pay good money, too. They can stay as long as they want and they pay tax, it's all official. The cartels bus people in too, but they go about it in a very different way. They pick up Mexicans close to the border and bring them up to Humboldt. They have bags over their heads until they reach the farms and their phones are confiscated. I'm told that conditions are pretty bad and the security is there to keep them in as much as it is to stop robberies.'

'Yeah, before I met you I had a run-in with some armed guys on the mountains. ATVs and shotguns.'

'That'll be cartel security,' he said. 'Or the Russians. Or Bulgarians. There's a lot of bad guys on the mountains.'

'And the cops don't intervene?'

'Not enough of them,' said Brett. 'They tend to stay away. It'd take a full-on DEA operation with SWAT and helicopters to take them on, and at the moment that's not happening. Down the road, maybe. At the moment they're using the legal routes to shut down the smaller growers. I get the feeling they'll fight the big battles down the line. Or maybe not.'

Standing frowned. 'Why do you say that?'

'It's this whole "war on drugs" sham,' he said. 'They're not winning the war, all they're doing is keeping the price up and putting a lot of people in prison. And when they're in prison, the government makes money. They sell food to the convicts, they charge for calls and emails. Prisons are big business. The more convicts there are, the more money the government makes.' He shrugged. 'In the short term it makes sense to have the legal cannabis provided by big pharma and have the cartels supplying the black market. That way everyone is happy. Then as state by state agrees to legalise cannabis, the legal market grows and the black market shrinks. Eventually there'll be no black market and big pharma will control it all.'

'You make it sound like a conspiracy,' said Standing.

Brett laughed harshly. 'Just don't get me started on the moon landings,' he said. 'Or as I call them, the alleged moon landings.'

Brett turned off the main road and on to a dirt track. It wasn't the same road that they had used the night they had driven to the farm from the bar. Standing wondered if Brett was deliberately trying to confuse him. He doubted that he'd be able to retrace either route. All the dirt tracks looked the same and the thick forest meant he could never see more than fifty feet or so ahead of him. After Brett had made three more turns, Standing had lost all sense of direction.

As they drove by a gate, Standing saw a man in camouflage gear with a rifle over his shoulder. Standing kept his head down, but Brett gave the man a cheery wave. 'That's the Williams place,' said Brett. 'He and his family have been here since the nineties. He was a Stanford English professor who gave up academia to grow pot.'

'Was that him?'

'No, that's one of his people. He's got quite a big operation, so he has a manager and a couple of security guys. He's trying to go the legit route but he's struggling.'

The track curved to the right. After a mile or so they passed a five-bar wooden gate with two large signs, one saying 'ARMED RESPONSE' and the other 'SURVIVORS WILL BE PROSECUTED'. 'That's not a joke,' said Brett. 'The McKinley brothers make a habit of shooting at any strangers who venture on to their property. The only upside is that they are both terrible shots, but you still wouldn't want to take the risk.'

'Do you know everybody on the mountain?'

'The old-timers, sure. You used to bump into everyone at the store or the bars eventually. And back in the seventies and eighties we used to hold festivals and stuff, there was a real community feeling to the place. But that's long gone. I know the old-timers but not the newbies, and certainly not the gangsters and the cartels.' He shrugged. 'You can't fight change,' he said. 'All you can do is accept it and adapt.'

The track curved to the left. There was an abandoned truck half on the road. Its wheels had been removed, along with the hood and one of the doors, and from the look of the rust and the moss on the truck bed, it had been there for several years. Brett drove slowly around it. In places the track was barely wide enough for one vehicle and by now Standing was certain that Brett had taken a different route to his farm. They drove for another thirty minutes before Standing recognised the gate to Brett's property.

Brett drove down the smaller track and parked in front of the containers. 'Come on. I'll introduce you to the girls,' he said. He climbed out and grabbed the holdall, then took Standing around the containers and over to a green canvas tent. One side of the tent had been opened and clipped back and inside two Taiwanese girls were sitting at a large metal table, clipping away at cannabis stems. They both looked over and smiled when they saw Brett, the smiles turning to frowns when they realised he wasn't alone. 'This is Dale,' he said. 'He's going to be staying with us for a while.'

The two girls smiled and nodded but continued to clip away. 'This is Angela,' said Brett, gesturing at the girl on the left, who had waist-length black hair tied in a ponytail and was wearing pink-framed spectacles.

'Pleased to meet you,' said Angela.

'And this is Amy. Her sister.'

Amy was plumper and had a round face framed by a pageboy cut. 'Pleased to meet you,' she echoed.

Both girls were wearing fleeces over polo-neck sweaters and Ugg boots. Each had two plastic boxes in front of them, one full of cannabis stems and one with the buds that they had snipped. As they finished each stem they dropped what was left into a large plastic bin on the ground between them. Their scissors were click-click-clicking like insects, and their hands moved so quickly that at times they were a blur.

'There's two ways of trimming, wet and dry,' said Brett. 'We use both here but the girls are experts at wet trimming so they tend to stick with that. With dry trimming we cut the plant and hang it up to dry for several days. Then you take the buds off and trim them. It's a lot easier, to be honest. Wet trimming is just plain messy. The trichomes get everywhere – on your scissors, on your hands, on your face.'

'Trichomes?' Standing repeated.

'They're the little bubbles of cannabis that coat the branches, leaves and buds. They're resin glands, they produce the cannabis wax and oil. There are all sorts of different types, different sizes and shapes and functions. Anyway, as the weed dries the trichomes harden and there's less stickiness.'

'So why trim wet?'

Brett grinned. 'That's what sets the professionals apart from the amateurs,' he said. 'Most farmers would take the easy way out and trim dry. But trimming wet gives you a more aesthetically pleasing product. And it's less damaging to the trichomes so you get a better flavour. That doesn't mean we don't dry trim here, we do, especially if we get shorthanded. But I'm a purist and so are Angela and Amy. Now grab a chair and the girls can show you the ropes.'

Standing took off his coat. He figured that Brett wanted to put his cash somewhere safe and that he didn't want him to know where that safe place was. Brett grinned. 'You'll be fine, I'm leaving you in good hands.' He walked away with his holdall over his shoulder.

Angela pointed at a stack of stem-filled plastic boxes. 'So, take a box and there are scissors in the cups over there.' She continued to clip as she nodded at a line of plastic cups on a bench, each of which had a pair of scissors in them. He went over and smelled the rubbing alcohol in the cups. He pulled out a pair and then took the top box of stems and put it on the table.

'And you need another box to collect the buds,' said Amy.

'Got it,' said Standing.

He grabbed an empty box, put it next to the stems box, and pulled up a chair. He sat down and grinned. 'Off to work we go,' he said. He clicked the scissors. They felt tiny in his hand. He picked up a stem and looked at it, then looked over at the two girls. 'I just cut off the buds, right?'

They giggled as they continued to snip away.

'You cut the fan leaves off first,' said Amy. 'That way you can see the buds more clearly. Put the leaves in the bucket. Then you snip off the individual buds.'

'That's called bucking,' said Angela.

Amy nodded. 'You keep bucking until you have a decent pile of buds to work on.' She held up one of her buds. 'You trim the stem as close to the bottom of the bud as you can get. But you mustn't go too close because then the bud will fall apart. Then you have to snip away the crow's feet, the tiny little branches that stick up from the bottom of the bud. Then you make it look pretty.'

'Pretty?' repeated Standing.

Angela laughed. 'It has to look good. It's like giving the bud a manicure, you have to trim away anything ugly. Anything that doesn't have trichomes on it has to go.'

'Okay, I think I've got it,' he said. He began to snip away at the stem, cutting off the leaves and tossing them into the bucket. With the leaves gone he could get a better look at the buds, and one by one he snipped them off and let them fall into the box. He threw what was left of the stem into the bucket. 'One down,' he said. 'How many more thousand to go?' He looked down at the buds he'd harvested. There were eight and they were so light he figured he'd need dozens to make an ounce, and hundreds to make up a pound. He grimaced as he realised that it wasn't going to be as easy as he'd thought.

He picked up a second stem and began snipping off the large leaves. He realised that his scissors were making a slow, steady click-click-click while those of the girls were clicking like Geiger counters gone crazy. He wasn't even halfway through taking the leaves off his stem by the time the girls had snipped off all the buds on theirs. 'It takes experience,' said Angela. 'Everybody starts slow.'

'I guess so,' said Standing. By the time he had finished taking off the leaves, the girls had taken all the buds off two more stems apiece. Their hands were constantly in motion and the scissors attacked the buds from every direction. He began to snip off the buds, but he couldn't come close to matching the speed of the girls. And the faster he tried to go, the shoddier his work became. He would either cut too close to the bud and it would fall apart, or he'd cut too far from it and leave an unsightly section of stem sticking out. He picked up a third stem and began working on it. Angela glanced in his direction and said something to her sister in Chinese, and both girls giggled. He was certain they were laughing at him and he could understand why. They were professionals and he was a rank amateur.

Time seemed to slow to a crawl. The girls were able to chat and laugh as they worked, but the moment Standing stopped concentrating he'd make a bad cut. His hands were annoyingly sticky and that made it much harder to use the scissors. His fingers were aching and his wrists were sore and his back was burning from sitting in one position for so long. The girls were clearly aware of his discomfort and flashed him the occasional sympathetic glance, but he was there to work so they just left him to it. The girls emptied one container of stems, and then another. Standing was still on his first box. He really wanted a coffee but he didn't want to stop, even for a few minutes. He ploughed on, snipping as quickly as he could. Leaves in the bucket, buds in the box, stems in the other box. The thumb of his right hand had gone numb. He wasn't sure if it was cannabis or the pressure of the scissor handle restricting the blood flow. Eventually it got so bad he had to stop. He put the scissors on the table and shook his hand to try to restore the circulation.

'Are you okay?' asked Angela.

'Just a bit numb,' said Standing.

As he was shaking his hand in the air, Brett returned, without his holdall. 'Taking a break?' he said. Three cats were following him; one was large and black, the others were black-and-white and not more than a few months old, presumably her kittens.

'No, I'm good,' said Standing, picking up the scissors again.

Brett walked over to the table and looked down at the buds in his box. 'Slow going?' he asked.

'I'm starting to get the hang of it.'

Brett grinned at Angela and Amy. 'What do you think, girls? Can he cut it? No pun intended.'

'It's his first day, right?' asked Angela.

'Oh yes, he's a virgin trimmer,' said Brett.

'He'll get better,' said Amy.

Standing smiled thinly. It wasn't exactly a resounding vote of confidence, but then he knew he hadn't put in an inspiring performance. He looked down at the buds. There were several dozen of them, but he doubted they'd weigh much more than an ounce or two. 'There's obviously a knack to it,' he said.

'It's a skill that takes time to acquire,' said Brett. 'Though to be honest, having hands the size of shovels doesn't help.' He grinned at the girls. 'Anyway I've got plenty of other jobs that need doing, plus he's a good cook. He can take over the cooking.'

'What do you girls like eating?' asked Standing.

'We usually eat noodles,' said Angela.

'I can do spaghetti ten different ways, and that's sort of noodles.'

'Sounds good,' said Brett. 'Come on, I'll show you around some more before you demonstrate your culinary skills.'

He took Standing away from the tent and followed a narrow trail through the redwoods. 'Those girls have got skills, I'll give them that,' said Standing. 'And in time I'll get faster. But surely there are machines that can do that work?'

'There are, there absolutely are,' said Brett. 'But they ruin the product. You lose flavour and you lose potency. It's like cheese.'

Standing grinned. 'You've lost me there.'

Brett patted him on the back. 'Can you make cheese in a factory? Hell yeah. You can have Kraft cheese slices whizzing off a production line and you can slap it on a burger and you've got a cheeseburger. Put it on a piece of processed ham between two slices of bread and you've got a ham and cheese sandwich. But if you really want cheese, real cheese, then you go to France and pick up a camembert or a brie. You're English, you know about cheese. How great is a good cheddar? And what's that cheese with the mould in it?'

'Stilton.'

'Yeah, Stilton. That mould thing is fucked up but it's a great cheese all the same. So if you like cheese, if you really appreciate cheese, you don't want it produced in a factory. You want it made with love and care. And that's why my weed is so damn good. Because I love it and I take care of it. Those guys we sold to at the motel – did you see their faces when they opened the bags and smelled my weed? Potheads, yes, but connoisseurs. They wouldn't buy production-line weed.'

'So you sell to the top end of the market at a premium price? That makes sense.'

'So long as there are people out there that are prepared to pay for good weed, I'll be okay. But big pharma doesn't give a shit about quality, all that matters to them is the bottom line. So they mechanise where they can and they market the fuck out of it and the public just goes along with it.'

They reached a structure ten feet across and fifty feet long, made of aluminium hoops supporting a plastic cover. A makeshift greenhouse. Brett took him inside. There were hundreds of cannabis plants and the smell was almost overpowering. 'This is my flowering tent,' he said. 'They start in the nursery, then the veg room, then we bring them here. They'll be ready in two more weeks. I planned to do some trimming here tomorrow, you can help.'

'I thought we were trimming out there?'

'We trim the plants while they're growing. That leads to bigger and better buds.' He grinned. 'It's a lot easier than what you were doing, don't worry. It's basically just snipping a few leaves off each plant.' He reached over and pulled one of the plants towards him, then nodded his approval. 'It's a nice crop.'

'And when it's ready you clip the stems and take them to the trimming tent?'

'It depends whether I bring in any more trimmers, and whether they're okay with wet trimming. You've seen how messy it gets, not everyone is up for it.'

Standing's hands were sticky with resin and he'd transferred some of it to his neck and face. It was an annoyance and he hadn't been able to rub it off on to his jeans.

'If we can't get extra wet trimmers, we'll dry it.' He pulled another plant towards him and examined the buds, then smelled it. 'This is my own strain. It took me almost twenty years to get it to this stage and I don't really think I'll be able to improve it. It's as close to the perfect weed as you can get. I love the colour. That's a result of the homozygous dominant. It's got thick stems so the buds can get plenty of water. Short internodes. Strong veins. Tight bud clusters. The THC content is more than twenty-five per cent.'

'You sound like you're in love,' said Standing.

Brett laughed. 'Reckon I am,' he said. 'I love the frosty look.' He pointed at the buds, which glittered in the sunlight and looked as if they had been dusted with ice crystals. 'That glitter is the trichomes, they contain the THC. The more the sparkle, the greater the high. This strain has a very high THC level and a sweet, hashy taste with a spicy fruit finish, a bit like Christmas cake.'

'It's the THC that gives you the high, right?'

'Yeah, and it can vary widely. You can buy weed on the street with a THC level of five or less. Waste of time and money. This variant here, one pull on this would have the same effect as five or six bongs of the street crap. If they gave out Michelin stars for pot, this would be three stars, no discussion or argument.'

Brett took Standing out of the greenhouse and along another trail. In a small clearing were more cannabis plants. 'This is one of our outdoor plots,' said Brett. 'There's a dozen or so on my land. I keep them split up so they're less obvious from the air.' He went over to one of the plants, which almost came up to his chest. He pulled one of the stems towards him and sniffed it. 'It's good weed, but because they're exposed to the elements the buds get knocked about a bit and generally they're smaller than the greenhouse buds.'

On the far side of the clearing was another container covered in camouflage netting and surrounded by towering redwoods. Unlike the containers that were being used for sleeping and storage, this one was in its original condition with two doors at one end. Two cats were lying close to the open doors, basking in the sun. Inside were lines of wooden racks, mesh baskets hanging from the roof and a large dehumidifier. 'We cut the stems and bring them here to dry for six or seven days,' said Brett. 'We have to run a generator so there's an extra cost, but the trimming is a bit cheaper.'

He pointed at one of more than a dozen multi-layered baskets hanging from the roof. 'Once the buds have been trimmed they're dried out here. There's a whole skill to the drying side. The big firms use machines to speed up the drying process, but again that makes for inferior weed. Slow and steady wins the race.' He took Standing back outside and the two men closed the doors.

'All this camouflage, what's that about?' asked Standing, pointing at the netting that covered the container.

'They're using satellites to monitor the farms in Humboldt County, so we try to look as small as possible. The smaller we look, the less likely they are to come out. They still send helicopters and I've heard tell that they use drones.'

'By "they" you mean the DEA?'

'It used to be, but these days it's the federal and state licensing authorities.' He took Standing along another trail through the trees to a second outdoor cannabis field, slightly smaller than the first, then the trail looped back in the direction of the camp.

As they walked, Standing heard geese honking. 'Wild geese?' he said.

Brett chuckled. 'Guard geese,' he said.

The honking intensified as they rounded a bend and were faced with a six-feet-high chain link fence around another shipping container covered in camouflage netting. In the grassy space between the fence and the container were half a dozen large black-and-white geese, flapping their wings and honking angrily.

'Guard geese? Are you serious?'

'Hell, yeah,' said Brett. 'In ancient Rome it was geese that gave the alarm when the Gauls invaded. They're territorial, fearless and kick up a hell of a noise.' He reached into his pocket, pulled out a handful of pellets and threw them through the fence. The geese immediately started to gobble them up. Brett took a keychain from his pocket and unlocked a large padlock so that he could pull open the gate. He threw more pellets on the ground and waved for Standing to follow him inside. 'You'll be all right so long as you're with me.' He closed the gate behind them and walked slowly to the container as the geese continued to peck at their food. Brett opened another padlock and Standing helped him pull the doors open.

The container was packed with rows of wooden shelving. The shelves on the right were filled with empty wide-mouthed glass jars, the ones on the left had the same type of jars filled with cannabis buds. Brett picked up one of the filled jars.

'These here are the famous Mason jars. Most growers use them. You can buy them online and in Walmart. In fact they're one of Walmart's best sellers in California.' Brett gave the jar to Standing. 'This is where we cure the buds, and it's where we separate the men from the boys. It's what raises my weed to the next level.'

'By putting it in a jar?'

Brett laughed. 'It's all about drying them just the right amount. Not dry enough and you'll get mould and the weed is ruined. Dry the buds too much and they fall apart and you lose all the flavour. It's a skill, it really is. Drying and curing breaks down the chlorophyll, which makes the smoke smoother and improves the flavour. When the buds are first harvested all you really smell is the "cut grass" fragrance. Curing gets rid of that and allows the more subtle fragrances to come through. And it takes out the harshness, it makes it a much smoother smoke. Most of the downsides of smoking weed that people talk about – the headaches, the anxiety, the paranoia – are the result of not getting the drying and curing right.'

Standing held up the jar. 'How much is in here?'

'It's what they call a thirty-two ounce jar, but that's the volume. We usually get about an ounce in, that's filling it up three-quarters. I did try it with bigger jars but they're more likely to go mouldy. Smaller works but the one-quart is optimal. And you can use different types of jars, but in my experience they don't seal as well.' He took the jar from Standing and shook it so that the buds moved around. 'You do that on a regular basis. If they're sticking together it means they're too wet, so you take the lids off a while. Once they've dried a bit you reseal. For the first week or so you air them every day and check the humidity. After a few weeks if they stay in what we call the cure zone, then you can start opening once a month. Assuming everything is okay, the quality should improve week by week for the next six months or so. After that it pretty much plateaus so that's when we sell it. We can sell earlier if we're pushed, but ideally you want to cure it for six months.'

'And you sell everything you produce?'

Brett nodded. 'At the moment, yes. The problem is that they're making it harder for us to sell to the dispensaries, so we have no choice other than to sell on the black market. But it's holding up. Worst comes to the worst we can repackage for long-term storage, but so far so good.'

'Does weed go off?'

'Providing it's been dried and cured properly, it won't go off but it will gradually lose its potency.' He took the jar from Standing and put it back on the shelf.

Standing looked around. 'So how much is this lot worth?'

Brett laughed. 'Enough for me to keep the guard geese outside,' he said.

'Wouldn't dogs be better?'

'Dogs take a lot of feeding, and they need exercise. You couldn't keep the dogs penned up twenty-four-seven. Plus any dog, no matter how well trained, is going to bolt down a piece of prime steak. And if the steak is drugged, the dogs are out like a light.'

'Couldn't robbers bribe the geese?'

Brett shook his head. 'You'd have to know what they eat, and they're fussy. And they'd be making a racket long before you got near the container. You can hear the noise from half a mile away.'

They walked out to find the geese lined up like soldiers on parade. Brett chucked them a handful of pellets. 'Stand at ease, boys,' he said. As the birds pecked at their food, Brett closed and padlocked the container doors and then slipped through the gate with Standing. 'Okay, let's head back and you can impress the girls with your culinary skills,' said Brett.

CHAPTER 15

B rett took a hit from his bong, then handed it over to Standing, leant back and put his feet on the coffee table. 'That spaghetti bolognese was pretty darn good,' said Brett. 'The girls were impressed.' There were two black cats curled up on the sofa next to him and he absent-mindedly stroked one behind the ears. It purred with contentment and rubbed its head against his hand.

'I've never used venison before, but it seemed to work okay,' said Standing. He had cooked the pasta and sauce in pans on the open fire and Brett and the girls had eaten the lot. It looked as if he'd nailed the job of camp cook.

'Meat-wise, I tend to kill what I eat,' said Brett. 'There's rabbits and snakes and every now and again I go out and shoot a deer. I'm about due to restock the larder. Maybe tomorrow we'll go out and do some hunting.'

Standing took a lungful of smoke, held it for two seconds, then exhaled. The euphoria hit him almost immediately, spreading out from his chest. He grinned. 'Wow.' He put the bong down on the coffee table and stretched out his legs.

'So you feel like staying here for a while?' asked Brett.

'You know that my only other option is to pitch my tent in the woods, right?'

Brett laughed. 'Guy like you, you'll find work easily enough.'

'My trimming skills, you mean?'

'Your military background. The way you carry yourself. You'd find a job on the security details of one of the bigger farms. Not the cartels because they use their own people, but there are a lot of other big operations out there.'

'I'm fine here if you'll have me.'

'There's plenty of work for you to do. I showed you the curing container, there's a big batch of jars that need opening and shaking every day. And you can help me with the trimming in the greenhouse. I've also got a few more deliveries coming up, and it would be useful to have you as my wingman.'

'Sounds like a plan,' said Standing.

'Let's say two hundred a day while you're learning the ropes. We can look at it again in a few weeks.'

'Perfect,' said Standing. He hated having to lie to Brett, but there was no alternative. The truth was that Standing was in Humboldt County to track down and kill a rogue Navy SEAL, and no matter how many bongs Brett smoked he wasn't going to take that news well. Brett clearly knew the area and most of the people who lived on the mountain, and would be a valuable source of intel providing that Standing could keep him on side.

'Do you have any long-term plans?' asked Brett.

'I'm just taking life day by day,' said Standing. 'Covid turned the world on its head. The cops forced you to stay home, you couldn't visit the dentist or get your hair cut, you were only allowed out to exercise or buy food. I realised then that it was all about controlling the population and I didn't want any part of it.'

'Covid never made it to the mountain,' said Brett with a smile. 'We've always had social distancing here. Nothing really changed. They put a sign on the door of the general store saying you had to wear a mask but nobody really did. It was business as usual. In fact business actually boomed because during the lockdowns, potheads tended to increase their consumption.'

'Seems to me that it's only the start,' said Standing. 'They took away all our freedoms once, they'll do it again, for sure. I could see the writing on the wall and figured I'd be better off in the land of the free and the home of the brave.'

'In the bar you said you had a friend out here.'

'Yeah. Frenchy. But I haven't heard from him for a while. He made it sound like there was money to be made out here.' Standing grinned. 'Looks like he was right.'

'You won't make a fortune, but you won't starve,' said Brett. 'Not sure what the long-term prospects are but at my age long-term isn't really an issue.'

'You're fit and healthy, I don't see that changing in the near future,' said Standing. 'Hell, you're living proof that cannabis is good for you.'

'That and Jack Daniel's,' said Brett. He took a deep breath and exhaled slowly, looking at the bong, clearly trying to decide if he wanted another hit or not. 'This Frenchy, you got a picture?' he asked.

'Yeah, in my bag.' Actually the photograph was in Standing's coat pocket but it might appear strange to be carrying it around with him. 'I'll dig it out tomorrow.'

'Navy SEAL, you said?'

'Yeah. He packed it in, though. Same as me, didn't like following orders. Said he was happy enough in combat, it was being back at base that used to drive him crazy.'

'They wore jeans in Vietnam, did you know that?'

'Who did?'

'The SEALs.'

'You're kidding.'

Brett shook his head. 'Hand to God,' he said. 'Levi's. They reckoned they stood up to the jungle better than fatigues and were protection against mosquitoes and leeches. What the SEALs didn't tell you was that under the Levi's they usually wore pantyhose.' He chuckled. 'Now that didn't quite fit with the gung-ho image, did it?'

Standing laughed. 'What about you, Brett? What did you do in Vietnam?'

'I didn't wear pantyhose, that's for damn sure.' He chuckled. 'Me, I was a tunnel rat. Based in Saigon but they ran us back and forth to the tunnels of Cu Chi. You heard about them, right?'

Standing nodded. 'I've been there.'

Brett's jaw dropped. 'No fucking way.'

'Every fucking way,' said Standing. 'I was out in Cambodia on a training operation a few years ago and a bunch of us did a side trip to Thailand and Vietnam. We did two days in Saigon and went on a trip to the tunnels. You know it's a tourist attraction now?'

'Are you fucking joking?'

Standing laughed. 'Swear to God,' he said. 'They widened some of the tunnels and put in electric lights and they let you crawl through. For a few dollars they'll rent you VC black pyjamas so you can look the part. Then afterwards you can fire an AK-47 or an M60. They give you the whole Vietnam War experience.'

Brett shook his head in amazement. 'I bet getting shot in the dark wasn't part of the experience?'

'No, but I can imagine what being in those tunnels must have been like.'

'It was interesting, man. The tunnels were tiny and all we had was a flashlight and a .38 revolver. They were full of booby traps and you never knew what was around the next corner.' He shuddered. 'It wasn't no tourist thing.'

Standing had learnt about the tunnels during his trip. The Viet Cong had used a network of them across the country to travel undetected and to store military supplies. Troops were able to sleep underground and treat their wounded. There were some seventy-five miles of tunnels in Cu Chi, around fifteen miles north-west of Saigon, and they were part of a much larger network that covered most of South Vietnam. 'How did you get to be a tunnel rat?' asked Standing.

'I was a lot smaller in those days,' said Brett. 'They were looking for volunteers and I just put my hand up.' He grinned. 'What can I say? The impetuosity of youth.'

'And why the revolver? I'd have thought you'd want something like a Colt .45.'

Brett shrugged. 'They were quieter, and there was less of a flash. Also it was wet and muddy underground and revolvers are less likely to jam.'

'You must have been scared to death. I got claustrophobic just crawling along with a group of tourists.'

'It was scary, but it was the ultimate game of hide and seek. I was too young to know any better. But provided you kept your wits about you, you could minimise the risks. If there were any VC down there, there'd usually hear you coming and nine times out of ten they'd scurry off like rats. That just left the booby-traps to deal with. Scorpions, snakes, punji sticks, explosives. You worked slowly and methodically and cleared the tunnel section by section, gathered any intel and then you'd blow it up to seal it.'

'I don't think I could ever have done that.'

'Yeah, we were a special breed. We had a motto: *Non Gratus Anus Rodentum.* "Not worth a rat's ass". That sort of summed up how we felt. But we volunteered. Nobody forced us. Even so, not everyone could handle the pressure. What about you? You enjoy combat?'

Standing screwed up his face as he considered the question. 'Enjoy' wasn't the right word. You might enjoy a cold beer or a hot meal, or a session in the gym or a game of football, but enjoyment didn't really describe how he felt when people were trying to kill him. Adrenaline kicked in, of course, along with endorphins, serotonin, dopamine, oxytocin and all the other chemicals that the body needed to gear itself for a fight. That gave him a high, there was no doubt about that, but he hadn't joined the SAS to get high.

'No easy answer, right?' said Brett, sensing that he was having trouble coming up with one.

'You've been there, you've walked the walk, it's not about enjoying, is it? But you never feel more alive than when you're close to losing your life. I just feel so connected with myself when I'm in combat. It's as if my body knows exactly what to do to protect itself. I don't have to plan, I don't have to think, it just happens. I can be in a firefight and I automatically know where the threats are coming from and the best way to neutralise them. It drove my officers crazy. They'd work out a strategy based on what they'd been taught – covering fire, linear ambush all that good stuff. Then the shooting would start and I'd do my own thing. The officers would be pissed off but I was never hurt and I never lost a man. If they said anything I'd tell them to go fuck themselves. There's no way I was going to ignore my instincts, which I know are always right, to follow the orders of a man who learnt everything from a textbook.' He grinned. 'But that's not answering your question, is it? I don't enjoy the combat, I don't take any pleasure in killing, but when I'm under fire it's as if I'm totally connected to the universe. I can see everything, I can hear everything, I can feel everything, time seems to almost stop and I'm just there in the middle of it. And there's the satisfaction of knowing that I'm surviving this and the enemy isn't.'

'As good as sex?' said Brett.

'Better,' said Standing, without hesitation.

'Yeah, I could see something of that when you faced up to those bikers at The Shack. The guy who came at you from behind, you didn't turn to look at him, you just knew he was going to push you. And watching as you took them down, hell, it was like watching a game of chess, but with a grandmaster playing a kid. Every move they made, you had the counter ready. It didn't matter what they did, you were ready. I guess I did wonder what you'd do if they had a gun, but you were lucky on that score.'

Standing shook his head. 'They didn't have guns, I checked them out when they were in the bar. There was a shotgun on one of the bikes but they didn't make a move to get it. I saw the knife but the chain was a bit of a surprise.'

'And the other thing I noticed was that you were totally calm. You weren't angry or tense, you just did what you had to do to get the job done.'

'I don't get angry in a fight,' said Standing. 'I almost never do. I just react. There's no real emotion in it.'

'And no fear?'

Standing laughed. 'At the time, no. It's like there's no time for fear. It's like when you parachute. As you're getting ready to jump there's always the apprehension, the knowledge that something could go wrong and it'll be your last jump, but as soon as you're out of the plane there's no fear. Combat's the same for me. Before it kicks off, sure, I'm as nervous and jittery as the next man. Probably because there's nothing I can do, nothing I can react to. But once the action starts, I'm too busy to be scared.'

Brett chuckled. 'Man, I wish I was like that. Every second I was down the tunnels I was scared shitless.'

'That's what you do in the military. You face the danger, you walk towards the rounds. I'm just lucky that for some reason I'm hard-wired not to feel fear.' He laughed. 'I'm also hard-wired to react instinctively. That's great in combat, but not so great when the bullets aren't flying. I've punched a few officers in my time because they shoved me or got in my face. My therapist says I should count to ten, and I do most of the time.'

'Therapist? You serious?'

'Yeah, it was either that or be dishonourably discharged.'

'Did it work?'

'I'm not in the army any more, so I guess that answers your question.'

Brett leant forward and picked up his bong and lighter. Standing genuinely liked the man and he had been so open and helpful that he didn't deserve to be lied to. But if he told Brett that he was still in the army, his story would make no sense. One lie always leads to another, and Standing was already having to think carefully about every statement he made. Even telling Brett about the trip to Vietnam had raised the question of what exactly he had been doing in Cambodia, which might at some point lead to more lies.

Brett lit the cannabis and filled the bong with smoke. He put down the lighter, took out the bowl, and inhaled the smoke. He started to chuckle and handed the bong to Standing. Standing grinned. 'Yeah,' he said. 'Don't mind if I do.'

CHAPTER 16

Standing woke to the sound of knocking on his door. He rolled out of bed and padded across the container. 'Wakey wakey, rise and shine!' called Brett. Standing looked at his watch. It was six o'clock in the morning. He pulled back the bolt and opened the door. The sky was streaked with red, dawn was only minutes away. Brett was wearing a jacket in a camouflage pattern and a matching baseball cap. Over his shoulder was a rifle.

'Sorry, mate,' said Standing. 'I completely forgot.'

Brett laughed. 'Yeah, the weed can do that,' he said. 'The best laid plans and all that. Get dressed, the coffee's on.'

Standing closed the door. Brett had said they'd go deer-hunting at dawn at some point the previous evening, but Standing hadn't realised it was a firm arrangement. He dressed quickly and pulled on his boots, then joined Brett at the camp-fire. Brett poured coffee into a mug and gave it to him. Standing got a better look at the rifle that Brett was carrying. It was a Remington Model Seven, a bolt-action gun with a low-power scope. Brett smiled when he saw Standing checking it out. 'Yeah, I'm old school,' he said. 'Most hunters these days turn their noses up at bolt-action, but to be honest, if I can't bring a deer down with one shot then I shouldn't be out hunting in the first place.'

'I hear you,' said Standing. 'And in the forest you're never going to be shooting more than a hundred yards or so.'

'Exactly,' said Brett.

'Does it take the Winchester .308 cartridge?'

'You know your guns.'

'The reason I remember that is because the .308 round is pretty much identical to the 7.62x51mm NATO cartridge. In fact the rounds are interchangeable, though the .308 packs more of a punch. I actually met a SEAL out in Afghanistan who went out on operations with a Model Seven. He used to carry his sidearm in a cowboy holster, too.'

Brett passed the rifle to Standing. 'I'm not sure it would be my weapon of choice in the desert, but it's perfect for the forest. It's light and the barrel is short so that it doesn't get caught in the undergrowth. And like you said, I'm not going to be taking super-long shots.'

Standing put down his coffee and checked the action of the rifle. It was decades old but had been well maintained. He nodded his approval and gave it back to Brett. 'Speaking of SEALs, here's that picture I mentioned.' He took the photograph from his coat pocket and gave it to Brett.

Brett studied it thoughtfully. 'What did you say his name was?'

'French. Ryan French. Everyone called him Frenchy.'

Brett shook his head. 'Nah, I've not seen him. Not up close, anyway. But I'll keep my eyes open.'

Standing took back the picture. 'What's the plan?' he asked, picking up his coffee.

'We'll take a walk through the woods and see what's on offer. We're not trophy hunting, we just need to replenish the larder. I've seen tracks about a mile north of here and it looks like they're from a couple of yearlings, but we'll take what we can get.'

They finished their coffees and then headed along the track that led to the drying container. A smaller track led off to the left and Brett followed it. The track was so narrow that they had to walk in single file. Within minutes they were swallowed up by the trees. They walked for half an hour and reached a small clearing. Brett stopped and took a water bottle from his belt. He offered it to Standing, who shook his head. 'I'm good,' he said.

Brett unscrewed the cap and took a long swig. 'So is this still your land?' asked Standing.

'No, my land ends about a hundred yards beyond the drying container,' said Brett. 'We don't bother with boundary markings out here.'

'So you have to get permission from the landowner, right?'

Brett chuckled. 'In writing, yes. That's the law. And you have to apply for a licence. In theory. But out here no one really pays much attention to the law when it comes to hunting. The California Department of Fish and Wildlife has a comprehensive deer management programme, but you won't see hide nor hair of their people. We don't hunt for trophies out here, we hunt to eat, and no bureaucrat is going to tell us what we can and can't put in our larder.'

'So the land we're on now, who owns it?'

Brett looked around the clearing. 'To the right is a thirty-five acre parcel that's owned by some accountancy firm in Seattle. They've never done anything with it. To the left and ahead of us is a fifty-acre plot that they say is owned by a dentist in San Francisco who likes to hunt, but I've never seen him. Some plots are owned by families who moved away years ago.

When I came here land was so cheap they were practically giving it away, so if someone packed up and left it was hardly worth trying to sell it. There was a lot of squatting back then because the land just wasn't being used. You could just pitch a tent or build a cabin and no one would bother you. Even now there's hundreds, maybe thousands, of acres that no one would lay claim to.' He clipped his bottle back on to his belt and began walking again. They crossed the clearing and were soon surrounded again by redwoods.

Brett stopped and held up his hand in a clenched fist. Standing paused. Something was rustling through the undergrowth to their right. Brett chambered a round and brought the gun up to his shoulder. He peered through the scope as the rustling got closer. Just as Standing realised that the sound was too small to be a deer, a grey rabbit hopped into view. It sat back on its hind legs, its nose twitching as it sniffed the air. Brett laughed. 'It's your lucky day, bunny,' he said. The rabbit flinched at the sound of his voice and disappeared into the undergrowth.

Brett lowered his rifle and began walking again. Standing followed. There were insects clicking and whirring, and the occasional flutter of a bird up in the tree canopy. The sun was still low in the sky, so the forest was still gloomy with long shadows rippling along the ground. The air was damp and earthy and cobwebs on the trees were dotted with dew.

Brett stopped again and held up his fist. Standing paused. Something was coming through the forest towards them, something much bigger than a rabbit. Brett grinned at Standing and nodded, then raised his rifle.

Standing moved his head slowly, trying to look through the trees. Forests and jungles were the same, they forced the eyes to only see things close up so the brain began to see just a wall of green or brown. The trick was to relax the eyes and try to focus further in the distance, and to keep the head moving so that peripheral vision would kick in. Brett was doing the same, focusing on the part of the forest where the noise was coming from but moving his head from side to side.

Standing saw a flash of brown among the trees. And he heard a whimpering sound.

Brett leant against a tree to give himself extra stability as he peered through the scope.

Whatever was moving through the undergrowth suddenly stopped. Standing could hear his own breathing. Brett was totally focused on the forest ahead of him, his finger tightening on the trigger.

A twig cracked and then there was a rustling of leaves. Something moved in the distance, brown and black, then there was a flash of white. It was coming towards them. More twigs cracked. Whatever it was, it was big. Standing wanted to ask Brett if it could be a bear, but he figured the man had lived in the area long enough to know what the dangers were and he didn't want to risk throwing him off his shot.

It was moving faster now, crashing through the undergrowth. Another flash of brown. And black. And blue.

'Hold your fire!' shouted Standing.

'Are you kidding me?' yelled Brett, still peering down his scope, his finger tight on the trigger.

'It's not a deer!'

Just as the words left his mouth, a young woman burst through a bush, her eyes wide and her mouth open, her face streaked with tears. She had long brown hair, a black sweatshirt with a marijuana leaf on it and blue jeans. 'Please help me!' she cried.

She staggered towards them, her arms outstretched. She was in her early twenties, her face and hands covered in scratches, and there were damp patches on the knees of her jeans. Standing hurried towards her and just as he reached her the strength went from her legs and she collapsed. He caught her and picked her up. Her eyes were closed, so he lowered her to the ground and sat her down with her back to a tree.

Brett started to move towards him. Standing shook his head, pointed his first and second fingers at his eyes and then pointed them in the direction the girl had come from. If she was being chased by anything then Brett needed to keep his eyes open. Brett swung the rifle up to his shoulder and kept a look out as Standing checked the girl. She didn't seem to be injured but she was trembling and clearly exhausted. 'What happened?' he asked.

'They were keeping me prisoner,' she gasped. 'They were making me work and they were doing things to me.'

'Who? Who was doing that to you?'

'Their names are Anton and Stanislav.'

'Russians?'

She shook her head. Her eyes were still closed. 'Bulgarians.'

Standing looked over at Brett. 'All clear,' said Brett. 'She okay?'

'Exhausted, but nothing serious.' He put a hand on the girl's shoulder. 'My name is Dale. What's yours?'

She opened her eyes. They were pale blue, almost grey, and they were brimming with tears. 'Brianna,' she said.

'Okay, Brianna, can you walk? We need to go to our place. It's three miles away.'

She nodded. 'I can walk. But you have to help my friends. They're still prisoners.'

He helped her to her feet. 'We need to get you somewhere safe first,' he said. He put his arm around her so that she could lean against him as they walked. Brett followed, cradling the rifle. He handed her his water bottle and she gulped some down greedily.

'Were they chasing you?' asked Standing.

'I don't think so,' she said. 'I mean, I didn't hear them. But they would have noticed that I'd gone.'

'You were on a farm?' asked Brett.

'Yes. I've been there for two months but they wouldn't pay me and they were making us do stuff.' She shuddered.

'How far away is the farm?' asked Standing.

'I don't know. I was lost, I didn't know where I was.'

'What time did you run away?'

'Just after it went dark.'

'So half past eight? Nine?'

'I guess. They kept my phone and I don't have a watch so I don't know what time it was. But the sun had gone down.'

'And did you keep moving all night?'

'I couldn't, it was too dark. I got as far from their camp as I could and then I curled up in a bush. I didn't sleep, I was too scared, I thought they would come after me.'

'So you waited until dawn?'

She nodded. 'As soon as I could see where I was going, I started running. I drank from a stream, that was the only water I had.'

Standing looked over at Brett. 'What do you think? Ten miles? Fifteen?'

'It a tough call because she probably wouldn't be moving

in a straight line. She'd be following the terrain most of the time.'

Brianna stumbled and Standing had to hold her up. They continued moving, but after about a mile she was having trouble walking so he picked her up and piggy-backed her. He was able to move faster with her on his back than walking with her, and half an hour later they were back on Brett's farm.

'Put her in the room you're using,' said Brett. He went to put his rifle away as Standing helped the girl around the containers and through the door to his room. She collapsed on one of the lower bunks and curled up into a foetal ball with her back to him. Standing covered her with a blanket.

Brett appeared at the door. 'Is she okay?'

'She's exhausted.'

'Okay, let her get some sleep. We need to talk.' Brett threw more wood on the fire and made a fresh pot of coffee.

Standing dropped down on to one of the deckchairs and stretched out his legs. 'Does this happen a lot?' he asked.

'It's the first time I've had it happen to me, but I've heard of people running away from farms where they've been abused.'

'And we call the cops, right?'

'It's not as easy as that. The sheriff's department has four patrol stations – Garberville, McKinleyville, Trinity River and the main one in Eureka. Now Garberville is the closest but they're only open between the hours of eight o'clock and four-thirty, Monday to Friday. But even if we go right now, there's no guarantee that there'll be a sheriff there to take a report. The lovely Carla on reception will put out a call, but they cover a lot of area. And if they do find a sheriff to take a report, he's not going to do anything. He's not going to drive out to the farm and start asking questions, not on his own.

He'd need back-up before driving into the forest and his bosses almost certainly won't authorise said back-up. They just don't have the resources.'

'Brett, the girl says she was abused. I'm assuming that means rape.'

'I hear you, I really do. But what seems to have happened to that girl happens all the time. They came here to work thinking they're going to make a small fortune and then they don't get paid. The cops can't help because usually the work is illegal anyway. But even if the work was legal, the cops would say not getting paid was a civil matter. So far as the rape goes . . .' He shrugged. 'Look, I'm not defending what's happening, if it was up to me I'd toss them in jail and throw away the key. But it's the Wild West out here and a lot of time these kids get out of their depth. Someone spins them a line and takes them into the wilderness and then who knows what happens? Pretty girl comes and says she wants to work, it doesn't take much for one of these guys to put pressure on her to do other things for him. Sometimes the girls are willing, sometimes they just say no and it's accepted, but yeah, there are some mean motherfuckers out here who won't take no for an answer. It's not just the girls that get abused, plenty of young men do too.'

'So what are we going to do?'

Brett scratched his chin. 'I don't know yet. Let her rest and then we'll talk to her. In the meantime, we've still got to fill the larder. Make us fresh coffee and we'll head on out again.'

CHAPTER 17

They eventually found a small deer about three miles north of the farm. Brett despatched it with a single shot, then hung it head down from a low branch and expertly skinned and gutted it with a large knife, before taking off the head. He wrapped the meat in a sheet of plastic and gave it to Standing to carry. 'That'll last us a week or two,' he said.

Standing put it over his shoulder and followed Brett as they headed back to the farm. 'Any idea where Brianna might have been working?' he asked as they walked.

'There's a number of small farms up that way, no big operations so far as I know,' Brett replied.

'Bulgarians, she said. Is that unusual?'

'There's been a long-running problem with organised crime in Humboldt and Bulgarians keep coming up. Don't ask me why. So yeah, it's possible they're Bulgarians.'

'You come across them?'

'No, they keep to themselves. The Russians too. They don't use the local store, you never see them in the bars.'

They reached the farm and Brett took him around the back of the containers where there was a solar-powered freezer and a metal table. Standing dropped the carcass down on to the table. Brett unwrapped it and then used his knife to cut it into manageable pieces, which Standing placed into the freezer.

When they were finished they were both splattered with blood. 'We should shower,' said Brett.

'Not together, right?'

Brett laughed. 'Damn right. I'll get you a towel and you can go first.'

'That's okay, I've got my own towel.' He went around to his room and eased the door open. Brianna was still curled up and snoring softly. Standing tiptoed over to his rucksack and pulled out clean clothes and a towel and let himself out.

Brett was waiting for him and took him around the container. At the far end there was an open-topped canvas tent below a large plastic barrel that had been placed on the top of the container. There was a small length of hose with a tap on it, connected to a plastic shower head. 'This works just fine,' said Brett. 'I've never been able to work out a way of getting the water up there without climbing up and pouring it in myself. But now that's another job you can do for me at some point.'

'No problem,' said Standing. As Brett walked away he stripped off his clothes and showered. There were plastic bottles of shampoo and soap on the ground and he lathered himself up before rinsing and turning off the water flow. He dried himself off and put on clean clothes.

He dropped off his dirty clothes and the towel in his bedroom, taking care not to disturb Brianna. Brett was back in his deckchair. 'Coffee's on,' he said nodding at the fire. Standing picked up the pot. Brett grinned at him. 'Pour me one while you're up,' he said.

Standing poured two coffees and gave one to Brett. 'Why don't you get started on dinner,' said Brett. 'See what the deer tastes like.' He stood up and gestured with his mug. 'I've got a few vegetables and stuff over here, come and have a look.'

He took Standing across the track and through a group of redwoods to a clearing, which had been dug over and planted with neat rows of vegetables. Brett pointed out his various crops. 'Potatoes, carrots, onions, cabbages, turnips,' he said. 'I've got garlic growing here and various herbs. Rosemary, basil, mint, sage, coriander and chives.'

'That's awesome, Brett,' said Standing, genuinely impressed. 'Green fingers.'

'When it was just me I only ever had to buy the essentials from the store,' said Brett. 'Jack Daniel's and beer. Everything else I either grew or shot. Bit different now that the girls are here, because they need rice and noodles and breakfast cereal. Anyway, take what you need from here, throw in some venison, and see how you get on.'

As Brett headed over to shower, Standing picked some vegetables. He found a wooden basket and pretty much filled it, then took it over to the table in the washing-up area. For the next half an hour he cleaned and chopped vegetables and prepared the venison, placed it all in a metal pot and carried it over to the fire. Two black-and-white cats appeared and they sat and watched him work. Eventually Brett reappeared, drying his hair with a towel. He stood over the pot and sniffed. 'Smells good,' he said. 'Okay, let's see how the girls are getting on.'

They walked over to the trimming tent where Angela and Amy were hard at work trimming individual buds. If anything they were snipping away even faster than when they had been working on the stems. It was close to two o'clock so they had probably been working for six hours but there was no sign of them flagging. The plastic box on the table in front of them was almost full and there were three full boxes stacked on the floor. 'You'll be glad to hear that Dale is cooking again,' said Brett.

'Great, what are we having?' asked Amy as she worked on a bud the size of a small lemon.

'Venison casserole,' said Standing. 'Or stew. Maybe even goulash. Where I'm from we call it pot luck.'

'Sounds delicious,' said Angela, and Standing couldn't tell if she was being serious or not.

'Grab those,' said Brett, nodding at the boxes on the floor. As Standing picked them up, Brett took the box of buds from the table and replaced it with an empty one. They headed down the track to the drying container. Standing followed him inside. Brett began placing the buds on the net racks, close together but not touching. 'The buds stay here until they're dry to the touch,' said Brett. 'You have to check them every day. If it's too humid and they're not drying then I bring in a fan or a dehumidifier. It should take between three and seven days. You can just dry the whole stem and clip the buds off later, but in my experience you tend to get more mould that way so I always prefer to dry the buds individually.' He picked up a bud that had been drying and gave it to Standing. 'This is about right. You want them dry, but not too dry. On the big farms they might use ovens or even microwaves to speed up the process – for a good product, you need to do it slowly.'

They finished putting the buds on to the racks and took the empty boxes back to the trimming tent. The two girls had already half-filled the box on the table. 'We'll eat here,' said Brett. 'In about half an hour.' He looked over at Standing. 'Let's go talk to our mystery girl.'

On the way, Brett grabbed a bottle of water from his room. Brianna was still sleeping but she rolled over and opened her eyes when she heard them walk in. At first she flinched as if she was about to be struck, but she relaxed when she saw who it was. 'I thought this was a dream,' she said. She sat up and looked around, then put her hands over her face. 'I can't believe I actually got away.'

Brett handed her the bottle of water and pulled over a wooden chair. He sat down. Standing sat on his bunk. 'Are you okay? How do you feel?'

She drank some water and wiped her mouth with the back of her hand. 'I'm just exhausted.'

'You were in the woods for more than twelve hours, right?' said Standing.

'I told you that? I don't remember.'

'Tell us again what happened,' said Brett.

She sniffed and stared at the end of her bunk. 'I was trimming on a farm with my friend Olivia. We got the job on the internet and it sounded great. Two hundred dollars a pound and they said most trimmers could do two pounds a day. So we got the bus to Eureka, and Anton and Stanislav met us in their van. We had to sit in the back. There were no windows, so we couldn't see where we were and they didn't let us out until we arrived at the farm.' She sniffed. 'We knew right away there was something wrong. They'd been sending us pictures of this amazing place with a rec room and a TV room and they said they had parties every weekend and there was great Wi-Fi. What we saw was two dirty shacks surrounded by piles of garbage and burnt-out cars. They said we would have our own room but all we had was a broken down shack with metal beds in it. It smelled so bad and there were rats and cockroaches and spiders everywhere. And we were the only trimmers. They said more were coming. In the emails they sent us photographs of loads of guys working. All happy and smiling and having fun.' She sighed. 'I can't believe we were so stupid.'

'It happens,' said Brett.

'Olivia wanted to leave straight away but they said we had agreed to work and they weren't going to drive us back to Eureka. So we started trimming. They made us work from dawn to dusk and all we had to eat were cans of soup and sardines. After a week we asked if we could get paid and they said no, they would pay us after a month. The month came and they said they only paid at the end of the second month. We said we wanted to go and that's when they started chaining us up at night. They chained us to the beds. We had to shout if we wanted to use the bathroom but they got angry if we disturbed them so we tried not to go.'

'And you said they abused you?'

She shuddered and closed her eyes. 'I don't want to talk about that,' she said.

'Okay, no problem,' said Standing. 'But you're safe now. No one can hurt you here.'

She opened her eyes. 'But the others? The others are still there.'

'So how many girls were on the farm?' asked Standing.

'Me and Olivia arrived together and then they got a new girl, Emma, a few weeks ago.'

'Whoa!' said Standing. 'Emma Mackenzie?'

'I don't know her full name. She's from Sacramento.'

Standing got up and hurried over to his coat. He pulled out the flyer and showed it to Brianna. She gasped. 'Yes, that's Emma.'

Standing sat down and looked at Brett. 'I met her mother outside the general store. She's worried sick.'

Brett took the flyer and read it. 'Poor kid,' he said.

'How did you escape, Brianna?' asked Standing.

'They chained us to the bed with this handcuff-like thing, with about three feet of chain. My feet are quite small and they didn't always fasten them tightly. I started not washing my hands and kept them covered in cannabis residue and I'd rub it around my ankle. Last night I could slip it off. I didn't want to leave the others but they said I had to get help.' She looked at Standing, her eyes brimming with tears. 'We have to rescue them. Can we call the police? Do you have a phone?'

'Phones don't work out here, Brianna.'

Standing looked at Brett. 'We could drive into town.'

'Go to the cops about the missing girl? They wouldn't care. In fact we'd be telling them that she's alive so she'd be one less missing person to worry about.'

'They wouldn't visit the farm?'

'You can try if you want. But I'd rather you didn't mention me or my place. The whole point of being under the radar is that I stay there.'

'But you don't think they'd go and look for her?'

'If you tell them that Bulgarian gangsters are involved, they'll definitely not come out on their own. They might put in for a SWAT team but I don't see them doing that for a missing girl. If she was underage, maybe. But she's an adult who just made a bad decision in a county that's full of bad decisions.'

'You can't just leave her and Olivia there,' said Brianna. 'I promised them I'd get help.'

'We'll get them out of there, don't worry,' said Standing.

'You promise?' she asked him earnestly.

'Cross my heart.'

'When?'

Standing looked across at Brett. 'What do you think?'

Brett's eyes narrowed. 'About what?'

'We need to rescue those girls, Brett. If the cops won't do it, then we have to.'

'We?'

Standing grinned. 'I'm happy to go on my own,' he said.

'You would too, wouldn't you?'

'Who dares wins,' said Standing. He felt his stomach lurch as he realised his mistake. Would Brett know that 'Who Dares Wins' was the motto of the SAS? He forced a smile. 'Somebody has to get those girls out. And the sooner the better.'

'Tonight?' said Brett.

'That's what I was thinking.'

Brett nodded slowly. 'Okay,' he said, 'Count me in.'

'So you'll rescue them?' asked Brianna.

'We'll do our best,' said Standing.

CHAPTER 18

'This is not half bad,' said Brett, popping another chunk of venison into his mouth. They had cleared the trimming equipment and they were all sitting around the table eating Standing's casserole with rice.

Brianna grinned. 'This is the first real food I've had in two months,' she said.

Angela and Amy nodded in agreement. 'It's good,' said Amy.

'It tastes a bit like the bolognese you made last night,' said Angela.

'I'm a cook rather than a chef,' said Standing.

'What's the difference?' asked Angela.

'Flair, I guess,' said Standing. 'Chefs prepare food to impress people, cooks just do it to feed them.'

'So you've been trimming, Brianna?' asked Amy.

Brianna nodded. 'Yes, but it wasn't a good experience. What's it like working here?'

'Brett beats us if we don't work hard enough,' said Angela.

Amy nodded in agreement. 'With a big stick.'

Brianna's mouth opened in shock and she stared at Brett in horror until the two Taiwanese girls burst into giggles. 'Sorry, Brianna, we're just kidding,' said Amy.

'Mr Mullican is a great boss,' said Angela. 'We've worked

with him three times and he's always been a sweetie.' She looked at her sister. 'Is that right? Sweetie?'

'Yes,' said Amy. 'That's exactly what he is. A sweetie.'

'Maybe Brianna can show you her trimming skills, after we've eaten,' said Brett.

Brianna looked at him in surprise.

'Is that okay?' Brett asked her. 'It's fine if you don't feel like it.'

'No, I think I need to work,' she said hurriedly. 'I just didn't expect you to be offering me a job, that's all.'

'Well you have to work for your supper,' said Brett. 'We all do. There are no free rides here.' He finished his stew and put down his knife and fork. 'Okay, well give it a go and see how you get on. When you're done you can move in with Angela and Amy. I'm sure you'd rather bunk with them than with Dale.'

'Where are you going?' asked Brianna.

'To see what we can do about your friends. Don't worry, everything's going to be okay.'

He stood up and patted Standing on the shoulder. 'Time to hit the road, Kemosabe.'

'Doesn't that make me the Lone Ranger and you Tonto? I mean, I'm fine with that if you are.'

The girls looked at them in confusion, not getting the reference. Standing opened his mouth to explain but decided it wasn't worth the effort so he just grinned, got up, and hurried after Brett.

Brett took him to the middle container, where he stored his weapons, along with cases of tinned tomatoes and beans, and bags of pasta and rice.

'I didn't want to say anything in front of the girls, but isn't there a chance the Bulgarians are going to come looking for Brianna?' asked Standing.

'If they were, they'd probably be here already,' said Brett. 'I don't think the Bulgarians are renowned for their tracking abilities. It would depend on that and on how much trace she left. If we're right and she covered ten miles, that would put her anywhere within a four-hundred-square-mile box. That's a lot of ground to cover.'

'The worry is they might do something to the two other girls. Get rid of the evidence.'

Brett nodded. 'I was thinking that.'

Standing looked at his watch. It was close to three o'clock in the afternoon. 'How sure are you that we can find this place?'

'She gave us a pretty good description. And we know the direction she came from.'

'Would it be worth driving to where we can get a phone signal and checking out a satellite view on Google Maps?'

Brett shook his head. 'The resolution isn't high enough and there's too much tree cover. But we saw her this morning coming from the north. And she says she came in a straight line.'

'Except we both know how difficult it is to walk in a true straight line, especially in rough terrain. Even on the straight and level, differences in leg length come into play.'

'True,' said Brett. 'But I'm a pretty good tracker. I'm fairly confident I can follow her back to the farm.'

'And then what? Lie up until dawn? I'm not sure we can do anything at night. What do you think?'

Brett grinned. 'I can help with that,' he said. There was a green metal trunk on the floor and he flipped it open. Standing's eyes widened when he saw what was inside. There were two sets of night vision goggles and half a dozen batteries, and underneath them several bulletproof vests, extendable batons, flashlights and various knives and scabbards. 'I'm a bit of a hoarder when it comes to military equipment,' he said.

Standing took out one of the sets of goggles. He put them on and pressed the 'on' button. They hummed and flickered into life.

'I give the batteries a boost every few months so they should be good to go,' said Brett. 'The way I see it, we do the tracking while there's still light, we find the farm, then we go in when it's dark.'

'Sounds like a plan,' said Standing. He switched off the goggles. 'And we bring the girls back in the dark?'

'I'm thinking we take flashlights with us. Depending on what happens when we get there, we could use the lights on the way back.' He took out four rugged flashlights, checked that they worked, and placed them on the floor.

'And what about the Bulgarians?' asked Standing.

'Yeah, we need to talk about that. There's a limit to what I'm prepared to do.'

'I hear you.'

'You're sure? I don't want to go to war over this. They might be slow to investigate murders out here but they do get investigated eventually.'

'I'm not planning on shooting anybody, Brett,' said Standing, though even as the words left his mouth he knew it was a lie. He had every intention of taking the life of Ryan French if he got the chance. But he agreed with Brett – killing the Bulgarians would be a mistake.

'Good, so let's just take pistols with us,' said Brett. 'I don't see the need for anything high-powered.'

'What about bears?'

'I've got bear spray. Spray is a lot more effective at keeping bears at bay than guns.'

'And we'll need bolt-cutters for the handcuffs.'

'I've got that covered.'

'Seems to me that if the girls are in a separate cabin we might be able to get them out of there without waking up the Bulgarians. If we can, then that's the way to go.'

Brett nodded. 'We could make heavy tracks to the north-west and then double back south, maybe send them in the wrong direction if they do decide to follow.'

'Excellent,' said Standing.

Brett opened the mesh door to his arms cache and took down two Glocks. He handed one to Standing, then opened a wooden drawer. 'Nylon or leather?' he asked. He grinned when he saw the look of confusion on Standing's face. 'Holster,' he said.

'I'll take nylon,' said Standing.

Brett took out a nylon holster and belt and gave it to Standing. He took out a leather set for himself. 'Like I said, I'm old school,' he grinned. He took four spare loaded magazines from the drawer, then closed it.

They took the gear outside and Brett fetched two backpacks from his container. They loaded their gear into the backpacks and took two bottles of water each. 'Good to go?' asked Brett.

Standing nodded. 'Bring it on.'

CHAPTER 19

It took them just over an hour to reach the spot in the woods where they had first stumbled on Brianna. They both had compasses but the direction didn't matter so much as her tracks. Brett took the lead, moving his head from side to side to keep them in focus. It was the complete opposite of regular tracking where the longer you followed, the closer you got to the quarry. Following Brianna's trail meant going back in time, and the further they followed her, the older the tracks. But they were helped by the fact that she hadn't been trying to hide her progress – there was plenty of broken vegetation and footprints in the forest floor.

Brett moved quickly and confidently, and Standing followed. There were places where there was no trace but by assuming she was moving close to a straight line Brett was quickly able to find her again. After a couple of hours they heard the crack of a rifle off to their left. Brett froze and Standing followed his example. A few seconds later there was a second shot. 'That'll be a hunter,' said Brett. 'Three miles away. Maybe four.'

They carried on moving. As the sun began to dip down to the horizon, the forest darkened, making Brett's task more difficult, but he kept up the pace. They reached a large clearing and they broke into a jog, assuming that she had cut directly across it. When they reached the far side Brett found a footprint almost immediately and they were off again through the trees.

They covered another mile. And another. Darkness fell and Standing figured that at some point they would have to start using the night vision goggles. Brett seemed to be okay though, and didn't appear to be moving any slower. They went up a steep slope, and then crossed a small creek. Brett stopped and pointed at muddy prints on a rock in the middle of the babbling water. 'That's her,' he said.

They continued up another slope, then the ground levelled off and they came across a clearing of cannabis plants. Brett stopped and waited for Standing to join him. 'We're close,' he said.

Standing nodded. They kept within the treeline as they skirted the clearing, taking care where they placed their feet to keep noise to a minimum. In the gloom ahead of them they saw the hulk of a rusting truck on its side. It was on a track that came from the left and further down was another abandoned vehicle, this one a saloon that had been stripped of its doors, windows and tyres. They continued to move through the trees, heading to the right. They stopped when they saw the two cabins. The one on the left was in darkness but there was a soft yellow glow coming from the windows of the other one. Brett pointed that they should go back the way they had come and Standing nodded. They retraced their steps and went back into the forest. When they were about a hundred yards in, they sat down at the base of a massive redwood. 'We should wait until they're asleep,' whispered Brett.

'Agreed,' said Standing. He took off his backpack and placed it between his legs. He took out one of his bottles of water and drank. They sat in silence as the seconds and minutes ticked by. Soon it was pitch black and the tree canopy was so dense above Standing's head that even when his night vision had kicked in he could only make out vague shapes. Sound carried at night and there was no way of knowing where the Bulgarians were. The mission was simple enough – to get into the cabin, release the girls and get them back to Brett's farm. Standing tended not to over-think before going into action. He was aware of the task, he had considered the options, now it was just a matter of waiting to see how it went down. He trusted his instincts and was confident that he would be able to deal with whatever came his way. He sat with his back to the tree, breathing slowly and evenly, as relaxed as if he was settling down on the sofa for a night of Netflix. He wasn't sure what was going through Brett's mind but he seemed equally composed. Nothing much seemed to faze Brett, though Standing wasn't sure how much of that was down to the man's daily cannabis intake. Standing had watched closely as Brett had despatched the deer that morning and he had been rock steady when he'd made the shot. And his tracking skills had been spot on. Fifty years of regular cannabis use didn't seem to have affected his motor skills, and his mind was sharp and clear most of the time. He did always get the giggles after his second bong and had a tendency to tell long, wandering anec-dotes that never really went anywhere, but then Standing had been known to waffle a bit after his fifth or sixth pint of lager.

Standing was able to keep track of time by the luminous dial of his Rolex Submariner. Nine o'clock. Ten o'clock.

'I'm going to check the cabin,' whispered Brett. 'You stay put. No reason for both of us to go.'

'Okay,' whispered Standing. He heard a rustle and a few

seconds later a high-pitched whine as the goggles were switched on. After a few seconds the whine stopped and Standing heard Brett move through the trees.

Standing took another drink from his bottle. He heard the occasional rustle around him as insects went about their business, and a couple of times he heard a brushing noise, which was probably a snake. Standing didn't know much about the snake situation in California, though he was fairly sure they had rattlesnakes. So long as he heard slithering and not a rattle, he wasn't overly concerned.

He kept looking at his watch as the seconds ticked by. Then he heard something big moving towards him, brushing against leaves and cracking twigs. It was disconcerting not knowing what was making the noise, though he doubted a bear would be going to the trouble of treading carefully. A dark shape loomed over him and a hand gripped his shoulder. 'The lights are off,' whispered Brett. 'Get your gear on.'

Standing ran his hands over his backpack to find the zipper, then opened it and took out his goggles. He'd used night vision goggles hundreds of times, in training and in the field, so had no problem pulling them on. He turned them on and heard the familiar whine. Within seconds the image had stabilised. Brett, now a ghostly green, was looking down at him. Standing flashed him an okay sign, then zipped the backpack closed and stood up.

They moved as quietly as they could through the trees. Walking while wearing night vision goggles was a skill that had to be learnt. They restricted the view directly in front of the wearer, which meant that you had a tendency to be constantly looking down at your feet. That left you vulnerable in combat, so you had to learn to keep looking ahead and to remember where obstacles were so that you could avoid them. Rookies who hadn't acquired that skill tended to walk by lifting their feet extra high with each step, looking like a dressage horse. Brett was clearly very familiar with the equipment and he moved confidently through the trees.

They reached the track with the abandoned vehicles and took up position behind the overturned truck. Both cabins were in darkness. They were pretty much identical; single-storey wooden buildings with shingle roofs. Each cabin had a small wooden porch reached by three steps. The cabin used by the Bulgarians had two lawn chairs on it and the area around the steps was littered with empty beer cans and bottles. There was a stack of barrels off to the right, some labelled 'PESTICIDE', the others 'FERTILISER', and all were stamped with hazard warnings.

They stayed where they were for several minutes, listening intently. There were no sounds from either of the cabins. Brett patted Standing on the shoulder and headed for the cabin on the left. Standing had no problem with Brett taking the lead, he had a quiet confidence and clearly knew what he was doing. It was hard to believe that his only military experience was as a conscript in Vietnam more than fifty years ago.

Standing followed him to the steps and waited while Brett went up, placing his feet close to the edge to minimise any squeaking. Standing drew his pistol. He wasn't planning on shooting the Bulgarians, but if for any reason they appeared with guns blazing he'd have no choice but to return fire.

Brett reached for the handle. Standing looked over at the other cabin, his gun at the ready. Brett grunted but nothing happened. Then he grunted again. Standing looked up the steps. Brett was clearly having trouble opening the door. He looked down at Standing and shook his head.

Standing pointed at the upturned truck and headed over to it. Brett came slowly down the steps and tiptoed after him. They crouched down behind the truck and put their heads close together.

'It's locked,' whispered Brett. 'Brianna didn't say anything about them being locked in.'

'Maybe they did it because she ran off,' whispered Standing. 'Is it a padlock? Can you use the cutters?'

'No, it's a deadbolt. The door doesn't look too strong, we could probably force it but we'll make noise.'

'Let's check around the back, see what our options are.'

They edged their way around the truck and headed to the side of the cabin. There was a small window but it was high up and fitted with a screen. The rear of the cabin had no windows or doors. There was just one way in. They crouched down. Brett was breathing heavily but Standing felt totally relaxed. 'I don't see we've got any choice,' whispered Brett. 'We're going to have to pop the door.'

'With what?'

'A crowbar would do it.'

'I don't suppose you brought a crowbar with you?'

Brett grinned and shook his head. He pointed to a ramshackle shed beyond the cabins. 'Let me have a look around, these guys don't seem to be the type to put things away.'

'I'll keep a watch on their cabin.'

Brett nodded and patted him on the shoulder, then started moving towards the shed.

Standing went back to the track and crouched behind the upturned truck so that he had a good view of the Bulgarians' cabin. If they did wake up there was a good chance they would switch their light on, and if they did the night vision would be ruined. And he and Brett would be silhouetted against the light when they opened the door. He kept his gun at the ready.

He saw Brett off to the left, moving towards the shed before disappearing from view. The seconds ticked by, then the minutes. Eventually he saw Brett emerge from the shed and move around the rear of the cabins. Standing met him at the bottom of the steps. He was holding an axe. 'They were using this to chop wood,' whispered Brett. 'I figure if I can get the leverage I can force the door away from the frame without making too much noise.'

'Worth a shot,' said Standing. 'You do what you can and I'll stand by the door in case they come out.'

'We don't want any shooting,' whispered Brett.

'If there's any gunfire, it won't be me,' said Standing.

Brett nodded and went carefully up the steps. Standing bent double and moved over to the Bulgarians' cabin. He stood looking up at the door. The hinges were on the right and the door opened inwards, which was the worst possible combination for him because when they opened the door they'd get a perfect view of the porch, leaving him with nowhere to hide. He could stand some distance away but if he did that he'd have no choice other than to shoot. There was a small area of the porch to the left of the door which was probably his only option, but he wouldn't be able to see them until they appeared through the doorway. Plus they'd be looking towards the other cabin, which meant they'd be looking straight at him. He took a quick look over at Brett. He was trying to force the head of the axe into the door jamb. If the door had been set into masonry it probably wouldn't work, but the cabin was all wood and had seen better days.

Standing went slowly up the steps, holding his breath. He

reached the porch and flattened himself against the wall to the left of the door. He looked across to the other cabin. Brett was forcing his weight against the handle of the axe. Standing could hear the sound of wood ripping for a couple of seconds, then silence. Brett took the axe away, looked over at Standing and flashed him the 'okay' sign.

Standing relaxed. Brett disappeared into the cabin and almost immediately there was a loud piercing scream from one of the girls, followed immediately by a second scream, even louder than the first. Standing tightened his grip on his Glock but kept his finger off the trigger. The screams stopped as quickly as they had started; obviously Brett had explained who he was and why he was there. But the damage had been done. Standing could hear muffled voices inside the cabin and the sound of bare feet slapping against the wooden floor.

He put his gun back into its holster. They would have to come through the door one at a time and they'd almost certainly be armed. He had the element of surprise on his side but he would have to act quickly. He pressed himself harder against the wall. They were talking now.

The lights came on and Standing flicked his night vision goggles away from his eyes.

The door rattled and then it was thrown open. The smell of stale sweat, urine, cannabis and alcohol billowed out. One of the men growled something in Bulgarian, then there was the flash of metal in the doorway. The barrel of a rifle or a shotgun. The man would step out and then turn, and would immediately see Standing. Standing pushed himself away from the wall and turned towards the man, both hands reaching for his weapon. It was a pump-action shotgun, lethal at close range. Standing pulled the weapon and twisted. The Bulgarian was so shocked that he yelped like a startled dog. He was a big man, a good two inches taller than Standing, with a shaved head and a pig-like nose. Standing wrenched the shotgun from his grasp, then slammed the stock into the man's groin. He bent double, screaming in pain. The second man was directly behind him holding an assault rifle to his chest. He was as shocked as his colleague and his mouth was working soundlessly. He was young, in his early twenties maybe, with pale skin and a dyed blond mullet. Before he could react, Standing hit him in the face with the stock of the shotgun. The man's nose splattered and blood erupted over his face. He staggered back, in shock but still holding the rifle.

Standing took a step back and brought the shotgun crashing down on the first man's head, then kneed him to the side and rushed into the cabin. The man with the busted nose was trying to bring his gun up. His eyes were watering and the tears were mixing with the blood that was gushing from his nose. Standing hit him in the stomach with the shotgun stock and the breath exploded from his mouth in a red mist. As the man's head came down, Standing smashed the stock against his temple. The man went out like a light and fell on top of his rifle.

Standing looked around the cabin. It was a disgusting mess. There were single beds with stained duvets at either side of the room, and a ripped plastic sofa in front of a wooden coffee table hidden under magazines, beer bottles, bongs and overflowing ashtrays. There was a plastic box full of empty beer cans and whiskey bottles, and empty crisp packets strewn across the floor.

He picked up the assault rifle. It was an AR-15, and from the look of it, the weapon had never been cleaned. Standing tossed the two weapons on the sofa, then dragged the bald man inside. There was a roll of duct tape on a table under the window and Standing used it to bind the ankles and wrists of the two men. He slapped pieces of the tape across their mouths, though he was fairly sure there would be no one to hear their shouts when they came to.

He picked up the guns, switched off the light and pulled the door closed behind him. Brett was still inside the second cabin, with the lights off. Standing flicked his night vision goggles back into position, jogged over to the treeline and threw the weapons into a large bush. He was fairly sure that the Bulgarians would have other guns but there was no point in making it easy for them.

He made his way back to the second cabin and went up the steps. The door was open. Brett was standing next to a metal bed, using his bolt-cutters. A young girl sat on another bed, she was wearing a T-shirt and jeans and was hugging herself. She stared at Standing. All she could probably see was a dark blur in the doorway. 'Brett, I'm going to turn on the light,' he said.

He and Brett flipped up their night vision goggles and Standing turned on the light. The two girls were blinking and rubbing their eyes.

'The guys are out cold, bound and gagged,' said Standing. 'They'll free themselves eventually but we'll be long gone by then.' He recognised the girl sitting on the bed. 'Emma?' he said.

She nodded fearfully.

Standing smiled. 'I met your mother two days ago.'

'Really?' she gasped.

Standing nodded. 'She's come out to look for you. She's going to be so happy to see you again.'

Emma burst into tears and buried her face in her hands.

There was a loud click from Brett's bolt-cutters. 'There you go,' he said to the second girl. She had long blonde hair and her eyes were red from crying.

'You're Olivia, right?' Standing said to her.

She nodded.

'I explained that we were taking them to Brianna,' said Brett. 'Just after they screamed the place down.'

'Yeah, that put the cat among the pigeons,' said Standing.

'I'm sorry, we thought they were coming to . . .' Olivia started to cry and couldn't finish the sentence.

'Okay girls get all your stuff packed and then we are out of here,' said Brett.

The girls nodded tearfully and got off their beds. They grabbed rucksacks and began stuffing their clothes into them, along with what few possessions they had.

'Do you think we can risk the flashlights?' Brett asked.

'There only seems to be the two of them, so we should be golden,' said Standing. 'But to be on the safe side let's get well away from the farm using the night vision, then when we're sure we're clear we'll switch to the flashlights.'

'Where are we going?' asked Emma, shoving a pair of trainers into her rucksack. The handcuff was still around her ankle; Brett had cut the chain as close to the foot as he could.

'Brett has a farm about twelve miles away,' said Standing. 'Once you're safe I'll get you to your mom.'

Olivia finished packing her rucksack. She was wearing a denim shirt and blue jeans and she sat on her bed to pull on socks and lace her boots. Like Emma she still had the handcuff on her ankle. 'Is Brianna okay?' she asked.

'She's fine,' said Brett.

'She didn't want to leave us but I told her our only hope was for her to go and get help.'

'It was the right call,' said Standing. He noticed bruising on her left cheek and her lip was split. 'Are you okay?'

'I wasn't, but I am now,' she said. She stood up and pulled on a jacket. 'Can we just get the hell out of here?'

Brett shrugged off his backpack and shoved it into her rucksack. He zipped it up and put the rucksack on his back. 'I can carry my own bag,' said Olivia.

'I'm sure you can, but you'll have enough problems with the dark.' He looked over at Standing. 'Good to go?'

Standing nodded. He followed Brett's example and put his backpack into Emma's rucksack. He put on the rucksack as she pulled on her Nikes. 'Are you okay?'

She looked tearfully up at him and nodded but didn't reply. 'Don't worry, we'll get you home,' he said. He went over to the light switch. 'The best way is for you to put one hand on the rucksack. Emma goes with me and Olivia, you go with Brett.

We won't move too quickly, just keep hold and keep up. Once we're sure we're in the clear we'll switch to the flashlights. Okay?'

The two girls nodded. Olivia seemed a lot more enthusiastic than Emma.

'Right, so get into position and I'll switch the light off.'

Olivia went to stand behind Brett and Emma stood up and reached for one of the straps on her rucksack. She held on with her left hand and wiped away her tears with her sleeve. 'Trust me, it's just a crazy game of follow-my-leader,' he said. 'The Bulgarians are out for the count, they won't ever hurt you again.'

'Thank you,' she whispered.

Standing flashed her a reassuring smile and reached for the light switch. He nodded at Brett, and turned off the light. As the cabin was plunged into darkness, the two men switched on their night vision goggles. He saw the look of terror on Emma's face. 'It's all right, Emma, I'm here and I can see everything.'

She bit down on her lower lip as she looked around fearfully.

'Right, out we go,' said Standing. 'Be careful on the steps.'

He walked slowly out on to the porch. Emma followed him. He went slowly down the steps, giving her time to feel her way down with her feet. 'Good girl,' he said. They moved a short distance away from the steps and waited for Brett and Olivia. They came down slowly and then Standing gestured for Brett to lead the way.

Brett headed west into the treeline. As he walked past a spreading bush he reached out and broke a couple of stems. It was unlikely that the Bulgarians were proficient trackers so he wanted to make sure they knew which direction they had taken. Would the Bulgarians follow them? It was a tough call for Standing to make. They'd lost three trimmers but there were plenty more available for hire. But with gangsters it was often more about face and image than it was about practicalities, and there was every chance that once they woke up and freed themselves they would want revenge. From the state of the cabin it was clear they were disorganised and either stoned or drunk most of the time. They were both overweight and had zero combat skills, and as Brett had pointed out, they probably weren't trackers. So long as they didn't know which way he and Brett had gone, the chances of them ever finding Brett's farm were pretty slim.

Emma was breathing heavily behind him, panting like a dog. 'It's okay, Emma,' he said. 'We're on fairly flat ground and so long as you stay right behind me you'll be fine.'

'Okay,' said Emma, but it was clear from the hesitation in her voice that she wasn't convinced.

'It might be easier if you put both hands on the rucksack,' said Standing.

She did as he suggested. The trees were closer together now but there was still plenty of room to walk between them. The main obstacles were roots that had erupted through the soil and several times Standing had to warn her to be careful where she put her feet.

He smelled the cannabis crop before he saw the plants, more than a hundred yards off to their right. They were still quite small, just coming up to chest height. Brett waited for Standing to catch up. 'I think we should walk through the plants, damaging a few as we go in but then slowing down and moving carefully. With any luck they'll lose our trail there.'

'Sounds like a plan.'

Brett nodded and led Olivia into the crop, breaking a few stems with his hand as he went. Standing followed with Emma. They moved slowly, but Emma was still breathing heavily. They reached the far side of the crop and entered the forest again. The ground was stonier now and they hardly left any footprints. In the distance, Standing heard a stream, and after a minute or so they reached a small creek, barely six feet wide.

Brett turned to Standing. 'This is perfect,' he said. 'If we walk in the creek we'll leave no tracks. We can cut south here and stay in the stream for a hundred yards or so.'

'That'll work,' said Standing. 'And we should start using the flashlights.'

Brett nodded in agreement. They both shrugged off their rucksacks and pulled out their backpacks.

'What's happening?' hissed Emma.

'We're getting our flashlights,' said Standing. 'Don't worry. Everything's okay.'

He took two flashlights from his backpack and handed one to Emma. As she turned it on, he switched off his night vision goggles, pulled them off his head and stashed them in the rucksack. Brett did the same. The four flashlight beams cut through the darkness, illuminating the trunks of the redwoods around them and the tree canopies overhead.

'Keep the beams low,' said Brett. 'At the ground.'

He and Standing put the rucksacks on their backs and walked into the creek. The girls followed. They began to walk in single file through the shallow water. Brett took the lead, followed by Olivia and Emma, with Standing bringing up the rear. The stream was only a couple of inches deep but was freezing cold. Standing's boots kept him dry for a few minutes but then the water began to seep in. A few minutes after that and his feet began to feel numb. He knew Emma must be feeling the cold even worse than him because she was wearing trainers.

They were walking upstream and the stones were slippery, so they had to tread carefully. The forest closed in on them and then they reached a clearing. 'Let's get out here,' said Brett. 'Wash the mud off your feet before you get out and try to stand on stones for as long as you can.'

He shook his right foot in the water, placed it on a large stone at the side of the creek, then washed his left foot. He took a long stride to another large flat stone and then shone his torch back into the creek. One by one they left the stream and made their way on to the rocks. Brett took his compass from his pocket, and pointed in the direction they were to go.

CHAPTER 20

The sky was reddening as they reached Brett's farm. The last few miles had been tough going and the girls were exhausted, but they had never complained. Standing's feet were still cold and wet from the walk in the stream and the rucksack had chafed his shoulders, but compared to what he'd done in the past with the SAS, it was a walk in the park. He'd been impressed with Brett; he was in his seventies but had kept going with an equally heavy rucksack. His navigation skills were first class, too.

Brett shrugged his rucksack off in front of the room where Angela and Amy slept. 'You girls can sleep here,' he said to Olivia and Emma. 'If you're hungry, we can get you some noodles or something.'

'I just want to sleep,' said Olivia.

'Me too,' said Emma.

Standing took off his rucksack and pulled out his backpack. He opened the door, switched on the light and took the rucksack inside. The two Taiwanese girls sat up, rubbing their eyes. 'Sorry to wake you,' said Standing. 'We've got visitors.' Brianna was curled up on one of the lower bunks, fast asleep.

He put the rucksack down next to one of the bunk beds. Olivia came in, flashed a smile at Angela and Amy, then pulled off her boots and socks and dived into the vacant lower bunk, pulling a blanket over her head.

Emma came in, carrying her rucksack. 'Grab any free bunk,' said Standing. She dropped her rucksack on the floor and climbed the ladder to sleep on the bunk above Olivia. 'We'll sort out the cuffs on your ankles tomorrow.'

Standing switched off the light and went outside. 'I need a bong to calm myself down,' said Brett.

'I'll join you,' said Standing. He followed Brett inside his container. He took off his belt and holster and put the gun on the coffee table, then dropped down on to the sofa. Brett prepared the green bong and gave it to Standing for the first hit. A calico cat emerged from underneath Brett's bed, arched its back and then walked stiffly over to the sofa. It jumped up and lay down next to Brett, watching Standing suspiciously through narrowed eyes.

Standing took a lungful of smoke, then passed the bong back to Brett and pulled off his boots and socks. Brett put the bong on the table and went to a cupboard to get him a towel. He tossed it to Standing, then sat down and took a hit from the bong. 'That was fun,' he said. 'It shouldn't have been, but it was.'

'It was fun because it went our way,' said Standing. 'It wasn't fun when the girls started screaming and the Bulgarians came out with their big guns.'

Brett chuckled. 'I forced the door easily enough, but before I could tell them that I came in peace they just let loose. My heart was pounding.' He patted his chest and chuckled again.

'Yeah, it got my heart racing, too. I wasn't expecting it. But they were amateurs, and I'm pretty sure they were stoned.' He put his bare feet up on the table and wriggled his toes. 'I'm surprised the girls went with them in the first place, they looked like trouble.'

'They get blinded by the money,' said Brett. 'All they're thinking about is the four hundred bucks a day. Once they're on the farm, miles from anywhere, it's too late.'

'And chaining them up? Have you heard of that happening?'

Brett nodded. 'Yeah, there was a case a couple of years back. A young couple, teenagers. They were picked up off the bus at Eureka and taken to a farm somewhere in Humboldt. They were chained and worked for going on four months, then they were drugged and dropped off by the side of the road. But at the end of the day, they were lucky. At least they were released eventually. They could have just as easily been shot in the head and buried out in the redwoods.' He copied Standing by taking off his boots and socks and putting his feet on the table. 'It never used to be like this,' he said. 'Back in the day it was hippies and free love and everyone just got along.'

'Times change,' said Standing.

'They do, ain't no doubt about that. But you'd hope that things would change for the better. Can you tell me that the world's a better place now than it was fifty years ago?'

Standing laughed. 'Mate, how old do you think I am?'

'You know what I mean. In terms of the way we treat each other. Back then, the hippies ran their own schools, they helped each other, we had gatherings where everyone came together and shared their weed.'

'I thought you came out here because you wanted to be away from people.'

'I'm not a hermit, Dale.'

'No, but wasn't it the hippies who were giving the GIs hell for serving in Vietnam?'

'In Washington and New York and Chicago, maybe. But out here, all anyone cared about was the weed. The hippies started coming about ten years before I arrived. Back then the logging industry had pretty much collapsed and cleared land was selling for a few hundred bucks an acre. The hippies were just planting Mexican seeds and the cannabis they produced was pretty low quality. They were the trailblazers. They experimented selective breeding and brought in strains from Southeast Asia. They began boosting the THC levels of the female plants by taking away the male plants and using light deprivation to make them flower prematurely. They were producing weed that the whole country wanted to buy and that started the whole Green Rush thing. That's when the rot set in. Back in the day, the hippies were more about being self-sufficient. Like me, they grew most of their own food. They grew weed because they liked to smoke it, and then they realised they could sell the weed that they didn't smoke. Then when it took off, the newcomers arrived. They were a whole different breed. They diverted the water from streams and rivers, they used all sorts of chemical fertilisers and pesticides and allowed them to get into the water. They didn't give a shit about the environment. You saw the state of the Bulgarian farm. Garbage everywhere, the place was a mess. And the pesticides they were using . . .' He shuddered. 'Their weed would be pure poison.' He began to laugh. 'I'm talking too much, right?'

'Nah, it's all good.'

Brett sighed. 'Man, I like being on my own, I'm happy with my own company, but sometimes it's good to have someone to talk to.'

'You ever get married, Brett?'

Brett nodded. 'Twice.'

'Twice? What happened?'

'They died. Both of them.'

'Serious? They died?'

Brett shrugged. 'Yeah. It was just bad luck, I guess.'

'Bad luck? What happened?'

'First wife, she ate some bad mushrooms. The poisonous kind.'

'Wow. That's terrible. And the second wife? What happened to her?'

Brett grimaced. 'She got hit over the head with a baseball bat.'

Standing's jaw dropped. 'What? How come?'

Brett shrugged again. 'She wouldn't eat the mushrooms.'

Standing stared at him open-mouthed until the penny dropped. 'Oh you bastard, you had me going there,' he said, laughing. He slapped his leg. 'That was funny. I'll remember that.'

'Your face was a picture.' Brett reached for his bong. 'I was engaged before I went to Nam, but my tour of duty put paid to that. Had another girlfriend when I came back but she had trouble with my mood swings and the fact that most nights I woke up screaming.' He shrugged. 'It's better if I sleep alone.'

'Good to know,' said Standing.

Brett chuckled. 'Man, you are definitely not my type.'

Standing laughed out loud. 'Well that is definitely good to know.'

CHAPTER 21

Standing woke to the sound of women screaming. He sat bolt upright. His gun was still in its holster on the coffee table and he grabbed it. He'd passed out on Brett's sofa, surrounded by empty instant noodle containers and biscuit packets. Brett had been asleep on his bed but he too was instantly awake and grabbing for his gun.

Standing leapt up and rushed barefoot to the door. The screaming continued and he slipped his finger over the Glock's trigger as he pulled the door open.

The screaming was coming from the next-door container, where the girls were sleeping. He held the gun up and went in. Brianna was jumping up and down, clapping and screaming. Olivia and Emma were out of their beds and were screaming just as loudly. Amy and Angela's beds were empty. Standing assumed they were already working.

The three girls began to hug and finally quietened down.

Brett put his hand on Standing's shoulder. 'I guess the girls are happy to be back together,' he said.

Brett and Standing went back to Brett's container, where they put down their guns and pulled on their socks and boots. The girls were still hugging when they went back outside. Tears were streaming down Brianna's face.

Angela and Amy appeared, looking to see what all the

noise was about, then grinned when they saw the girls hugging.

'You did it!' Brianna said to Brett and Standing tearfully. 'I can't believe you did it. I woke up and there they were. Like a miracle!'

'Piece of cake,' said Brett. He picked up the coffee pot and threw some logs into the fire pit. 'You girls hungry?' He nodded at Standing. 'Dale here makes a mean breakfast. Or we've got noodles.'

'Breakfast sounds good,' said Brianna. 'I could eat a horse. Obviously not literally, because I'm a vegetarian.'

The other two girls nodded. 'I could definitely eat,' said Olivia.

'Me too,' said Emma.

'We might as well eat now that we're here,' said Amy.

'Definitely,' said Angela.

'Okay, Emma, you and Olivia sit down and I'll get a hack-saw,' said Brett. 'I'll cut those cuffs off your ankles while Dale cooks.'

Standing went to get potatoes and onions from Brett's vegetable garden, added eggs and garlic and had half-decent Spanish potato tortillas ready by the time Brett had sawn the handcuffs off and made the coffee. Standing cut the tortillas up, put them on plates and handed them out with forks. The girls devoured them hungrily.

Brett sat down on one of the deckchairs and tucked in. After a couple of mouthfuls he nodded his appreciation. 'Damn, that's good.' He turned to the girls. 'So, ladies, we have to decide what we're going to do with you,' said Brett. 'I know you've all had a tough time, so maybe you just want to get the hell out of Dodge. And I know Emma's mom is going to want to see her.'

'I just want to go home,' said Emma. 'I've had enough.'

'I understand,' said Brett. 'As soon as we're done here, Dale can take you to where there's phone service and you can call her.'

'And I can go, right?' she asked him anxiously.

'Of course,' said Brett. He looked over at Olivia and Brianna. 'What about you girls? If you need taking to the bus station, we can do that.'

The two girls looked at each other and something unspoken passed between them. 'Could we work here?' asked Brianna. 'We came to Humboldt to work, I don't want to go home with nothing.' Olivia nodded in agreement.

'I pay two hundred bucks a pound, and you stay and eat for free,' said Brett. 'The food's got a lot better since Dale arrived.'

Brianna and Olivia exchanged another look, then they both smiled and nodded. 'We'd love to work here,' said Olivia. She looked over at Emma. 'Why don't you stay? You can earn some money to take back with you.'

'I don't want to,' she said. She shuddered and folded her arms. 'I just want to get as far away from here as I can.'

Brett sipped his coffee. 'Do you girls want to talk about what happened with the Bulgarians?' he asked.

'I don't,' said Emma, quickly.

'The sheriffs aren't great out here, but if you want to report it, I can take you there.'

Olivia shook her head. 'I don't ever want to see them again,' she said.

'At the end of the day if we do talk to the police, it won't change what happened,' said Brianna. 'I just want to forget about it.'

'I couldn't face them in court,' said Olivia. 'I couldn't look at them again. And what if the jury didn't believe us? There's no DNA. No CCTV. It's just our word against theirs.'

'There's three of you,' said Standing. 'You corroborate each other.'

'There's two of them,' said Olivia. 'Three against two isn't great odds. And most people here don't like trimmigrants. They'll probably think it's all our own fault. And if they do go to trial and they're found not guilty, what happens then? They'll know who we are and they'll come after us.'

'I don't think that'll happen,' said Standing.

'You don't know what they're like. They made us give them our phones and we had to show them all our messages and numbers and pictures. They said if we ever went to the police they'd track us down and kill us and kill our families.'

'They're only bullies,' said Standing. 'There's no way they'd carry out their threats.'

'You can't say that,' said Emma. 'You don't know what they're capable of. People do terrible things sometimes. The best thing to do is to pretend it never happened.'

Standing wanted to reassure her, but at the end of the day it was her decision. 'Okay, it's your call,' he said. 'I'm just the cook.'

They finished their food and Standing collected the plates.

'Emma, you should get your things together,' said Brett.

Emma headed off to fetch her rucksack while Standing took the plates behind the container. He washed up and by the time he'd finished, Emma was back at the fire pit with her rucksack packed. Olivia and Brianna hugged her and they all promised to stay in touch. Standing was pretty sure that wouldn't happen. Emma had made it clear that she wanted to forget what they had been through and the other girls would always be a painful reminder of what had happened.

Angela and Amy wished Emma well, then she hugged Brett and thanked him. 'You saved my life,' she said, and kissed him on the cheek.

'You take care of yourself, young lady,' said Brett, patting her on the back.

Brett went through the directions with Standing, who did his best to memorise them. Then Standing picked up Emma's rucksack and took it over to his truck. He put it in the back and climbed into the driving seat. Emma gave Olivia and Brianna a final hug and then joined Standing. She waved as he started the engine and drove slowly along the track away from the containers.

Standing drove at walking pace to the entrance of the farm and on to the track that led down the mountain. The track was wide enough but riddled with potholes, so he kept the speed down as they wove between the redwoods.

As they turned on to the road to Alderpoint, Standing gave Emma his phone. 'As soon as you get a signal, call your mom. Tell her we'll meet her where I first saw her, outside the general store.'

Emma stared at the screen as Standing drove. After a couple of minutes she nodded excitedly. 'Yes!' she said. 'A signal.' She tapped out the number and grinned at Standing as it rang out. 'Mom, it's me!' she said. Standing could only hear half the conversation, but it was clear that Mrs Mackenzie was relieved to hear from Emma, and whatever she said made tears well up in Emma's eyes. 'I love you too, Mom,' she said, then arranged to meet at the store. She gave the phone back to Standing and wiped her eyes. 'She's in Garberville, she'll drive over,' she said.

Standing put his phone in his pocket. She looked at him solemnly. 'Dale, could you do something for me?'

Standing looked across at her. He never liked questions like that. How could he agree to doing something until he knew what it was? But he could see that she was close to tears so he smiled and said yes, sure, whatever.

'When we see my mom, could you not tell her what happened?'

'What do you mean?'

'I don't want her to know that they kept me prisoner. Can we just pretend I had a job and there was no phone coverage, something like that?'

'She's your mother, Emma. She can help you get over this.'

Emma shook her head. 'If she knows what happened, she'll never look at me the same way again. Everything we do, every conversation we have, she's going to be thinking about what happened to me.' She shook her head. 'I don't want that. I want everything to be the same as it was before.'

'What about your father?'

'He left when I was small. He lives in Boston with his new family. I hear from him at Christmas and on my birthday. He's not part of my life. But my mom is and I want things to go back to the way they were.'

'Okay, that's fine. Whatever you want. But I can tell you from experience, when bad things happen to you, talking about it can make it easier to deal with.'

She flashed him a sideways look. 'People have hurt you?'

'Yes. And I've hurt people. And bottling it up doesn't help you deal with it.'

'So tell me something bad you've done. Something really bad.'

Standing's teeth clenched. He'd killed people, often in combat but sometimes because they deserved it. Some of the killings he could speak about, some he couldn't. He didn't want to say as much to her but in fact she was right – sometimes the only thing you could do was bottle it up. Some secrets weren't for sharing.

She sensed his discomfort. 'See?' she said. 'Sometimes it's better to keep secrets.'

Standing sighed. 'You're right,' he said. 'Sometimes it is. But your mom loves you and maybe she can help you.'

'It's too late for that,' she said. 'What happened, happened. There's nothing that anybody can say or do that will change that. I can deal with it, but I'm going to deal with it by never thinking about it or talking about it ever again.'

Standing caught the flash of a headlight in his rear-view mirror. There was a motorbike behind them. A second one appeared. Two bikers with long hair and denims, riding what looked like Harleys.

'That's your call, Emma.'

'I know it is. It's my life.'

The road straightened and two more bikes came into view, riding next to each other, a short distance behind the first two. It was the Outlaws from The Shack.

'It's better for me, and it's better for her,' said Emma.

'Then you'll need to get your story straight,' said Standing. 'She's going to have a lot of questions for you and you'll need to have answers.'

'Okay,' she said.

'For instance, she's going to want to know why you didn't call.'

'I'll just say there was no phone service.'

'And where's your phone now?' The bikers were closing on the pick-up truck. He wasn't sure whether they would remember his vehicle. They had all been out for the count when he had driven away from The Shack. But they might well have seen him when they arrived and parked.

'What do you mean?'

'The Bulgarians took your phones, right? Your mom'll notice so you'll need to have an explanation ready.'

'I'll just say I lost it.'

The bikers were about twenty feet behind the pick-up truck. The man on the right had a large plaster across his nose and a black eye. He was the one who had attacked Standing with the knife. The one on the left had a bandaged hand. He was the one who had started it all, the one who had taken Standing's pork chop.

'And she'll want to know why you left early. And why you weren't paid.'

'I'll think of something.'

Standing looked in his side mirrors and then at the rear-view mirror. The front two bikers were shouting at each other. Then they accelerated and moved apart. One came up on his right, the other on his left.

'I'm sure you will,' said Standing. 'But that's a lot of lies to tell.'

'But I'll only have to lie once and then she'll forget about it. If I tell her the truth, if I tell her what really happened, then it's always going to be there between us. She's never going to look at me without remembering.' She shook her head. 'I'll be okay, really.'

'It's your call,' said Standing. The biker on the right had drawn up next to the window. Emma hadn't noticed. Standing pressed himself back against his seat, hoping that Emma would block the biker's view. 'You've got to do what works for you.'

There was the roar of an exhaust to his left and a Harley appeared. It was the biker with the plaster across his nose. His long hair was flailing around his head as he looked across at Standing. Standing looked straight ahead and accelerated. The bike kept pace with him. Standing still didn't look to the side. There was an outside chance that the man wouldn't recognise him, but that now seemed unlikely in the extreme.

The bike accelerated and Standing saw the 'OUTLAW' colours on the biker's jacket. There was a shotgun in a leather holster affixed to the seat. The bike on the right also overtook the pick-up. The driver looked over his shoulder.

The two bikes moved together and then accelerated until they were about fifty feet ahead of the truck. 'Emma, we've got a bit of a problem here,' Standing said. 'But I don't want you to worry, all right?'

'Who are they?' she asked. 'Do you know them?'

'I ran into them a few days ago. They might bear grudges. Just open the glove compartment and pass me the gun that's in there.'

'Can't we call 911?'

'Just give me the gun, Emma.' He pressed the button to wind down his window.

She did as she was told. The two bikers behind the truck had moved closer. Standing recognised one. He was the guy who'd been swinging the chain at The Shack.

Standing held the gun in his right hand and kept it low.

'Open your window, Emma,' he said.

She opened it and her hair began to whip around in the wind. She was biting down on her lower lip.

'Don't worry, everything's going to be fine,' said Standing. His eyes flicked to the rear-view mirror. The two bikes were closer now. He moved his left foot over to cover the brake pedal. 'I need you to get down in the footwell, Emma,' he said.

'What?'

'Just put your seat back as far as it will go and then crouch down on the floor.'

'Are you going to shoot them?'

'Not unless I have to.'

He eased his left foot down on the brake pedal and at the same time pressed his right foot on the accelerator. The two bikers slowed the moment they saw his brake lights go on. The truck powered forward, narrowing the gap with the bikes ahead of them.

Emma put her seat back and slid down on to the floor.

The biker ahead of him on the left moved over and slowed. He kept his left hand on the handlebars and reached for his shotgun with his right.

Standing eased his foot off the accelerator and the pick-up truck began to slow. The bikes behind him moved closer.

Emma buried her head in her hands.

Standing pressed the brake pedal again as he accelerated. The bikes behind him braked, then accelerated as they realised what he was doing.

The biker on his left had the shotgun out now. The biker on the right had a revolver in his bandaged hand. A big one. A Smith and Wesson 500. A beast of a gun.

Standing's eyes flicked to the rear-view mirror. The two bikers were closing again. The one directly behind him had a sawn-off shotgun. It would do a lot less damage than the Smith and Wesson but it was still a threat. Though firing a shotgun one-handed was never a good idea, especially when driving a motorbike.

The biker on his left was swinging his shotgun around. He was still ahead of Standing's truck so he was going to have to slow before he could take his shot. The biker with the Smith and Wesson was totally out of position, he'd have to twist around a hundred and eighty degrees to stand a chance of hitting anything. And the recoil of the massive gun made firing one-handed problematic at best.

Standing's eyes flicked to the side mirrors, left and right, and then to his rear-view mirror. The biker with the sawn-off was about to shoot. The spread from the barrel would be so wide that it wouldn't do much damage beyond fifteen feet or so, but it would be enough to take out one of his tyres, and at the speed he was travelling there was a risk that the pick-up would overturn.

The biker on his left had slowed and was level with the front wing of the pick-up now. The smart thing for him to do would be to shoot at the tyre, but the biker was grinning savagely and clearly wanted to fire at Standing. He was a big man but the shotgun was heavy and the slipstream made the weapon vibrate wildly.

Emma was sobbing, her hands pressed against her face, her hair whipping around in the wind that roared through the cab like a living thing. 'It's almost over, Emma,' he said. 'Don't worry.'

The biker with the sawn-off was now just ten feet behind the truck and was aiming at Standing's nearside tyre. Standing stamped on the brake, hard, and the tyres squealed on the tarmac. The biker with the sawn-off screamed as he realised what was happening but there was no way he could steer the bike one-handed and he hit the back of the truck with a sickening thud. The shotgun flew skywards and the bike ploughed into the road, throwing off the biker who span through the air like a marionette whose strings had been cut.

The other biker behind him just managed to avoid Standing's truck, but he ran off the road and when the bike hit the grass it fish-tailed and flipped over, throwing him into the air. His arms and legs flailed but then he hit the trunk of a redwood and went still.

The biker with the shotgun was now twenty feet ahead of the truck. He was twisting around and the weapon was pointing up in the air. The biker with the Smith and Wesson was looking over his shoulder, trying to see what was going on.

Standing accelerated. He quickly transferred the gun from his right hand to his left. The biker with the shotgun started to lower his weapon, trying to get a bead on the truck's front tyre. Standing accelerated and raised his Glock. The biker saw the movement and then saw the gun. His eyes widened in shock and then Standing pulled the trigger and fired twice, aiming at the bike's rear wheel. He missed, so he fired again and kept firing until the tyre exploded. The bike flipped over and scraped along the road in a shower of sparks as the biker somersaulted into the trees.

The remaining biker was about to twist the throttle when Standing stamped on the accelerator and clipped the rear of the bike. It span out of control and the biker flew through the air, the revolver still in his hand. Standing wrenched the wheel to the left to avoid hitting the bike, then straightened up and floored the accelerator again. He glanced in his rear-view mirror. One of the bikers was sitting up, shaking his head as blood streamed from his nose. Beyond the crashed bikes, the road was clear. He smiled to himself and eased back on the accelerator. 'It's okay, Emma, you can get back in your seat now,' he said.

'Is it over?' she asked through her fingers.

'Yes,' he said. 'It's over.'

CHAPTER 22

Standing pulled up in front of the general store and parked. He looked around but couldn't see Mrs Mackenzie. 'Do you want a coffee or a soda?' he asked.

Emma forced a smile. 'I'm good, thanks. Can I ask you a question?'

'You can ask, I can't promise I'll answer.'

'Okay, that's fair enough. I guess I'm wondering what you're doing in Humboldt.'

'I just wanted to work. The Green Rush. Same as you.'

'But you're English, right? England is the other side of the world.'

'People come from all over the world to work on the farms here. Look at Angela and Amy. They've come all the way from Taiwan.'

'Except you're not a trimmer, are you? The girls said you were a bit clumsy.'

Standing chuckled. 'I've got big hands. The scissors are tiny. What can I say?'

'Exactly. It's not an obvious career choice for you, is it?'

'Well, to be fair, I do other things for Brett.'

'Security?'

Standing shrugged. 'I'm an extra pair of hands.'

'You rescued Olivia and Brianna. They said you went all MMA on Anton and Stanislav.'

'That's a bit of an exaggeration.'

'They said you didn't even use your gun. You just knocked them out.'

'They were in a different cabin. They didn't see what happened.'

'But you did knock them out, right? They were big guys. Strong.'

'They were fat pigs,' said Standing. 'They were fine when it came to terrorising girls, not so great when confronted by someone who can fight back.'

'That's what I mean,' she said. 'You're not the same as most of the guys here. And you're not a pothead.' She shrugged. 'You don't have to tell me if you don't want to,' she said. 'I'm just being nosey.' Before he could say anything she spotted a blue Ford Explorer turning off the road and began bouncing up and down on her seat. 'That's Mom!' she said excitedly.

They watched as the Explorer parked. The door opened and Mrs Mackenzie got out. She was wearing the same blue fleece, pullover and high-heeled boots that she'd had on last time he'd seen her. This time she had a wool beanie hat. She looked around, then took out her mobile phone. Emma opened her door and called out to her mother. 'Mom!' she shouted.

Mrs Mackenzie looked up from her phone and her face broke into a smile. Emma ran over and hugged her so hard that Mrs Mackenzie gasped.

Standing got out of the truck and retrieved Emma's rucksack. He waited until they had finished hugging before walking over.

'I can't believe you found her,' said Mrs Mackenzie.

'I wasn't really lost, Mom,' said Emma. 'There was no cell phone coverage on the farm and no Wi-Fi, it was only when Dale turned up that I realised you were looking for me.'

'Where is your phone?' asked her mother. 'It's usually always in your hand.'

'I dropped it and it broke,' said Emma, not missing a beat. 'Totally trashed.'

'Honey, that was an iPhone 12,' said Mrs Mackenzie.

'I know, I was really upset but like I said, there was no signal anyway.'

'Where was this farm?'

'About twenty miles away. In the middle of nowhere.'

'Was it okay? What was it like?'

'It was fine, Mom. There were a dozen other trimmers and they were a great group, but the work was really boring and I was pretty fed up. Then Dale arrived and said you were worried and I just thought, you know, I'd had enough.'

'Oh honey, you don't have to leave. I was just worried about you. I was being stupid. I've been putting up flyers all around the place. I should have just trusted you.' She hugged her daughter. 'I'm sorry I over-reacted.'

'No, Mom, I'm the one who's sorry. It was a stupid idea to come here, I see that now. The work is just so boring and you're stuck in the middle of nowhere. There's nothing to do other than work and all you're doing is clipping away with scissors from dawn to dusk. I want to go home. Is that okay?'

Mrs Mackenzie hugged her again. 'Of course it's okay.' She realised that Standing was carrying Emma's rucksack, so she stopped hugging and opened the rear door of the Explorer. Standing put the rucksack in the back.

'I can't thank you enough for finding Emma,' she said.

'It was just dumb luck,' said Standing.

'The Lord moving in a mysterious way, more like,' she said. 'And He certainly worked a miracle today.' She closed the door.

'Can I ask you something, Mrs Mackenzie?' he said.

'Sure.'

Standing took the photograph of Frenchy and showed it to her. 'While you were out looking for Emma, did you ever come across this guy?'

She took it from him and frowned as she looked at it. 'I think so, yes.'

Standing's jaw dropped in surprise. 'Seriously?'

She nodded. 'He was in a diner with two other men. I showed them Emma's pictures and they weren't very nice. They said a few nasty things about girls who were trimmers.' She waved the picture. 'This man actually shut them down. He was quite pleasant. He said he hadn't seen Emma but that he'd keep an eye out for her and he took a flyer.'

'Where is this diner? What's it called?'

'Morty's, it's on the road up to Phillipsville.' She gave the picture back to him. 'Is he a friend of yours?'

Standing nodded. 'Yeah. I'd just like to know he was okay.'

'He seemed fine. They were drinking and making passes at the girls there. As I said, his friends weren't very nice but he seemed okay.' She looked at her watch, then flashed him a smile. 'I am so grateful to you, Dale. I'll never be able to thank you enough.'

'I'm just glad that Emma's back with you.'

'Yes, thank you so much,' said Emma. She hugged him and stood on tiptoe to kiss him on the cheek. 'And thank Brett for me.'

'I will.'

He watched as they climbed into the Explorer and drove off. Mrs Mackenzie beeped her horn and Emma waved. Standing waved back.

Once they were on the road, Standing took out his phone. There were a dozen messages, all from Charlotte Button, and most of them telling him to call her back. The last one was just three letters and he smiled. 'FFS'.

He called the number and she answered almost immediately. 'Where the hell have you been?' she asked.

'Off the grid,' he said. 'This isn't Hampstead or Knightsbridge, the phone service is patchy at best. It's a ten-mile drive to get a single bar on my phone.'

'Have you made any progress?'

'I've a possible lead, yes. I'll check it out ASAP.'

'You need to pull your finger out, there's chatter that he has another job in the offing.'

'It's not a question of pulling my finger out, this place is a wilderness. And if I say the wrong thing to the wrong person there's every chance I'll end up buried out in said wilderness.'

'If it was easy, I wouldn't have needed you, Matt.'

'You need me because I know Frenchy and he knows me. That's the only reason you used me.'

'Don't sell yourself short. Look, I appreciate the difficulty of the task you've been set, but I'm sure you'll get the job done. I just need you to know that the clock is ticking and that you're aware of the consequences of failure.'

'Fuck you very much.'

'The clock is ticking, Matt. Tick tock.'

Standing ended the call and glared at the screen. He wanted

to throw the phone on to the ground and stamp it into little pieces, but he knew that wouldn't achieve anything so he took a deep breath and began to count to ten.

CHAPTER 23

Brett was sitting in one of his deckchairs with a beer in his hand and a camouflage-pattern baseball cap pulled low over his eyes when Standing drove up. The calico cat was curled up in his lap. 'You deliver her in one piece?' asked Brett as Standing climbed out of his truck.

'Yeah, she's on her way back to Sacramento,' said Standing. He walked around to the back of his truck and took out a case of Budweiser. He took it over to Brett and put it down next to his deckchair. 'Emma says thanks.'

'Did she buy the beer?'

Standing laughed. 'No, that's from me.' He gestured at the truck. 'I bought some provisions. We were running low on eggs so I bought a couple of dozen. Speaking of which, why don't you see if you can get the geese to lay?'

Brett chuckled. 'They're fighters, not lovers.'

Standing went back to the truck and pulled out a large cardboard box. 'They had a delivery of croissants just in, so I grabbed a few.'

Brett grinned. 'Give me one and see if the girls are hungry. They're all trimming.'

Dale took out one of the croissants and gave it to Brett, then he took the box and put it in the middle container. He took out the bag of croissants and walked around to the trimming tent. Angela, Amy, Brianna and Olivia were snipping away at cannabis stems. The big bucket of waste was almost full and they all had large piles of buds in front of them. Brianna and Olivia weren't as fast as the Taiwanese girls, but they were close. They all squealed with delight when they saw the croissants. He took one for himself and that left two each for the girls.

'Is Emma okay?' asked Brianna as she grabbed a croissant.

'She's fine. We met up with her mom and she's on the way home.'

'Dale, you don't think the Bulgarians will come looking for us, do you?' asked Olivia.

'It's very unlikely,' said Standing. 'If anything they're more likely to pack up and go if they think you've gone to the cops. They almost certainly wouldn't be able to track you to Brett's farm, but even if they do Brett and I are more than a match for them.'

The girls stopped snipping and began to munch on their croissants. Standing went to sit next to Brett, who had finished his croissant and had both hands on his beer bottle. 'Thought I'd show you the ropes in the curing room,' said Brett.

'Sounds good,' said Standing, breaking off a chunk of croissant and popping it into his mouth. 'Hey, have you heard of a diner called Morty's? On the road to Phillipsville?'

'Yeah. Everyone knows Morty's. I think the plan was to capitalise on the tourists driving to the Avenue of the Giants but it's ended up as a bit of a dive. Quite a few growers come down from the mountain to eat there and they tend to be a bit rough and ready and not too particular about their personal hygiene. But the food's okay.'

'Emma's mother thinks she saw my friend there while she was handing out flyers. I thought I'd swing by.'

Brett grinned and raised his bottle. 'Maybe I should be your wingman,' he said. 'After what happened to you in The Shack, I think you could do with somebody to watch your back.'

'It's a date,' said Standing with a grin.

Brett drained his bottle and stood up. 'Right, off we go,' he said. He eased the calico cat off his lap and disappeared into his container. He came back with a ziplock bag containing brown pellets, which he gave to Standing. 'You can feed the guard geese,' he said. He took Standing along the trail to the curing container. Standing threw handfuls of the pellets through the chain link fence as Brett unlocked the padlock. They went through and the geese continued to peck at the ground as Brett closed the gate and unlocked the container. Together they pulled the doors open and then went inside.

Brett pointed at the shelves closest to the door. 'So, these are the newest in and these are opened, shaken and checked every day.' He nodded at the shelves further along. 'These have been in for five days so they have to be done daily for maybe another week. Sometimes it takes a couple of weeks.' He picked up one of the bottles and showed him a handwritten label on the top. 'When they come into the container they're dated, along with a note of what strain it is.'

He put the bottle back and moved inside the container to the next rack. He picked up a bottle and gave it to Standing. 'You can see by the date that this one has been here for six weeks. At that stage it's to be opened once a month. I try to get them synchronised so they can all be done on the first of the month. It just makes it easier to keep track.' He took it back from Standing and unscrewed the top. He sniffed and smiled. 'Perfect,' he said. 'You can usually smell if there's a problem.' He moved the buds around with his finger. 'You're looking for the buds to be like popped popcorn. If you give them a gentle squeeze they should pop back into shape. Too wet and they'll stay crushed, too dry and they'll crumble into dust. And you definitely don't want them damp because that's when you get mould, and if you get mould then it's game over. The buds should feel slightly sticky to the touch, and they should move independently when you shake the jar. You don't want to see them clumping together.' He replaced the lid, shook the jar gently, and put it back on the shelf. 'Now the unscrupulous farmers will just spray the buds with a fungicide, which stops the buds going mouldy, but that's not good for the customer. That's why people keep buying from me – they know that my product is as pure as it gets. I don't use fungicides or pesticides and I don't allow artificial fertilisers anywhere near my plants. I'm one hundred per cent organic.'

'Aren't there health and safety rules about what you can and can't put on the plants?'

'For the legal farms, sure. Pages and pages of regulations. But the farms that aren't regulated, they can use whatever they want. All sorts of poisons are used and they don't care because their stuff ends up on the streets being sold to people who don't know any better. They're the same farmers who pour chemicals into the streams and who dump their garbage in the forest. Like those Bulgarians. No respect for the land.'

'And once you're on the once-a-month cycle, how long do you keep that up?'

'That's really up to the grower. Most would cure their weed for a month, some for two months. Me, I think the longer the better. Like wine.' He picked up another of the jars. Inside, along with the buds, was a black plastic rectangle, about four inches long and an inch wide, with a digital readout showing two numbers. 'I went hi-tech a few years ago,' said Brett. 'I started using these digital hygrometers. They give a reading of the temperature and humidity inside the jar, which takes a lot of the guesswork out. You're looking for humidity between sixty and sixty-five per cent. That's the zone as far as I'm concerned. I know some farmers who swear by fifty-five per cent. When it's that low there's less chance of mould, but it makes the weed less potent in my experience. Okay – so the job is to open the jars that need daily opening, then shake the monthly jars and check the hygrometer readings. Unless it's the first of the month, in which case the monthly jars need to be opened and allowed to breathe.'

He went back to the first rack. 'We'll do it together this time and tomorrow you can handle it yourself,' he said.

Brett began opening jars and swirling the buds around. Standing followed his example. They did all the daily jars and then moved on to the monthly section. It wasn't difficult work and they were done within half an hour. Brett looked at his watch. 'How about I run you down to Morty's now?'

'Cool,' said Standing.

They locked up the container and Standing fed the geese as Brett opened the gate. They headed back to the trimming tent, where the girls were still hard at work. Brett explained that he and Standing would be away for a few hours and that they should cook for themselves when they were hungry.

They climbed into the Jeep. Brett started the engine then drove slowly down the track. The Jeep was perfect for handling the rutted ground but it was still a rough ride. They joined the wider trail. 'This was a logging road, back in the day, long before I came to Humboldt,' said Brett. 'They've been logging here since the 1850s. When the first settlers arrived they found trees thirty feet wide and four hundred feet tall, the oldest living things on the planet. So of course they began chopping them down and taking them to mills on Humboldt Bay to turn them into houses, railroad ties and fence posts. The lumber was loaded on to ships and sent around the world. Back then a logger was allowed to buy up to a hundred and sixty acres of forest for two dollars fifty an acre and by the end of the 1800s all the redwood forests were owned by loggers and ranchers. Even after the war, a logger could still buy a square mile of virgin redwood forest for twenty thousand bucks. Cut down the trees and you had timber worth ten million dollars, and that was back in the 1940s. It's all different nowadays.'

'Why's that?'

'Conservation, mainly,' said Brett. 'The tree-huggers pretty much brought an end to cutting down the old-growth trees and even second-growth trees require state approval and permits. It's still a big industry, but it's nowhere near as big as it used to be.' He grinned over at Standing. 'You know it's because of the logging industry that cannabis is illegal, right?'

'Is this one of your conspiracy theories?'

Brett laughed. 'It could be, but there's a ring of truth to it,' he said. 'You know they can make paper from hemp?'

'I didn't know that.'

'Hell, yeah. It's faster to whiten than wood pulp, it can be reused and is way more recyclable, and it hardly deteriorates or yellows over the years. You can get five tons of pulp per acre easily and with some strains up to twelve tons. Much more than from trees. So in terms of paper production, hemp would be the natural choice, right? Why use trees to make paper when hemp is so much better suited?'

'Okay,' said Standing, not sure where the argument was going.

'So, you go back to the 1930s, before my time obviously, and who was one of the biggest owners of forest and timber in the US of A?'

Standing shrugged. 'No idea. Sorry.'

'A guy called William Randolph Hearst. One of the richest men in the world, back then. The equivalent of Bill Gates and Mark Zuckerberg these days. Now, Hearst owned vast tracts of forest and made a fortune chopping down the trees for timber, and for paper. And he realised that he stood to lose a fortune if everyone switched to paper made from hemp. Now, as well as owning all those trees, he owned the largest media chain in the world.'

'So Rupert Murdoch as well?'

'Exactly,' said Brett. 'So Hearst used his newspapers to start campaigning against cannabis. He demonised it, and the people who used it, who back then were mainly black or Mexican. He printed a barrage of anti-cannabis propaganda and started calling it marijuana instead of cannabis because marijuana sounded more foreign. He got his way and in 1937 the government passed the Marihuana Tax Act. Cannabis was made illegal and his timber fortune was safe. It was never about cannabis being dangerous, it was all about money.' He shrugged. 'The world never changes,' he said. 'The rich get richer and the poor get screwed. You saw what happened during the Covid pandemic. The billionaires all made money hand over fist. Amazon, Facebook, big pharma, they were making fortunes as hundreds of thousands of regular folks lost their jobs.'

'So you reckon Covid was a conspiracy as well?'

Brett looked across at him and grinned. 'Don't get me started,' he said.

Standing switched on his phone as they reached the outskirts of Alderpoint. He got a signal straight away. There was only one text message – from Button. Just one word. 'SITREP?' He replied with: 'I'M ON THE CASE'.

'Your pal?' asked Brett.

'Nah, a woman in the UK.'

'Girlfriend?'

'Friend of a friend.' He put the phone back in his coat pocket.

They drove from Alderpoint to Garberville, then headed north on Route 101. The diner was about five miles from Garberville, a single-storey wooden building with a line of windows overlooking the road and a car park to the side.

There was a sign across the roof that said 'MORTY'S' and a neon sign that confirmed it was open. Brett parked his Jeep and they climbed out. They walked to the main entrance, Brett pushed open the glass door and they went inside. There was a sign on a metal pole that said customers should seat themselves. To the left was a line of stools at a counter, behind which a large man with bulging arms and a shaved head sweated over a griddle. There were eight booths by the windows. Two were occupied. There were four middle-aged men in hunting gear devouring burgers, and a couple of hipster guys with neatly-trimmed beards who were sharing a bowl of cheese nachos.

Brett went over to the booth at the far end and slid in with his back to the wall. At the end of the counter was a door leading to the toilets, and next to it was a large noticeboard with more than a dozen 'missing' posters on it. Standing went over and ripped off Emma Mackenzie's flyer.

'Hey now, what are you doing?' said a woman behind him. 'Don't go messing with that noticeboard, sugar. That there's private property.'

Standing turned to find a waitress holding up a pot of coffee. She was in her forties with dyed blonde hair and a name tag with 'DEBBIE' on it pinned on to her blue and white uniform.

'That's somebody's loved one so don't you be taking that poster down.'

Standing held it out so that she could see it. 'We found her, yesterday,' he said. 'She's back with her mom and on her way home as we speak.'

'Are you serious?'

'Very much so,' said Standing. 'She was on a farm with no cell phone coverage. I drove her to Alderpoint this morning and her mom picked her up.'

'Well, sugar, aren't you the hero?' She raised her coffee pot. 'I think that deserves a free cup of coffee. Where are you sitting?'

Standing nodded at the booth and her eyes widened when she saw Brett. 'Well hello there, Brett,' she said. 'Long time no see.'

'Hiya Debbie,' said Brett. 'You're looking good.'

She gave him a little curtsey and giggled like a schoolgirl. 'And did you help the good Samaritan here get the young lady back to her mom?'

'I played a small part,' he said.

'Then you both deserve hero coffee,' she said. Standing slid into the booth opposite Brett and she poured coffee into their mugs. 'Last time you were here you had the turkey sandwich, heavy on the cranberry sauce,' she said to Brett.

'I do like my cranberry sauce,' he said.

'Same again?'

'Please,' he said. 'And coleslaw on the side.'

'Good choice,' she said, and flashed Standing a beaming smile. 'And for you, sugar?'

'I'll have the same,' he said.

'Also a good choice,' she said.

As she walked away, Standing sipped his coffee. 'So are you a regular?'

Brett shook his head. 'Far from. Must be two years and some since I was here, but Debbie has a mind like a steel trap. You come back here at any time in the future – a year, five years, ten years – and she'll remember every word of the conversation you had and what you ordered. She never writes her orders down, either.'

'I know a guy like that,' said Standing. 'Eidetic memory they call it.' He drank his coffee and looked over his shoulder. 'The clientele looks okay,' he said. 'You made it sound like something out of *Deliverance*.'

Brett frowned. 'Deliverance?'

'It's a movie. Burt Reynolds.' Realisation dawned and he put down his mug. 'Of course, you'd have been in the woods then. Early seventies. So you've never seen a movie?'

Brett laughed and shook his head. He took out his phone and held it up. 'I've got a Netflix account, I watch movies. Just not when I'm on the farm because we've got no Wi-Fi. But I know what's happening in the world.'

'Of course you do, sorry.'

'No, it's a fair comment. Before smartphones and the internet, back then I really was in the dark most of the time. The Vietnam War had been over for nine months before I found out. Most of the time I didn't know who was president. I didn't care, either. But these days I'm a bit more informed.'

Debbie returned with their sandwiches. 'I took a chance that you'd want extra cranberry,' she said to Standing as she put the plate down.

'Perfect,' he said. He took Frenchy's photograph from his coat pocket and showed it to her. 'Speaking of missing people, do you by any chance remember this guy? He's a friend of mine.'

She took it from him, looked at it for less than a second, then shook her head. 'No. Never seen him.'

'He would have been here when Mrs Mackenzie put the flyer up about her daughter. She said he was here then.'

'Ah, okay, that flyer went up in the morning, so it was before my shift started. You'd need to talk to Ashley.'

'Ashley?' repeated Standing.

'Ashley Miller,' said Debbie. 'She usually does the breakfast shift.'

'Ashley Miller? Dominic's kid?' said Brett.

'That's her.'

'She's what, thirteen?'

'Nineteen,' said Debbie.

Brett's jaw dropped. 'Wow, time flies. Does she still live with her dad?'

'Yeah, she's not going anywhere, that one.'

'Is she in tomorrow?'

'She should be, bright and early.' She scribbled a bill and placed it on the table. 'Enjoy your sandwiches, heroes.'

'So you know this waitress?' asked Standing, as Debbie walked away.

'I knew her grandparents, and her father. It's a small world.' He took a bite of his sandwich. 'John and Betty Miller were pretty much the first people I met when I came to Humboldt. It turned out that I'd pitched my tent on their land, but they were cool about it. They were real hippies. Free love, they tried every drug that was available. They gave me my first LSD. First and only.' He chuckled to himself and took another bite of his sandwich. 'They were teachers, in San Francisco, and they decided to go back to basics and bought a few acres not far from here. They set up a sort of commune, I guess you'd call it. By the time I met them they had three families living on their land, and at the height of it there were a dozen. That was in the late seventies. They went through a phase of doing everything naked in the summer months. Looking after their crops, tending the land, building their houses, they did it all buck naked. The only time they wore clothes was when they went into town.'

'Nice.'

'They were good people. They're the ones who taught me about cannabis growing. I would help them trim when they were short-handed and I was always asking them questions. Bit by bit I learnt everything there was to know about pot-growing. Betty got pregnant in the early eighties. They wanted her to give birth out in the open, close to nature, but there were complications. Their son was okay but Betty died before they could get her to hospital. The commune pretty much fell apart after that and John lived there on his own with the boy. Dominic, his name is. John did a good job of raising the boy. I'd moved to my own place by then and didn't see them that often. Eventually Dominic grew up and got married and had three kids, and Ashley is the oldest. John died seven or eight years ago. He's buried out on their land.'

'And Dominic's a farmer?'

Brett nodded. He ate a few mouthfuls of coleslaw before continuing. 'Yeah, he took over the farm when his dad died. It's been a long time since I've seen him, though.'

'What's the plan? To go and see Ashley?'

'Might as well while we're in the area, right? Dominic's less than an hour away. How's the sandwich?'

'Good. The extra cranberry was a good call.'

CHAPTER 24

They finished their meal and Standing paid, leaving a big tip for Debbie. They went outside and climbed into Brett's Jeep. They drove north on 101 to Phillipsville and then turned east, heading for a town called Fort Seward. The road was narrow and winding and most of the time it was a struggle to get above twenty miles an hour. When they reached Fort Seward, Standing realised it wasn't a town at all, just a collection of a few single-storey wooden houses. They crossed a bridge over Eel River, then headed north for a couple of miles before Brett turned off the main road and on to a single track that wound its way through woodland. At times the tree canopy overhead was so dense that they were driving in near darkness. They turned on to a narrower track, then the trees began to thin out and ahead of them Standing saw a two-storey wooden house with a sloping roof. Brett beeped his horn. 'Always better to let them know you're coming in this part of the world,' he said. 'Saves any nasty surprises.'

There was a line of vehicles parked to the left of the house – three pick-up trucks, a white SUV and a blue Honda Civic. As Brett pulled up behind the SUV, a tall gangly man with an assault rifle walked out of the house. The weapon was down at his side but his finger was close to the trigger. He was wearing a plaid shirt and faded jeans and had round-framed glasses, and he peered over the top of them at the Jeep. Brett wound down his window. 'Dom, it's me!' he shouted. 'I come in peace.'

Dominic's face broke into a grin revealing a wall of grey teeth. 'Brett? My God!'

'Long time, no see,' said Brett.

Dominic leant the assault rifle against his house and hurried over to hug Brett. 'It's been years,' he said.

'Yeah, I'm sorry about that.' They hugged again, and then Brett introduced Standing. 'Dale has just started working for me.'

Standing and Dominic shook hands. 'What's the story with the gun, Dom?' asked Brett. 'What happened to peace and love?'

'We've had a few unwanted visitors,' said Dominic. 'Let's get a beer and I'll tell you about it.' He took them up on to the porch where there were two wooden chairs and a wooden swing large enough to seat three. 'Let's sit outside, I'll get the beers,' said Dominic. Standing and Brett sat on the chairs while Dominic went inside.

'This is a nice place,' said Standing, looking around.

'I helped build it,' said Brett. 'Part of it anyway.'

'When was that?'

'Must have been forty-odd years ago. Before Dominic was born. It was all built by hand from trees they cut down themselves. They were paying ten bucks a day to anyone who worked here, and they threw in as much weed as you could smoke. It was much smaller then, Dominic has extended it over the years.'

'Which bits did you do?'

'I was doing the roof mainly. I wasn't the best carpenter so I was fetching and carrying most of the time.'

Dominic returned with three bottles of beer. He handed them out and sat down on the swing.

'I was just telling Dale I built part of this house,' said Brett.

'You guys did a good job,' said Dominic. 'It'll stand for a hundred years. Dad was always so proud of it.' He looked over at Standing. 'There was nothing but trees here when Mom and Dad arrived. They lived in one of those VW camper vans, one of the original ones with the split windshield.'

'Hell, yeah, I remember that van,' said Brett. 'I remember how your mom and dad would head off for a nap and how it would be bouncing up and down.' He laughed and drank his beer.

Dominic chuckled. 'Too much information, Brett.'

'Come on, man, we both know you were conceived in that van.'

'That is true.'

'Whatever happened to it?'

'The van? It got stolen, when I was a kid. One of the trim-migrants hot-wired it and drove off with it, along with a couple dozen plants. You know what Dad was like, he trusted everyone.'

'Yeah, he was one of a kind, your dad.' Brett looked at Standing. 'The day he died he was as much a hippy as he was in the sixties. Peace and love. He trusted everybody. He believed in karma – that what goes around, comes around.'

'Most of the time he was right,' said Dominic. 'But every now and again someone would rip him off. He'd just shrug and say that if they needed something so bad that they had to steal it, then they were welcome to it. I mean, he loved that van, but he didn't even report it stolen. I think he believed that he'd get it back, eventually.' He grimaced. 'He was wrong, of course.'

They sipped their beers. 'Is Ashley around?' asked Brett.

'She's in the greenhouse, doing some trimming with her mom,' he said.

'Can we go and say hello? There's something we want to ask her.'

Dominic's frown deepened so Standing took out the photograph of Frenchy and showed it to him. 'I'm looking for a friend and we think he might have been in the diner where your daughter works.'

'Debbie thinks Ashley was working the morning he was in,' explained Brett.

'No problem,' said Dominic. 'Come on.'

They put down their beers and Dominic picked up his rifle and took them around the side of the house. 'I can't believe she's nineteen,' said Brett. 'Last time I saw her she was what, thirteen? Fourteen?

'It's been a while,' said Dominic. 'You know what it's like, a lot of the community things we used to do have fallen by the wayside. It's dog eat dog these days. Every man for himself.'

Ahead of them was a greenhouse with polythene sheeting over metal hoops, similar to the one Brett had on his farm. Off to the right was the shell of a building that had been destroyed by fire. Part of it was still standing but most of it had been reduced to ashes.

'What happened here?' asked Brett. 'Generator fire?'

'I wish,' said Dominic. 'As I said, we've been having a few problems recently.'

'What's going on, Dom?' asked Brett.

Dominic sighed. 'I've been made an offer I'm not supposed to refuse.'

'The mafia?'

'The Russian mafia. A couple of heavies came around last month and said they wanted to buy my farm. I said it wasn't for sale.' He started walking and Brett and Standing followed him. 'Two days later my barn burned down. There was a generator in there so my first thought was that we'd had an electrical fault, but then the Russians came back and said that I wasn't to worry, that they wouldn't be lowering the price because of the "accident". They were both grinning when they said that. I said the farm wasn't for sale and they went away again and the following week two of my dogs were poisoned. I don't know what else they've got planned but now the gun goes everywhere with me.' He held up the assault rifle for emphasis.

'This isn't good, Dom,' said Brett.

'I know. I don't know what to do. The cops'll be no help, you know that. What are they gonna do? Sit a man outside in a patrol car?'

'I hear you,' said Brett.

'Why would they want your farm?' asked Standing.

Dominic gestured over to the left with his gun. 'They already own thirty acres over that way. They've been there for a year or so. Then they bought old man Wainwright's place to the north a month or so ago. He'd been wanting to sell up for years. They obviously want to put the plots together. Economies of scale. But there's no way I'm selling. My dad built this farm. I was born in the field over there.' He gestured with his gun again. 'My mom and my dad are both buried here and I'm not leaving them.'

'So what's the plan?' asked Standing.

'The plan? I don't have a plan. I thought about buying in security but a half-decent guy costs more than a trimmer and it's just dead money.'

'Are you going legit?' asked Brett.

'That's the idea,' said Dominic. 'Tanya and I ran the numbers and because of our acreage we worked out we could make it pay. You know how good our weed is.'

'Almost as good as mine,' said Brett with a grin.

Dominic ignored the jibe. 'We've had all the surveys done and put in our paperwork, but if I have to pay tens of thousands of dollars for security then the numbers just won't work, we'll be running at a loss from day one.' He shrugged. 'It's a fucking nightmare, Brett.'

'Dale here could stay with you for a while, if that'd help,' said Brett. 'You'd be okay with that, right?' he asked Standing.

'Sure,' said Standing.

'I appreciate your offer, really,' said Dominic. 'But I'm not sure that one extra gun will make a difference. It's Tanya and Ashley and the boys I'm worried about. Those guys set fire to the barn, so what's to stop them burning down the house with my family in it?' He forced a smile. 'Don't talk about it in front of Tanya and Ashley. They know we've got a problem but I don't want them to know how bad it is.'

'You need help, Dom,' said Brett.

'Let me think about it,' said Dominic. 'Come on, they're in here.' He leant the rifle against a water barrel and led them into the greenhouse. It was similar to the one Brett had on his farm, but wider and twice as long. There were hundreds of plants, most of them up to Standing's chest. In the middle of the greenhouse were two women, snipping away with scissors. The older one was in her forties with blonde hair cut in a bob. She was wearing denim dungarees and bright red Crocs. The younger one was wearing a baggy white linen shirt over tight white shorts and had her chestnut hair tied back in a ponytail. She had a phone in her back pocket playing rock music, and they were both dancing as they worked.

'Guys, look who's here to see you!' shouted Dominic.

The girl pulled out her phone and switched off the music as the woman turned to look at them, her scissors in her hand. Her face broke into a grin when she recognised Brett. 'Well hello, stranger,' said Tanya. She hurried over and hugged him. 'This is a surprise.'

'Yeah, I'm sorry I've been out of touch for so long. You just get caught up with work and time passes.'

'Ashley, do you remember Brett?' asked Dominic. 'It's been a few years.'

'Of course,' she said. She gave him a small wave. 'Hiya Uncle Brett.'

'Hi Ashley. Looks like I've missed a few birthdays.' He nodded at Standing. 'This is my friend Dale.'

'Do you and Dale want to stay for dinner?' asked Tanya. 'I've got coq au vin on the stove and there's more than enough to go around.'

'Tanya, I would love that,' said Brett.

'We were just about done here,' said Tanya. 'Why don't you guys grab a beer and Ashley and I will set the table.'

Dominic collected his rifle and took them back to the house. They went up on to the porch and inside the house. It had high ceilings and bare wood floors, and the furniture was handmade but of very high quality. It was hard to believe that they were in the middle of a redwood forest. There were two large sofas and a La-Z-Boy reclining armchair around a coffee table that appeared to be a slice of redwood trunk, six feet across. 'Sit,' said Dominic, and Standing and Brett dropped down on to one of the sofas while he went into the kitchen.

'Does this sort of thing happen a lot?' Standing asked Brett. 'Gangsters trying to force people off their land?'

'Unfortunately, yes. Didn't used to be that way because land around here was so cheap. Now big pharma is snapping up a lot of the legal sales so the gangsters and cartels have to get heavy if they want to expand. Dom's right to be worried. If they came here at night, who's going to stop them?'

'Do you know these Russians?'

Brett shook his head. 'No, but I know the type. And they won't hesitate to burn him out if they have to.'

Dominic returned with three more bottles of beer and he handed them out before dropping down on to the La-Z-Boy. They clinked their bottles and drank. 'So what brings you out here, Dale?' asked Dominic.

'Change of pace, pastures new, a desire to try something different.' He shrugged. 'I just got fed up with England, I guess.'

'Humboldt isn't like it used to be,' said Dominic. 'You could come here and start a new life if you wanted. Nobody would bother you, we were off the grid, no taxes, no rules, no regulations. We were like one big family. We all helped each other. We had our own schools, we lent money if a family was short. My dad would've hated what's happened to the place.' He took a drink and wiped his mouth with the back of his hand. 'Between them, the gangsters and big pharma have ripped the soul out of Humboldt. Maybe I should just sell to the Russians. Maybe it's time to call it a day.'

'What are they offering?' asked Brett.

'About three quarters of the market price.'

'Bastards,' said Brett.

'But how can I sell to them after this? They burned down my barn and killed my dogs. You can't let bullies win.'

'Sometimes you have to,' said Standing quietly.

'What do you mean?' asked Dominic.

'There are some nasty bastards in the world and you can't fight them all.' He sipped his beer.

'This is my home. It's my family's home.'

'Then you have to fight. But when you fight, there's the risk of collateral damage and then any victory is pyrrhic.'

'I don't want my family hurt, that's for sure,' said Dominic. 'But I can't let them walk all over me.'

'How many of them are there?' asked Standing.

'Four of them in an SUV. The car was black with blacked-out windows. They were obviously trouble, just from the look of them. It was the same four that came back after the fire. But I don't know how many there are on their farm.'

'What sort of operation do they have?'

'I've never seen it.' He gestured off to the east. 'My land runs about half a mile in that direction and there's thick forest there. Their farm is about three miles further on.' He looked at Brett. 'It was the old Hanks place. Remember Bill Hanks?'

Brett laughed. 'Crazy Bill? Hell yeah. He pretty much smoked everything he grew. He used to talk to himself, all the time. He wasn't dangerous or anything, and he was always polite to the ladies. He used to wear this leather cowboy hat and he'd raise it every time he saw a woman and wish her a good day.'

'Bill passed away a couple of years ago and his farm was empty. I don't think he had any relatives. Then I was told someone had moved on to the farm about six months ago. I never saw them but I heard they were Russians. They're far enough away that you never see or hear them, so I've no idea what sort of operation they've got over there. But whatever it is, they're expanding.'

'If it's just four then it's not too big a problem, I guess,' said Standing. 'I guess we need to find out for sure.'

'So now it's "we" is it?' said Brett.

'We could pop over and carry out a recce,' said Standing.

'There's that "we" again.'

'You guys don't have to get involved,' said Dominic.

'Involved in what?' asked Tanya, appearing in the doorway.

'Just talking about the crop,' said Dominic.

'Well your dinner's on the table,' said Tanya.

'Great,' said Dominic, getting to his feet. They followed Tanya through the hallway into a dining room with a table set for seven. There were plates of coq au vin and serving bowls of mashed potato, carrots and peas. As Standing and Brett sat down, Dominic fetched fresh beers from the kitchen.

There were two young boys sitting at the table. The elder was the spitting image of Dominic, the younger one was more like his mother. 'This is Jacob and Ethan,' said Tanya.

Standing and Brett said hello to the boys and sat down opposite them. 'No school today, boys?' asked Standing.

'We homeschool them,' said Tanya, taking her place at the head of the table. 'The nearest school is Garberville, so even if we wanted them to go there we'd be spending hours in the car.'

'Homeschooling is the better option,' said Dominic. 'The school system is going completely woke these days. The rubbish they teach them, it's shameful.'

'You've got such a nice place here, Tanya,' said Standing, looking around the room. On one of the walls were a dozen or so framed photographs of the farm, including several of the house being built.

'As opposed to my converted containers, you mean?' said Brett.

'I love your containers,' said Standing. 'But this is a real home.'

'Thank you,' said Tanya. 'Dominic's parents built it. They were naked most of the time. Brett helped them, but he never admits to taking his clothes off.'

'Mom!' said Ashley. 'Not everyone wants to hear that story.'

'The world was a different place back then,' said Dominic.

They tucked into their food. 'You raise chickens here?' asked Standing.

Tanya nodded. 'We've always been self-sufficient for food,' she said. 'There's not much we need to buy.'

'Dom says you're going legit,' said Brett. 'How's that working out?'

Tanya grimaced. 'It's been a nightmare,' she said. 'Every time we fill out one form they come up with two more. And the costs? It's as if they're going out of their way to put us out of business. What about you?'

'It's not worth it for me,' said Brett. 'But I've been through this before. I got through the whole war on drugs thing, this isn't much different.' He turned to look at Standing. 'Back in the early eighties when Reagan was in the White House and Nancy was pushing her "just say no" line, they declared war on the drug industry in general and the cannabis farmers of Humboldt County in particular. We had DEA helicopters flying in every other week, we had armed SWAT teams terrifying the kids.'

Dominic grimaced. 'They burned down our school,' he said. 'We had what they called attack drills, as soon as we heard the helicopters we had to run and hide in the forest. They'd come in and destroy the crops and our equipment. Sometimes they'd set fire to buildings. It was terrifying.'

Brett nodded. 'I had more than my share of flashbacks, waking to the sound of helicopters,' he said. 'Back then I didn't have much to lose and most of the time I'd get overlooked. I just had a tent and a hundred or so plants growing wild. I'd hear them coming and grab what I could and head into the woods. It was like a game, except they were playing with people's livelihoods.'

'Does that still happen?' asked Standing.

'DEA raids?' said Brett. 'No. It's been a good few years since I've seen the DEA here. These days it's the cops and it's more about licence enforcement. They still destroy crops, but tend not to use helicopters these days. They'll come in a convoy.'

'With a chipper,' laughed Tanya.

'Hell yeah, the chipper,' said Brett. 'It wouldn't be a raid without a chipper.'

'Chipper?' repeated Standing.

'A wood chipper,' said Dominic. 'In the old days they'd helicopter in and use machetes to hack the crops, and then set fire to them if the plants were dry enough. But these days they're worried about global warming and pollution levels so they use a chipper. There are watchers along the main roads keeping an eye out for the authorities, and if they spot a convoy with a chipper in it then that means they mean business.'

They ate their coq au vin and Tanya fetched seconds from the kitchen. Standing waited until they had finished their meal and were drinking coffee before taking out the photograph of Frenchy. 'So, other than cadging a free meal, the reason we dropped by was to show this to Ashley,' he said. 'It's a friend of mine who's gone missing. I spoke to Debbie in Morty's and she said he might have been in there for breakfast, which would be your shift.' He passed the photograph across the table to Ashley. 'He was in the diner a couple of weeks ago. There was a woman who came in looking for her daughter. She put a flyer on the noticeboard and spoke to some guys in a booth.'

Ashley looked at the photograph and nodded. 'I remember that. She spoke to everyone in the diner. She even showed it to Eric on the griddle.'

Standing pointed at the photograph. 'And him?'

'Yes, he was there. Like you said, in a booth.' She looked at him and frowned. 'He's a friend, you said?'

'Yeah.'

'But he's American. His friends were foreign. But he was American.'

'Yeah, I met him overseas. He came to Humboldt and then I lost touch with him. Did he tell you his name?'

'No, I just took their order. They were there for breakfast. That woman went over to speak to them and the foreign ones gave her a hard time. I remember this guy telling them to behave. They were only joking but she was upset. I mean, she was looking for her daughter, right? So obviously she was upset.' She gave him back the photograph.

'Was that the only time he was there?'

'No, he's been in there a few times. Always for breakfast. He always has the same thing. Scrambled eggs, bacon, hash browns and toast.'

'And always with the same people?'

'Always with guys, but not always the same ones.'

'Americans or foreigners?'

She bobbed her head from side to side as she tried to remember. 'I've seen him four times in all,' she said. 'Twice with two other guys, twice with three other guys.'

'Did you see what vehicle he used?'

She laughed. 'You've got a lot of questions,' she said.

Standing smiled and held up his hand. 'Sorry, I'm just trying to track him down.'

'I didn't see what they were driving. You've tried calling him, right? He had a mobile phone. They all did. They had their phones on the table. And walkie-talkies, too.'

'Yeah, his old number isn't working and I think he's only got my UK number. The walkie-talkies make sense, because the phone service is so poor out here. You didn't hear any messages over the walkie-talkies did you?'

She shook her head. 'No, sorry.'

Standing waved away her apology. 'It's fine. It's a relief to know that he's okay.'

'How did you meet him?' asked Tanya.

'We were soldiers, out in Syria,' said Standing. 'We ended up being on a few missions together and we promised to stay in touch. Then I got a message saying he was in Humboldt and I thought I'd come over and meet up with him again. To be honest, I was worried that he might be living rough in the woods, but from the sound of it he's working.'

'Probably for one of the big companies, too,' said Dominic. 'Walkie-talkies means that has to be a professional outfit.'

'Could you do me a favour and give me a call next time he drops in?' Standing asked Ashley.

'Sure,' said Ashley.

Standing gave her the number of his US cell phone and she tapped it in.

'Actually I'm out of coverage most of the time, maybe send me a text.'

'I'm on it,' she said.

They were interrupted by the sound of a vehicle heading their way. Dominic frowned. 'Are we expecting anyone?' he asked his wife.

'I wasn't expecting Brett and Dale,' she said.

Dominic forced a smile and headed for the door. He picked up his assault rifle. Brett and Standing followed him.

A black SUV with tinted windows was driving towards the house. Dominic walked out on to the porch, flanked by Brett and Standing.

'Who is it?' called Tanya.

'Stay inside, babe,' said Dominic without looking around. 'Keep Ashley and the boys with you.'

The SUV came to a halt, facing the house. The engine continued to run.

'Have you got any more guns?' asked Brett.

'We should be okay,' said Standing. 'If they came here to shoot, they'd have started shooting already.'

'I hope you're right,' said Brett.

'There'd be more of them, too. I think we're good.'

The seconds ticked away as the three men stared at the SUV. Then the front passenger door opened and a heavy-set man in a black leather jacket climbed out. 'This guy was here before,' whispered Dominic.

The man's head was shaved and he had a diamond stud in his left ear and a chunky gold watch on his wrist. From the way the jacket was hanging, Standing was pretty sure he was carrying a gun in an underarm holster under his left arm. The man pushed the door closed. He had a thick scar across his neck and a smaller one on his left cheek.

The two rear doors opened and two more men climbed out. The one on the left was a giant, close to seven feet tall and broad-shouldered. He was wearing a San Francisco 49ers jacket that must have been an XXXL at the very least, and tight black jeans. He was in his thirties and had a thick brow over dark, brooding eyes that glared at Dominic as he slammed his door.

The one on the right had jet black hair, cut short. He was small in comparison, but was still over six feet tall. He wasn't muscled and he didn't glare threateningly at anyone, but Standing knew instinctively that he was the most dangerous of the three. He was wearing a grey fleece over a black polo-neck sweater, loose jeans and sneakers, and was hiding his eyes behind Oakley sunglasses. Unlike the giant, his loose clothing meant that he could move quickly if necessary and there was a casualness about his movements that suggested he was totally unfazed at being confronted by a man with an assault rifle. Standing was fairly sure that he didn't have an underarm holster but would have bet money that there was a gun in the small of the man's back. He had special forces written all over him. He closed the door with his right hand but his attention never wavered from the porch and, even with the sunglasses on, Standing was sure that the man was looking right at him and not at Dominic and his assault rifle.

The driver stayed where he was and the engine continued to throb. The three visitors moved forward and fanned out, then stopped when they were a few paces apart. 'Dominic, my friend, is that how you greet visitors?' said the man with the shaved head. 'Where is that American hospitality I'm always hearing about?'

'This is private property, Sergei, I told you that last time. I'm quite within my rights to shoot anyone who threatens me on my property.'

Sergei raised his hands and smiled, showing two gold teeth at the back of his mouth. 'No one is threatening you, Dominic.' He turned to look at the giant. 'Are you threatening him, Yuri?'

Yuri snarled and shook his head.

'What about you, Mikhail?' said Sergei, turning to his left. 'Are you threatening anybody?'

Mikhail grinned, showing brilliant white teeth. 'No yet,' he said, in accented English, as he continued to stare at Standing.

Sergei turned back to Dominic. 'There you are, my friend. No one is threatening anyone.'

'So why are you here?' asked Dominic.

'I don't think you've seriously considered my offer,' said Sergei. 'So I'm here to emphasise that you selling your property is the best option for everybody.'

'My land isn't for sale.'

Sergei laughed. 'Everything is for sale. Everything has a price.'

'I was born on this land and I intend to die here.'

'Now that can be arranged,' said Sergei. He was smiling but his eyes were hard.

'Are you threatening me?' said Dominic, bringing the gun to bear on the Russian's chest.

Sergei threw his hands in the air. 'There you go again, accusing me of threatening you.'

'Get off my land, Sergei.'

Sergei's eyes narrowed. 'Or else?'

'There's nothing more to be said. I'm not selling.'

'And how does your wife feel about that? And your delightful daughter. Your sons are probably too young to have an opinion, but does your family agree with you?'

'This is a family home and we're not selling.'

'But does your family appreciate the dangers of owning a property like this, in the middle of nowhere? It can be dangerous. There are all sorts of wild animals out here.'

'Well that's why I've got this,' said Dominic, lifting up the assault rifle.

'That is admittedly a nice weapon,' said Sergei. 'But is it any good against bears?'

'I'm not planning on shooting a bear.' He still had the weapon across his chest but his finger had slid across the trigger.

'And these new faces, who are they?' said Sergei, gesturing at Standing and Brett.

'Just friends.'

Sergei nodded. 'It's good to have friends. Real friends. Are they real friends, Dominic?'

'We're his friends,' said Standing.

'Ah, you are not American,' said Sergei.

'British.'

'You are a long way from home.' He looked over at Brett. 'And who are you, old man?'

Brett's jaw tightened but he didn't reply. Sergei walked

towards him. Standing moved to the steps and then went down, his eyes on Sergei. Sergei stopped and stared at Standing, clearly weighing him up. 'Do we have a problem?' asked Sergei.

'Not if you do as my friend asks, and leave.'

Standing heard footsteps behind him. He took a quick look over his shoulder. Tanya and Ashley had come out on to the porch. Sergei grinned up at them. 'Ah, the lovely wife and daughter. Why don't you see if you can talk some sense into Dominic? He needs to sell this farm before someone gets hurt.'

'Why would anyone get hurt?' asked Brett. He came down the stairs to join Standing.

'Ah, the old man speaks,' said Sergei.

'You carry on talking like that and this old man will teach you a lesson you won't forget.'

'Really?' said Sergei. He smiled. 'Are you not worried about falling and breaking a hip?'

'You and your knuckleheads need to get off this land, now.'

'I'm not here to talk to you, old man. What is it they say? I need to talk to the organ grinder, not his monkey.'

'Dom doesn't want you on his land. He's already told you, his farm isn't for sale.' Brett pushed Sergei in the chest. The Russian took a step back, glared at Brett, then reached into his jacket and pulled out a gun. It was huge, which is why Standing had spotted it so easily. It was a Desert Eagle, known as a Deagle to gun aficionados. With a man like Sergei it would all be for show, which meant that he probably had the gun chambered for the .50 Action Express. It was the largest pistol centre-fire cartridge on the market, so big that only seven rounds could fit in the magazine. The gun weighed almost four and a half pounds, so it pretty much had to be fired with both hands and had a recoil that was almost impossible to control. On the plus side it could hit a man-sized target at more than 200 yards, but not with any degree of accuracy.

As soon as he'd pulled the gun out, Sergei had to use his other hand to help keep it up. He sneered at Brett. 'Now what have you got to say, old man?' he said.

'Big gun, little dick, is the first thing that comes to mind,' said Brett. 'And then I guess I should mention that only a coward pulls a gun on an unarmed man.'

Sergei's finger tightened on the trigger. Standing couldn't believe that the Russian would shoot Brett in cold blood, but the man was angry and getting angrier by the second. Standing stepped towards Sergei, putting himself between Brett and the weapon. 'We don't want any trouble,' he said quietly. 'You've said what you wanted to say, now you need to go.'

Sergei pointed the gun at Standing's face. He was a big man and strong, but he was already having trouble keeping the gun steady. 'Fuck you,' he said. He jabbed the gun at Standing's face. Standing almost laughed out loud. The man was holding one of the world's most powerful handguns and he was using it like a club.

'Just go,' said Standing.

Sergei went to jab with the gun again. Standing's left hand came up and slapped the gun, knocking it away from him and Brett. Almost immediately he brought his right hand up to grab the back of the gun and slip his thumb over the hammer. That simple move effectively deactivated the weapon – even if Sergei pulled the trigger, the hammer was locked.

Standing twisted the gun with his right hand and pushed

Sergei's arm with his left. Sergei yelped as his wrist cracked and Standing pulled the gun away from him. Sergei lashed out with his foot but Standing twisted to the side and he missed. As Sergei's foot came down, Standing hit him on the side of the head with the butt of the gun. The Russian staggered back and Standing hit him with the gun again, this time across his chin. Blood sprayed from Sergei's mouth and his arms flailed in the air as he tried to keep his balance. Standing stepped forward and drove his knee into his groin, then as he bent over in pain, he brought the gun crashing down on the back of his head. The Russian fell to the ground and lay still.

Yuri was standing transfixed by what had happened, but Mikhail was already moving, reaching behind his back and pulling out a Glock as he dropped into a crouch.

Standing twisted the gun around and slid his finger over the trigger. He brought his left hand up to support his right as he aimed the Desert Eagle at Mikhail's chest. Mikhail was calm and unflustered. He followed Standing's example and used both hands to hold his Glock. 'Just so you know, I hit you anywhere with this and you're either dead or you lose an arm or a leg,' said Standing. 'Your Glock shoots nine millimetre rounds, so unless you get me in the head or the heart you're not going to do any major damage.'

'It'll be in your left eye,' said Mikhail. 'You'll be dead.'

'Your call, then,' said Standing.

Yuri was still confused, staring at Sergei who appeared to be unconscious, lying flat on his back with his eyes closed.

Mikhail's eyes flicked towards Sergei. 'If you've killed him, you're in big trouble.'

'He's not dead. And you're the one who's outgunned here, so truth be told you're the one who's in big trouble.'

Dominic walked to the edge of the porch. 'Tanya, Ashley, get back inside,' he said. He raised his rifle to his shoulder and aimed at Mikhail's chest.

Mikhail moved back towards the SUV but Standing moved with him, keeping the Desert Eagle trained on his chest. Mikhail shouted over at Yuri in Russian and the giant moved towards Sergei. Dominic swung his assault rifle around and aimed at Yuri's chest. 'Stay where you are!' he shouted.

'I told him to pick up Sergei,' said Mikhail.

'If he pulls out a gun, I will shoot him,' said Dominic.

'He doesn't have a gun,' said Mikhail. 'It's in the car.'

'Yeah, well forgive me if I don't take your word for that,' said Dominic. He kept his rifle trained on Yuri, who slowly walked towards Sergei, his hands in the air, palms open.

Mikhail started moving again, keeping his Glock aimed at Standing. When he reached the SUV he opened the passenger door. Standing moved to the side so that he had a clear shot, though the massive round in the Desert Eagle would rip through the door like paper if necessary. Mikhail kept his eyes on Standing as he spoke to the driver in Russian. When he had finished, he nodded at Standing. 'He will help Yuri put Sergei in the car. He has a gun but he won't draw it. Do you understand?'

'I understand,' said Standing. 'Dom, if the driver so much as reaches for a weapon, you shoot him.'

'Not a problem,' said Dominic.

Standing kept his eyes fixed on Mikhail. 'If I hear a shot I pull the trigger, come what may,' he said.

'And so will I,' said Mikhail. 'So let's hope everyone stays calm.'

The driver opened his door, put his hands in the air and

shuffled out. He was in his mid-thirties, the shortest of the group, with slicked-back hair that glistened in the sunlight. He was wearing a black bomber jacket. It was unzipped and Standing caught a glimpse of a holstered gun. The man moved slowly away from the SUV, his hands still in the air. Mikhail barked at him in Russian and he and Yuri walked towards the unconscious Sergei. Both men kept their hands in the air until they reached Sergei, then they knelt down and picked him up. Sergei groaned but his eyes stayed closed.

They half carried, half dragged him to the back seat of the SUV and laid him down. Yuri climbed in with him and slammed the door shut.

The driver put his hands in the air again and moved to his door. He climbed in slowly, then shut the door behind him.

Mikhail nodded at Standing. 'We will leave now.'

'Probably best.'

'I'm sure we'll meet again.'

'I'm sure we will,' said Standing.

'I don't suppose you'll give me Sergei's gun, will you? It's one of his favourites.'

'Get the fuck out of here,' said Standing.

Mikhail grinned, then smoothly slid into the front seat and pulled the door closed. Immediately the SUV pulled into a tight turn, the tyres kicking up dirt and dust, then it sped off down the track. Standing kept his gun trained on the vehicle until it was out of sight.

'Dale?' said Ashley from behind him.

Standing lowered his gun.

'Dale!' Ashley repeated.

Standing realised she was talking to him. He could never

gct used to being addressed by a different name. He turned to look at her. She was back on the porch with her mother.

'The guy who had the gun,' she said. 'The one with the sunglasses. I've seen him before.'

Standing frowned, not sure what she was getting at.

'He was with your friend. In the diner.'

CHAPTER 25

'I guess you're looking at Frenchy in a whole different light now,' said Brett. They were driving on the Avenue of the Giants, heading south.

'It's not what I expected,' said Standing. He was staring out of the side window, his arms crossed.

'He's obviously not fussy about who pays his wages.'

'It's possible he doesn't know what they're doing,' said Standing. 'He wasn't at Dominic's farm. He could just be working security at their base.'

Brett flashed him a sideways look. 'You really believe that?'

'I want to believe it, sure. But it's not looking good, is it?'

'On the plus side, you know where he is now. On the down side, you practically beat one of his colleagues to a pulp.'

'I really need to talk to him,' said Standing. 'I'm thinking the diner is the best bet.'

'That's not going to work, is it? There's no phone coverage so Ashley can't call you. And by the time you pick up her text message, he'll be gone.'

'I was thinking maybe I could move into a motel for a bit. That way I'd get any message straight away. I could drive in to your farm every day and leave late at night. She said he was there for breakfast so I could be at your place at ten.'

Standing already had the motel paid for, though it was an hour's drive from there to the diner.

The two men sat in silence for a while as they drove through the trees. The sky was cloudless and darkening as the sun went down. High overhead a red-tailed hawk hovered, seeking its prey.

'This French guy must be pretty important to you,' said Brett eventually. 'You're going to a lot of trouble.'

'I suppose so.'

'You're going above and beyond, that's what it seems like to me. You carry his picture with you, now you're going to start paying a motel bill every day just so you can receive a message about him.'

'I figure it'll only be a few days.'

'Yeah, but you were out here looking for work, right? Or was this Frenchy the main reason you're here?'

'Six of one,' said Standing. He didn't like the way the questioning was headed, but he couldn't very well refuse to answer.

'So me offering you a job, that doesn't count for anything?'

'No, Brett, that's not it at all. I'm grateful for the work, and I'll still be at the farm after breakfast.'

'I just get the feeling that you've been using me.'

Standing looked over at him. He was using Brett, there was no getting away from it. And the moment that Standing had done the job he'd been sent to do, he'd be off and he'd never see Brett again. He hated lying to the man, but didn't see that he had any choice. If Standing told Brett the truth, he'd want nothing to do with him. 'I needed work and I'm grateful for you taking me on,' he said. 'But I haven't told you the full story about Frenchy. He went off the rails while he was in Syria and they kicked him out of the army. PTSD was the cause, but he started self-medicating with pot and he failed a drugs test. Once he got Stateside he got worse, and then he told his sister he was thinking of killing himself. She knew I was a friend so she called me. That's why the urgency.' He shrugged. 'I should have been honest with you up front.'

'They've never looked after our troops,' said Brett. 'They didn't in my day and things haven't got any better. They reckon that more Vietnam vets killed themselves than died in combat. But if your friend is working, he can't be in too bad a state.'

'That's what I thought,' said Standing. 'But if he's okay, why didn't he contact his sister? And what's he doing working for the Russians?'

'There probably aren't many jobs going for someone with his skill set, especially if he was kicked out of the army.'

'That's why I want to talk to him. I can't believe that he knows what they're up to.'

'And if he does? If he does know?'

'I'll cross that bridge when I get to it,' said Standing.

'You saw what they were like back there. They're not going to quit until they've got Dominic's farm. You stood up against them today – if push came to shove would you stand up against this Frenchy?'

'Of course. No one has the right to steal another man's land. I like Dominic and his family and I was happy to help. I'll continue to help, you know that.'

'We'll see how it pans out,' said Brett. 'But I think you need to prepare yourself for the worst, Dale. If he's carrying a gun for the Russians . . .' He left the sentence unfinished. 'Look, I hear what you're saying, but moving into a motel seems to be a lot of trouble, especially as it's not guaranteed that they'll be going to the diner again. Why don't you stay at my place and just take a drive down to Alderpoint each morning until you get a signal? Or you could even drive out to the diner each morning and see if they drop by. They open at seven, you could stay there until ten and then drive back after that.'

'You'd be okay with that?'

'I don't see why not. You can cook breakfast when you get back.'

They drove in silence until they reached the road to Alderpoint. 'I know we talked about the police before, but is there nothing they can do?' asked Standing.

'Against the Russians?' He sighed. 'We can try. But look at it from the cops' point of view. The Russians want to buy Dominic's land. Dominic doesn't want to sell. His dogs got poisoned, his barn is burned down and they pulled guns on us. But it all happened pretty much in the middle of nowhere. The Russians obviously aren't going to admit to anything so what can the cops do? And even if Dominic asks them for help, if he tells them that his family need protection, do you think they're going to give him an armed guard, twenty-four seven? They don't have the resources for that. They'll probably tell him to move out for a while if he's worried, but if he does that the Russians might well burn his house down and take over his land. Even then the cops are likely to say that it's a civil matter. This isn't the big city. It's not even small-town America.'

'It's the Wild West.'

'As close as you'll get,' said Brett.

'So what's the answer?'

Brett shrugged. 'Dominic is going to have to increase his security. It's expensive but if he has a couple of guys with assault rifles on his property, the Russians might leave him alone.' He grinned over at Standing. 'Maybe you can persuade your friend to switch sides. That would simplify things.'

'I'll give it my best shot.'

It was dark by the time they got back to Brett's farm. The fire was burning and Olivia and Brianna were sitting in the deckchairs. They got up when Brett walked over but he told them to stay where they were. 'How was your first day?' he asked.

'Good,' said Brianna. 'We both managed two pounds each.'

'Are Amy and Angela asleep?'

Olivia nodded. 'They cooked us a Chinese rice thing so we said we'd do the cleaning up. They're really nice, aren't they?'

'They are,' said Brett. 'Do you girls want to smoke?'

'Do bears shit in the woods?' asked Olivia.

'The ones that live around here definitely do,' said Brett. 'Dale, there are a couple of lawn chairs behind your container. Bring them over, will you?'

Standing fetched the chairs and assembled them while Brett went inside to get a bong, a bag of cannabis and his Zippo. He brought them outside and sat down on one of the lawn chairs. 'Did you girls get to smoke with the Bulgarians?' asked Brett as he prepared the bong.

'For the first few days, yeah,' said Olivia. 'But only because they wanted us to get high so they could jump us. Then they started not to bother, they just . . .' She shuddered.

'Their weed was crap, anyway,' said Brianna.

'In that case, you're in for a treat,' said Brett. 'This is possibly the best weed in the county, if not the country.'

CHAPTER 26

Standing woke at exactly six o'clock in the morning. It was a trick he'd learnt as a teenager – before going to sleep he would bang his head on the pillow corresponding to the time he wanted to wake up. So, six o'clock, six bangs. It worked almost every time – the only time it didn't was if he'd had too much to drink the night before. He had even managed to use it to wake up at half past the hour, by making the final bang much softer than the rest. Standing had no idea how it worked, but it did.

He didn't bother showering, he just dressed and went outside and over to his pick-up truck.

The sun was just above the horizon and birds were singing high up in the trees. He climbed into the pick-up, started the engine and drove slowly along the track. He switched on his phone and as he reached the outskirts of Alderpoint he had a signal. There were three text messages, all from Charlotte Button, asking and then telling him to call her. There was nothing from Ashley but the diner wasn't open yet.

He pulled over at the side of the road and used Google Maps to work out his best route. Heading south and then across to Garberville and then north on Route 101 was a mile or so longer, but the roads were better and the journey time was showing as twenty minutes shorter than driving via Fort Seward.

Google Maps was absolutely right and it was five to seven when he saw Morty's ahead of him. There were two vehicles parked next to the diner, the blue Honda Civic that he'd seen outside Dominic's house and a grey Ford Escape, which Standing figured belonged to the cook. He knew that there was no way he could park next to the diner without being seen, so he drove off the road a couple of hundred yards away and parked up. As he switched off the engine, the neon sign flickered on, announcing that the diner was open.

Standing took out his phone and called Button. She answered almost immediately. 'I think I'm on to him,' said Standing. 'It looks like he's involved with some Russian mafia group. I'm hoping to find him within the next day or two.'

'Russian mafia? What's he doing with them?'

'I think he's just a hired gun.'

'You've seen him?'

'No, but I've spoken to a waitress at a diner he uses. And I've crossed swords with some of his colleagues.'

'What do you mean by that?'

'It's complicated. The Russians are trying to buy up farms in the area and they're using guys like French as muscle. I had a run-in with a few yesterday. Former Spetsnaz, I'd say. I told you before that the mobile phone coverage is patchy at best; it looks as if they take a run out to this diner for breakfast and to catch up on their messages.'

'And how are you equipment-wise?'

'I've hooked up with a guy who has enough kit to fight a small war, so I'm good. Look, Charlotte, I want to run something by you.'

'I'm listening.'

'It's possible that Frenchy doesn't know what these Russians are up to. I was thinking I could maybe talk to him, see if we can get him back on the straight and narrow.'

'You were told what your mission was, Matt.'

'Yes, I know. But he's one of the good guys. Or at least he was.'

'This isn't about what Ryan French was, it's about what he is now. And what he plans to do in the future. You know what your mission is, Matt. If you're not capable of carrying out that mission you need to tell me and I'll send someone else out to finish the job. Just so long as you realise the consequences of me doing that.'

'I just wanted to put forward another option.'

'There are no other options, Matt. Just get it done.'

Standing opened his mouth to reply but she ended the call. He gritted his teeth as he stared at his phone. He could feel his heart pounding and he was gripping the phone so tightly that his knuckles were whitening. He sat back in his seat, took a deep breath, and began square breathing to calm himself down.

CHAPTER 27

B rett was running towards the Huey helicopter, his MI6 clutched to his chest, as bullets zipped overhead. His feet were heavy and with every step the mud seemed to suck at his boots, sapping the energy from his aching legs. The helicopter was at the treeline, heading towards him. He could see the door gunner crouched over his M60 as he sprayed bullets over the paddy field. Brett's lungs were burning and every breath was agony. A hundred yards and he'd reach the helicopter. Eighty. Sixty. The helicopter was swooping down towards him. In a matter of seconds he'd be safe. But the mud was deeper now and he could barely pull his boots out. He opened his mouth to scream but then his eyes opened and he was awake. He could hear an engine outside. No, three engines. Four. Heading towards his farm. He was wide awake now. He rolled off his bed and knelt down, groping for the AR-15 assault rifle he kept nearby. He looked at his watch. It was just after seven. Dale would have left already. Brett cursed under his breath. He grabbed two spare magazines and tossed them on to his bed, then pulled on his jeans. He shoved a magazine in each pocket. The engines were louder now. He pulled on his boots but didn't have time to lace them before he ran to the door and flung it open.

Down the track he saw a black SUV with tinted windows.

There was an outside chance that this was a police or DEA raid, but they would almost certainly have announced themselves with flashing lights and sirens. These weren't cops, and the SUV was a close match to the one the Russians had been using at Dominic's farm.

He ran towards the container where the girls slept. He pushed open the door. 'Ladies, we have a problem outside. Can you all drop down on to the floor and stay down until I come back.'

Angela sat up and reached for her glasses. 'What's happening?' she asked.

'There's no time for questions, just do as I say. Get down on the floor and stay there.' He pulled the door shut and turned around. He could see a second black SUV now. And a third.

The first SUV made a sharp turn and came to a halt with a squeal of rubber. The rear doors opened and two men got out, holding assault rifles. Then the front passenger door opened and Mikhail climbed out. He was holding a pistol. A Glock. His sunglasses were on top of his head.

Brett brought his gun up. 'What do you want?' he shouted.

Mikhail was looking around, his pistol at his side. 'Where's your friend? The Brit?'

The second SUV screeched to a halt and three more men piled out, all with assault rifles.

'I don't want no trouble!' shouted Brett.

The third SUV pulled up behind the second. Sergei climbed out of the front passenger seat. He shouted over at Mikhail in Russian as two more men got out of the back. One of them was the giant, Yuri. This time he was holding an AR-15 that looked like a child's toy in his massive hands.

Mikhail pointed his gun at Brett and pulled the trigger. Brett ducked to the side and the round slammed into the container behind him. Brett bent double and ran around the side of the container, towards his shower. He turned, dropped into a kneeling position and fired three quick shots at Mikhail, but almost immediately there was a hail of bullets from the two men with him. Brett turned and ran.

He heard shouts in Russian behind him but he didn't look around. His only chance was to get into the trees.

He ran past the clearing of cannabis plants. Bullets thwacked into a tree to his left and he began to zig-zag, keeping his head down.

There were more shouts and he heard the slamming of car doors.

He ran behind a massive redwood, knelt down and quickly tied his boots, then turned, bringing up his rifle. He saw Yuri, ambling between the trees, and he took aim at the giant's chest and pulled the trigger. The round hit him dead centre and Yuri staggered backwards. Brett fired again, three shots in quick succession, all to the chest. Yuri swayed, but didn't go down. Instead, he raised his AR-15 and fired a short burst that hit a tree just above Brett's head. Then he started to jog towards him, shouting in Russian. Brett realised Yuri was wearing a bulletproof vest, and he cursed under his breath. He turned and began running again.

The guard geese were shrieking in the distance. Brett turned away from the curing room and ran through the trees. Someone off to his left fired a burst on automatic, more than a dozen shots, most of which hit a redwood behind him, kicking off chunks of bark. Brett veered to the right.

Several guns began firing behind him and suddenly his left calf felt as if it had been stabbed with a red-hot poker. He could still run, so he knew it was only a flesh wound, but it was bleeding heavily.

He ran around a spreading bush. Bullets whizzed through the leaves. He reached a large redwood, turned and brought up his rifle and started shooting again. There were four men moving through the trees towards him. Brett fired single shots, trying to avoid their chests, going for head shots or aiming at their legs. He caught one of the men in the thigh and he went down screaming. He saw Yuri hiding behind a tree and fired three shots at him, but the Russian ducked away and didn't appear again.

Brett heard the girls screaming in the distance. He doubted that the Russians would harm them but every fibre of his being told him to run back to the containers and protect them. It would be certain death though – he knew his only chance of survival was to lure the Russians further into the woods and take them out one at a time. Four vehicles. Sixteen men at most. He forced a smile. The odds weren't good but they weren't impossible.

A gun fired off to his right and a bullet hit the tree just inches from his head. He cursed and started running again, grunting every time his left foot hit the ground. More shots ripped into the vegetation around him, so he bent low and zig-zagged. He was breathing heavily and his leg was hurting like hell, and he knew he wouldn't be able to run for much longer.

He heard Sergei screaming at the top of his voice off in the distance. Brett didn't speak Russian but he got the gist. He reached a small clearing, fifty feet or so across. The ground sloped up beyond the clearing. A giant redwood had died and fallen on its side. He ran towards it, his chest burning. His left boot was filling with blood and making a squelching sound with every step. He had to veer around a bush, and as he did, bullets raked into the ground behind him, kicking up leaves and dirt.

He reached the fallen tree and ran around the exposed roots. He scrambled along the side of the trunk until he reached a point where he could rest the rifle on it and cover the clearing. His face was bathed in sweat and he blinked to clear his eyes. He caught a glimpse of a man moving between the trees, so he took aim and fired. The man's head crumpled and blood flew through the air. A second man appeared in the clearing and Brett fired again, but this time he missed and the man returned fire. Bullets smacked into the trunk. The man was firing low. Brett took a breath to steady himself, aimed at the man's head and squeezed the trigger three times in quick succession. The man fell like a sack of potatoes.

He heard more shouts, this time off to his left. He moved his gun, turning his head slowly from side to side so that his peripheral vision would kick in. He saw movement. A camou-flage-pattern jacket. He aimed and tracked the movement. A man in an LA Dodgers baseball cap appeared from behind a redwood. Brett squeezed the trigger and the cap flew off along with a big chunk of the man's skull. He fired again and what was left of the face blew apart.

Brett knew that he was going to have to change magazines soon. He'd lost count of how many shots he'd fired. There would have been thirty in the magazine when he started. How many had he fired? Fifteen? Twenty?

He heard a loud bang behind him and gasped as he felt something thump into his back. Blood sprayed across the tree trunk and when he looked down he saw a large ragged hole in his chest. His whole body went cold and his legs went weak. He twisted around and slowly slid down the trunk to the ground as his rifle slipped from his fingers. His mouth was open and he was panting, but he wasn't getting any air into his lungs. He needed to put something over the wound but he didn't have anything, so he pressed his hand over the hole. He was wasting his time, he knew that. The bullet had hit him in the back. A through and through.

A man was walking towards him. He was wearing camouflage pants and a webbing waistcoat over a denim shirt, and a camouflage-pattern boonie hat. He was taking his time, his gun at the ready, but Brett knew that he was finished and that he was no threat to the man. His gun was six inches from his right hand but it might as well have been six miles away.

Brett could feel his lungs filling with blood. Every breath was agony now. The man walked up to him. He was chewing gum, slowly and steadily. The assault rifle he was holding was a close match to the one Brett had been using. Brett stared up at the man and blinked his eyes as he tried to focus. He frowned. 'I know you,' he said.

The man looked down at him, still chewing. 'I don't think so.' He swung his rifle up and rested it against his shoulder.

Brett coughed and tasted blood in his mouth. 'Yeah. You're Ryan French. Former SEAL.' He coughed again and blood trickled from between his lips. 'Dale is looking for you.'

'Who the fuck's Dale?'

A shadow fell over Brett. It was Sergei. He was holding a huge revolver. A Desert Eagle. It couldn't have been the one that Standing had taken off him. The Russian probably had half a dozen of them. Brett wanted to repeat his 'big gun, small dick' insult but he was finding it too hard to breathe. 'Not so fucking tough now, old man,' he said. He sneered at Brett and then spat in his face.

'Fuck you!' grunted Brett. Blood was bubbling up in his throat now and red froth dribbled down his chin. Blood was also oozing through his fingers and running down his chest.

'Who's Dale?' said French.

'No, fuck you!' shouted Sergei. He pointed the gun at Brett's face and pulled the trigger, and everything went black.

CHAPTER 28

Standing sighed and looked at his watch. It was half past nine. He had been sitting in his truck for two and a half hours and while several dozen customers had come and gone, there had been no black SUVs and no one who had looked even remotely like Frenchy. The clientele appeared to be a mix of overweight men with beer bellies and hunting gear, and bearded hipsters who probably had the munchies. His phone had remained resolutely silent. His stomach growled and he realised it had been more than twelve hours since he had eaten anything. He started the engine and drove slowly to the diner, parking next to Ashley's Honda Civic.

She was standing by the cash register when he walked in. 'Dale!' she said, clearly surprised to see him. She looked over his shoulder. 'Is Brett with you?'

'No, I'm flying solo this morning.'

She picked up a menu and took him to the same booth he'd used the last time he was in the diner. She handed him the menu but he shook his head. 'I'll have scrambled eggs, bacon and toast,' he said. 'And coffee.'

'We've got a breakfast set that has orange juice and cereal included, and it's only a dollar more than what you ordered.'

'Sounds like a bargain,' he said. 'Let's do it.'

Ashley went to give his order to the cook and Standing

looked out of the window. A few pick-up trucks drove by. It was probably too early for tourists. Ashley returned with his coffee and orange juice. 'Dale, can I ask you something?'

'Sure,' he said, adding cream to his coffee.

'Those men who came to our farm yesterday, do you think they're dangerous?'

'What does your dad say?'

'He says that we're not to worry, that they're just trying to scare us.'

'He might be right.'

'You know they burned down our barn? And poisoned our dogs?'

Standing nodded. 'I don't know what to tell you. Your dad has lived here a lot longer than I have. He knows how things work here.'

She sat down opposite him. 'I told him that we should move out. He says that'd be running away and that if we did that we'd lose the farm.'

'I understand his point of view. It's your home, he doesn't want to give it up. You can't back down every time someone bullies you. If you do that, you end up with nothing.'

Tears were welling up in her eyes. 'I just don't want anything to happen to my family,' she said.

'I'm sure your dad feels the same way,' he said. 'He's just doing what he thinks is best.'

'And your friend. This man you're looking for. What's he doing with these Russians?'

'I don't know. If I see him, I'll ask him what's going on.'

'Who is he and why is it so important to you that you find him?'

Standing sipped his coffee as he tried to get his thoughts

in order. He hated having to lie to people that he liked, but he had no choice. There was no way that he could tell Ashley the truth, that his mission was to find Ryan French and kill him and that once he'd done that he'd be on the next plane back to the UK. 'He's an old friend who's having problems,' he said eventually. 'He was a Navy SEAL but he went through a lot out in Syria and he got PTSD. Post-traumatic stress disorder. His family thought he might end up hurting himself so they asked me to check that he was okay.'

'Well he was here and he looked fine. He didn't seem stressed out. Most of the time he was laughing and joking.' She wiped away a tear. 'I can't believe I served the guy who almost shot you. He was one of the men who was being nasty to that woman with the flyer. He told her that bad things happened to people in the woods and that she was wasting her time. Your friend told him to leave her alone.' She wiped her eyes again. 'And he asked me for my phone number.'

'Who did?'

'The Russian. The one with the gun. He said he'd take me out and show me a good time. He said once I'd been with a Russian man I'd never want to go with an American one again. He and his friends were saying that to all the girls in the diner, even the ones there with their husbands and boyfriends.'

'So there were four at the table?'

She nodded. 'Your friend, the Russian with the gun at our farm, and two more Russians.'

'But the other two weren't at the farm?'

'No, just the one with the gun. My heart was in my mouth, it really was. I was sure he was going to shoot you.'

'I don't think he ever meant to pull the trigger,' said Standing. 'Usually if someone's going to shoot you, they do it straight away. If they just point a gun at you, it means they're looking for a reason not to pull the trigger.'

'You weren't scared?'

He smiled. 'It wasn't the first time somebody's pointed a gun at me and I doubt it'll be the last.'

A bell dinged on the counter and Ashley slid out of the booth and went to collect Standing's meal. She placed it on the table in front of him. She was about to sit down and continue the conversation when the door opened and a group of three teenagers came in. 'I'll leave you in peace,' she said.

'Don't worry,' he said. 'I'm sure everything will work out.'

She flashed him a tight smile. 'I hope so,' she said, before heading off to deal with the customers. Standing picked up the ketchup bottle. He truly hoped that everything would work out for her, but he had a horrible feeling that things were only going to get worse.

CHAPTER 29

Two Russians dragged the four girls from the container and threw them on the ground where they lay, sobbing. Sergei and Frenchy appeared, with Yuri in tow. Between them they were carrying the weapons of the men who had been killed. Mikhail was standing by the fire pit, his Glock back in his holster in the small of his back.

'You got him?' asked Mikhail.

'He's dead,' said Frenchy.

'He got three of ours,' said Sergei. 'Lev, Mark and Erik. And Georgy has a bullet in his leg.' He looked around. 'Where's the fucking Brit?'

'He's not here,' said Mikhail.

'Well where the fuck is he?'

Mikhail walked along the track that led to the road, staring at the marks in the mud. 'There's another truck,' he said. 'He's probably gone somewhere.'

'Where the fuck would he go at this time of the day?'

Mikhail shrugged but didn't say anything.

Frenchy gestured at the woods. 'What do we do with the bodies, boss?' he asked.

'Just leave them,' said Sergei. 'They're not carrying ID and in a few days they'll just be bones.' Two men were helping

Georgy through the trees. 'He's the fucking problem. What do we do with him?'

'We could drive him to the hospital in Eureka,' said Frenchy.

'They'll call the cops.'

'He can say he shot himself by mistake.'

'He doesn't have a visa. They're going to have a lot of questions. We'll take him back with us.'

'He's lost a lot of blood, boss,' said French.

'That's his own fault for getting shot,' snarled Sergei.

'What shall we do with them?' asked Mikhail. He pointed at the four girls. They were now all kneeling. Two of the girls were hugging each other tearfully. The other two were staring at the ground, avoiding eye contact. Sergei rubbed the back of his neck. There were only two choices. Kill them or take them to his farm. Killing them would be the easiest option, but skilled workers had a cash value so it made more sense to put them to work. He could always kill them when the season was over.

'Take them with us,' he growled.

Yuri and three of the men went over to the girls, grabbed them and dragged them over to the SUVs.

Mikhail came back to Sergei. 'He's going to come back. I'm sure of it.'

'So we'll leave some men here. They'll take care of him.'

'I'll do it.'

Sergei's eyes narrowed. 'Are you taking it personally?'

'He pointed a gun at me. Anyone who does that needs to pull the trigger, because if they don't I'm going to kill them.'

'Okay. I'll leave a couple of guys with you.'

'I don't need a couple of guys. I'll handle it myself.'

The two men carrying Georgy arrived at the containers. They had tied a belt around his left thigh as a makeshift tourniquet. His jeans were wet with blood but he was conscious. 'I'm sorry about this, boss,' he said.

Sergei waved away his apology. He pointed at the Jeep Wrangler. 'We'll take that. Put him in the back, I don't want him bleeding in our vehicles.'

As they carried Georgy over to the Jeep, another of Sergei's men appeared in the doorway of the middle container. 'Boss, have a look at this.' It was Viktor Kozlov, like Mikhail a former member of the Spetsnaz, Russian special forces. Viktor was in his forties and had retired in 2005 after almost twelve years in the army, latterly running an assassination squad in Chechnya where his team were responsible for the deaths of several hundred Islamist fighters determined to create their own independent state. Sometimes, when he was drunk, Viktor would regale them with stories of killings he had personally carried out. Sergei was no stranger to violence, but some of the things Viktor talked about made even him feel queasy. Viktor was a big man, almost as large as Yuri. He shaved his head daily so that he could show off the shrapnel scars that peppered his skull.

Sergei went over and Mikhail followed him. Viktor showed him the collection of guns in the metal cage. 'Some nice guns here,' he said. He pointed at the boxes on a shelf to the right. 'Lots of ammo, too.'

Sergei examined the padlock. 'Mikhail, find something to break this open.'

Mikhail went out and returned less than a minute later with a spade, which he used to smash the padlock to pieces. Sergei pulled open the metal doors and grabbed one of the assault rifles. 'The old man has quite a collection,' he said, as he checked out the weapon.

Mikhail opened the metal trunk on the floor and they both looked inside. 'Night vision equipment, tactical vests, more ammo,' said Mikhail. 'Pity he didn't have it all to hand when we turned up.'

'A pity for him, good luck for us,' said Sergei. 'Viktor, we'll take all this with us.'

'Right, boss.'

There was a bolt-action rifle on the wall and Mikhail took it down. It was the Remington Model Seven. 'I'll have this,' he said.

Sergei took down one of the HKs. 'Heckler & Koch G3,' he said. 'This is the better gun, none of that single shot and fumbling to reload nonsense.'

Mikhail grinned. 'I'll only need one shot,' he said.

'I thought you liked your killings up close and personal.'

'I do, but there's something about that Brit.'

'Don't tell me you're scared.'

Mikhail's eyes hardened. 'I'm not fucking scared,' he said quietly. 'But that Brit knows how to handle himself. He's special forces, no question, and that means the SAS. You don't fuck around with the SAS.' He held up the rifle. 'So if it's all right with you, I'll use this to take care of business.'

Sergei grinned savagely. 'It's your kill so it's your call.'

'Just leave me with one of the cars. I'll drive back when I'm done.'

CHAPTER 30

Standing slowed as he approached the turn-off that led up the mountain, but he braked sharply when he saw the black SUVs heading down the track. The lead vehicle turned to the right and headed down the road. It was followed by another SUV, then Standing's stomach lurched as he saw Brett's Jeep Wrangler. It turned to follow the SUVs. They were too far away for Standing to see who was driving, but whoever it was they were white. He gritted his teeth. Another black SUV turned and followed the Jeep. He thought about following the convoy but dismissed the idea immediately. They'd see him on their tail. He stamped on the accelerator, drove off the Alderpoint road and headed along the rutted track, driving as fast as the pick-up would go. His heart was pounding and his breath was coming in ragged gasps.

The drive to Brett's farm seemed to take an eternity. But he didn't want it to end, because he knew when he finally got there his worst fears would be realised. As the track curved ahead of him something flashed and he immediately braked. In the distance, through the trees, he saw a black SUV. The sunlight had glinted off one of the side mirrors. They had taken Brett's Jeep with them, so why was the SUV still there? It only made sense if one or more of the Russians had stayed behind. He leant over, opened the glove box, and took out the Glock 22. He put the truck in park, eased open the door and slipped out. He kept low, turning his head from side to side, listening intently. If they were waiting for him they'd have heard him already, so he was going to have to move quickly. From where he was standing he could see the middle container and smoke rising from the fire pit. He could see the offside of the SUV but everything else was blocked by the trees. Hopefully that meant they also couldn't see him.

He bent low and moved into the trees, breathing slowly and evenly. He kept moving east, using the trees as cover. He looked to his left but nothing seemed out of place. He stopped and crouched down. Had he misread the situation? Just because the vehicle was a black SUV didn't automatically mean it was owned by the Russians. And maybe Brett had driven away of his own free will. His mind raced as he considered his options. As he stared at the containers he spotted movement on the top of the container on the left, the one where he had slept. He shaded his eyes with his left hand and moved his head from side to side. There was a barrel of a rifle and a bump under the camouflage netting, next to one of the solar cells. A sniper. Covering the approach to the farm. But was he alone? The sniper would be focused on the pick-up truck and hopefully hadn't noticed that Standing had left the vehicle. But the longer the truck stayed where it was, the more likely the sniper would realise what was going on.

As Standing moved through the trees around to the curing room, he realised that the guard geese weren't making any noise. He moved closer. The gate was open and the geese were dead on the grass, their feathers glistening with blood. The doors to the container were open and as he moved towards the gate he could see inside. All the jars containing cannabis buds had been taken.

He stopped and listened. In the distance he could hear the throbbing of the pick-up truck. He started moving towards the rear of the middle container, his gun at the ready.

At some point the sniper was going to realise that the truck wasn't going anywhere. At that point he would have a choice: to wait it out or change position. He was using a rifle, which gave him the edge over long distances, but in close-quarter combat it was less effective.

He stopped and listened again. If the sniper had back-up, they'd have moved towards the truck to check it out, so all the signs were that he was alone.

Standing moved to the right, using the trees as cover. Eventually he was able to see the rear of the container on which the sniper was lying. Next to the container was a pair of wooden stepladders that Brett used to fill the plastic barrel that supplied water to the shower. Standing moved across the grass towards the steps. He reached them and slowly went up, his gun at the ready. The steps were old and they squeaked as he put his weight on them. His breath caught in his throat and he paused, then he carried on upwards. His head reached the top of the container. The sniper was still aiming at the truck. Standing took another step and pointed his gun at the sniper, who was covered by the camouflage netting. 'Drop the gun or I'll put a bullet in your head!' he shouted.

The sniper didn't react and the rifle continued to point at the truck in the distance.

As Standing opened his mouth to shout again, he heard a twig crack behind him and he twisted around to see Mikhail coming across the grass towards him, a Glock in his hand, his

Oakley sunglasses pushed on top of his head. The Russian grinned as he pulled the trigger but Standing had already lost his balance and fell to the side, smacking against the canvas wall of the shower. Two rounds thudded into the container as Standing slid down the canvas. The stepladder fell with him and banged against his side. Mikhail fired again, another double-tap, but he was still firing one handed and both rounds hit the ladder, sending splinters spraying across Standing's face.

Standing rolled across the ground as bullets thudded into the grass next to him. He fired as he rolled, two quick shots that hit Mikhail in the centre of his chest. He carried on rolling and the Russian fired again. His rounds smacked into the base of the shower. Standing realised that the chest shots hadn't had any effect so he raised his aim and focused on the man's face. Mikhail dropped into a crouch and put both hands on the Glock, but before he could aim Standing fired again, two shots at the Russian's mouth. Both hit their target and Mikhail fell back, his finger pulling the trigger as he died, sending another bullet into the shower.

Standing stood up and went over to the Russian. He was dead but the gun was still in his hand, finger on the trigger. Close up, Standing could see the bulletproof vest he was wearing. He kept his pistol up as he walked around to Brett's container. It was empty. He went back outside and into the centre container. He saw immediately that the cage was open and all Brett's weapons and ammunition had been taken. He cursed under his breath. The Russians had taken all his weapons and his cured cannabis and his Jeep. So what had they done with the man himself?

He went outside again and checked the SUV. He saw dried

blood on the grass and bent down to look at it. Someone had been bleeding profusely. Had they hurt Brett and taken him with them? There was no sign of the girls. He shouted their names but there was no reply.

The blood trail came to a sudden end. Presumably the injured man, whoever it was, had been put inside one of the vehicles. He began following the blood trail the other way, back into the woods. The trail took him around to the rear of the containers.

He moved forward, his eyes on the ground. He saw boot prints, heading to where the vehicles had been. Two men holding another who had been carried and dragged.

He continued to follow the tracks. Broken twigs, bruised vegetation, footprints in the mud.

As he went deeper into the forest the trail led to a patch of earth where somebody had fallen. There was a pool of dried blood on the ground. He knelt down and stared at the footprints in the soil. One man had gone down, bleeding. Two men had carried him away so he was probably alive. But who had been injured? Was it Brett?

Standing straightened up. He saw more tracks, coming from the north, and he followed them. In the distance, on the edge of a small clearing, he saw a body, lying face down. He hurried over. As he got closer, he saw that it was one of the Russians. Most of his head had been blown away. Standing looked around but couldn't see a weapon. His colleagues had obviously taken the gun with them but had left the corpse.

There was a second body a few yards away. Another head shot. As Standing walked up to the body he realised the man was wearing a bulletproof vest. He frowned as he stared down at it. They had taken one man with them but left two behind.

So they had taken the injured man but left the dead. That wasn't how professionals worked – the SAS would never leave a man behind, alive or dead.

In the distance was a massive fallen redwood, lying on its side. The shots that had killed the Russians had almost certainly come from there. Brett must have found cover. His heart began to pound at the realisation that maybe, just maybe, Brett was still alive.

He cupped his hands around his mouth. 'Brett!' he shouted in the direction of the tree. 'Brett, it's me!'

There was no reply. Standing headed towards the tree and almost fell over a third body. This one was face down, wearing a camouflage-pattern jacket. Most of the top of the man's head was missing and a blood-spattered LA Dodgers baseball cap was lying on the ground a few feet away. As with the other two bodies, the man's weapon was nowhere to be seen.

'Brett, I'm heading your way!' he called. He walked around the root end of the fallen tree. 'Brett, it's me!'

As he reached the far side of the tree he saw Brett slumped on the ground. He hurried over but as soon as he got close he could see that the man was dead. There was a gaping wound in his chest and most of his head had been blown away. The wounds and the blood spatter told the story. He'd been shot in the back and the round had exited through his chest, then he'd fallen down and been shot at close range in the face. They'd taken his gun with them.

'Brett, mate, I'm so sorry,' he whispered. 'I should have been here with you.' He stood looking down at the body, considering his options. If it had happened anywhere else he would have called the police, but he knew that in Humboldt County that would be a pointless exercise. And even if they did take action, putting the killers behind bars wouldn't bring Brett back, or give Standing any feeling of satisfaction. Brett had never mentioned any relatives, so there would be no one clamouring for justice. And if Standing did go to the police, and if they did make any sort of move against the Russians, Frenchy would almost certainly vanish. Standing was all too aware of what Button's reaction would be if that happened. 'I'll make them pay for this, Brett, I swear,' he said out loud.

As he walked back to the containers, he put together a plan. The Russians had abandoned their dead and Standing didn't intend to waste his time burying them. Brett was a different matter. He deserved the respect of a decent grave, and Standing figured he would have preferred to be buried among his beloved plants than in a graveyard surrounded by strangers.

He went back to the camp and collected a large carving knife. Then he picked up Mikhail, threw him across his shoulders and carried him into the woods. After a couple of hundred yards he dropped the man on to the ground, pulled off his sneakers and used the knife to cut off all his clothing. He checked the man's pockets but there was no ID, just a wad of cash.

He figured there'd be plenty of predators in the woods who would be more than happy for a free meal. He picked up the sneakers and clothes, then retraced his steps and removed the boots and clothing from the other three Russians. He took the clothing and footwear back to the fire pit. The fire was still burning, so he tossed it all on to the embers and threw on a few more logs.

He grabbed the spade that the Russians had used to smash their way into Brett's arms cache and took it back to the fallen tree. Brett's body was covered in blood, so Standing had no choice other than to drag him to the clearing filled with cannabis plants.

He pulled the body to the middle of the field, then he dug up four of the plants, trying not to damage the roots. He put them to one side and spent the next three hours digging the grave. He wanted it deep because he didn't want the body being disturbed. It was to be Brett's resting place for eternity, so the job had to be done properly. He worked quickly and efficiently without any breaks and didn't stop until the grave was five-feet deep. When it was done, he climbed out, then carefully placed Brett in the hole, lying him on his back. He piled soil on top of the body. He wasn't sure if Brett was religious, but when he had finished he recited the Lord's Prayer and stood for a minute in silence. The last thing he did was to replace the four cannabis plants and pat the soil down with the back of his spade.

He went back to the fire pit. It was burning nicely. He tossed on a couple more logs and stared into the flames as he considered his options. He needed to find Frenchy. And he needed to find the Russians, because he was going to make them pay for what they had done to Brett. And he had to find the girls and release them. And he had to do it all single-handedly. As he stared at the fire he remembered the weapons he'd taken from the quad bikes when he'd first arrived in Humboldt. He hurried over to the container where he kept his things and smiled when he saw that his rucksack was still by his bunk. He unzipped it. The shotgun and the SIG Sauer were there.

He gathered up his clothes and wash bag and put them into his rucksack, then picked up a towel and wiped down everything he might have touched during his stay. He tossed the towel on to the fire, had a final look around, then went over to his truck and put his rucksack on the passenger seat.

He did a final walk around to make sure that he hadn't left anything behind, then climbed in and started the engine. He drove slowly down the track, deep in thought.

CHAPTER 31

It took him almost an hour to reach the Garberville motel where he'd left his bags. He was on high alert all the way, keeping an eye out for black SUVs, but he didn't see any. He parked outside his room, then took his rucksack inside. He stripped off his clothes. There was blood on his shirt and his jeans so he tossed them into the shower, then used wads of toilet paper to clean his boots, flushing it down the toilet when he'd finished.

He got into the shower and let the water play over his face for several minutes, then he washed himself and shampooed his hair. He washed his jeans and shirt and then draped them over the side of the bathtub before drying himself and changing into clean clothes.

His phone buzzed to let him know that he'd received a message. He picked it up. It was from Charlotte Button. 'SITREP?' He was tempted to give her a piece of his mind, but knew there was no point in antagonising her. He sent her a text back. 'ENDGAME SOON'.

He rolled on to the bed, put his Glock on the bedside table and stared up at the ceiling. His heart began to pound as he thought about what the Russians had done to Brett, chasing him through the woods and shooting him like an animal. And the girls, what had happened to the girls? He hoped that the

Russians had only kidnapped them and that they weren't dead in the woods. He could feel his whole body tensing so he counted slowly to ten and then began square breathing. There was nothing he could do, not right now. He had to wait. He was alone and the Russians were mob-handed and heavily armed. He needed a plan.

After two minutes of square breathing he was more relaxed. He decided to grab some sleep. He banged his head softly on the pillow six times, then closed his eyes and listened to his own breathing. He was asleep within seconds.

He woke up at six o'clock exactly. He swung his feet off the bed and went into the bathroom, where he splashed water over his face and brushed his teeth. When he was finished, he sat on the bed and checked his Glock 22. The magazine held up to fifteen .40 S&W rounds. Standing wasn't a fan of the cartridge, he found it produced a snappier recoil than a 9mm and didn't really do any more damage. There were only three rounds in the magazine.

He put the rucksack on the bed and unzipped it. He took out the shotgun and assembled it, then checked out the ammunition. There were twelve cartridges and they were all birdshot. It would be useless, he realised. It was an impressive-looking weapon but with birdshot cartridges it wouldn't do any serious damage beyond twenty or thirty feet. He disassembled the shotgun and put it back in the rucksack.

He took out the SIG Sauer and ejected the magazine. For many years the P226 was the favoured firearm of the Navy SEALs. Prior to adopting it, they had used the Beretta 92FS, known as the M9. The SEALs were notoriously hard on their guns and legend had it that one of the M9s had spectacularly failed during a demonstration for a visiting VIP. The slide flew off and hit a SEAL in the face. Not long after that, the SEALs switched to the SIG Sauer and used it for more than thirty years in Panama, Somalia, Haiti, the Balkans and across the Middle East. It was a good piece of kit and one that Standing was very familiar with.

He stripped down the gun and examined the components. It was in good condition and had been well maintained. He reassembled it and checked the magazine. It was full. He slapped it back into the grip. He took the two spare magazines out of the rucksack. They were both fully loaded. Each magazine held fifteen rounds in a double-stack configuration. It meant a lot of firepower but it needed a wider pistol grip, making it harder for individuals with smaller hands. The SEALs weren't known for having small hands so it was never an issue. In 2015, Naval Special Warfare Command decided to introduce the Glock 19, but many SEALs preferred to stick with the SIG Sauer. Not that Standing had a choice. His Glock was almost empty and he had forty-five rounds for the P226. It was a no-brainer.

His stomach rumbled and he realised it had been almost twenty-four hours since he had eaten. He took his hand luggage down from the top of the wardrobe. In one of the side compartments he found two energy bars, a bar of chocolate and a packet of peanuts. He wolfed them all down with a bottle of water.

When he'd finished he tidied up the room and put on his coat. He put the P226 in his right coat pocket and the magazines in the left, and tucked the Glock into his belt. He left a 'DO NOT DISTURB' sign on the doorknob and locked the door.

He climbed into the pick-up truck and put the Glock in the

glove compartment. It wouldn't be much use with only three rounds in the magazine, but it would be better than nothing in an emergency.

The diner was a fifteen-minute drive from the motel and again he parked down the road to give himself a good view of the car park. Ashley's Honda was already there and shortly afterwards the cook arrived.

The minutes ticked by. A dozen pick-up trucks came and went, a few saloons, and several farm vehicles. The only SUVs that arrived were white and none had tinted windows. But just after eight-thirty a black SUV drove from the direction of Phillipsville. It turned off the road and parked close to Ashley's car. The windows were tinted so Standing couldn't see who was inside, but his heart raced when he recognised the man who climbed out of the driving seat. Ryan French. He was wearing a camouflage combat jacket over khaki pants. Yuri the giant eased himself out of the passenger door and a third man with blond hair climbed out of the back. The three men walked over to the entrance, laughing about something as they went inside. After a couple of minutes, Standing's phone beeped and he looked at the screen. It was a message from Ashley. 'YOUR FRIEND JUST ARRIVED WITH ONE OF THE MEN WHO WAS AT OUR FARM.'

Standing texted back. 'OK. THANKS.'

A few seconds later she messaged him again. 'ARE YOU COMING?'

Standing grimaced. He didn't want to confront Frenchy and the others inside the diner. What he had to say and do had to be done without witnesses. But he didn't want to raise Ashley's suspicions, and he definitely didn't want her to say anything to Frenchy.

'PROBABLY NOT TODAY,' he sent back. 'PLEASE DON'T SAY ANYTHING TO HIM. I NEED TO FIND OUT WHAT HE IS DOING WITH THE RUSSIANS.'

After a minute she replied. 'OK', with a sad face.

'TEXT ME WHEN THEY LEAVE.'

After another minute she replied with another 'OK' and a happy face.

Standing drove slowly to the diner and parked next to the black SUV, pulled a camouflage-pattern baseball cap down over his eyes and sat slumped in his seat as he waited. After forty-five minutes his phone beeped. 'THEY ARE LEAVING NOW.'

He texted back. 'OK.'

She sent him a smiley face.

Standing tucked his P226 into his belt and climbed out of the pick-up truck. He heard the diner door open and deep voices emerge. Then a laugh and more voices. He kept his head down and his back to the entrance. He heard the SUV beep and saw its lights flash as Frenchy pressed the key fob. Standing walked around the back of his truck, taking out his gun and holding it at his side. Frenchy pulled open the driver's door and got in. Yuri climbed into the front passenger seat and slammed the door. The third man walked around the back of the SUV. As he pulled open the passenger door he said something in Russian to Yuri.

Standing moved behind him and hit him on the side of the head with the gun, then hit him again as he went down. He yanked the man's transceiver off his belt, pulled his cell phone from his back pocket, then hit him again.

Frenchy and Yuri twisted around in their seats to see what was happening, but before they could react, Standing had climbed in, slammed the door, and pointed his gun at Yuri's head. 'Drive,' he said to Frenchy.

'What the fuck?' said Frenchy.

'Drive!' shouted Standing.

'Okay, okay,' said Frenchy. He turned around, started the engine and reversed away from the diner, taking care not to run over the unconscious Russian.

'Back to your farm,' said Standing. 'Yuri, pass me your phone and your radio. Do it nice and slowly because I have a very itchy trigger finger.'

Frenchy drove on to the road and headed north towards Phillipsville, chewing gum and trying to get a good look at Standing in his rear-view mirror. Yuri did as he was told and Standing put the radio and transceiver on the floor.

'Now do the same with Frenchy's.'

Frenchy twisted around, frowning. 'How do you know . . .?' He left the sentence unfinished as he recognised Standing. 'Matt?' he said. 'Matt Standing? What the fuck are you doing here?'

'Just drive,' said Standing. 'Yuri, give me his radio and phone. Slowly. Really slowly.'

Yuri passed Frenchy's phone and radio back and Standing dropped them on to the floor with the others.

'Okay, where do we stand gun-wise?' Standing asked.

'Matt, what the fuck is going on?' asked Frenchy.

'Keep your eyes on the road. Yuri, where's your gun?'

'Glove compartment,' he said.

'Okay, so you're going to open the glove compartment and you're going to take out your gun with your left hand, just using your finger and thumb and holding the barrel. If I even think your finger is going over the trigger I will shoot you in the back of the head. Do you understand?'

Yuri slowly followed Standing's instructions and passed back the gun, a Glock 19. Standing took it and shoved it into his coat pocket. 'What about you, Frenchy?'

'I'm not carrying. What are you doing in Humboldt County, Matt? You're a long way from home.'

He twisted around in his seat but Standing gestured with his gun and told him to concentrate on the road. 'You think I didn't see the bulge under your left armpit?' he said.

'Can't blame a guy for trying,' said Frenchy.

He took his right hand off the steering wheel but Standing told him to keep it where it was. 'Yuri, reach over and take out his gun. Finger and thumb only and move very, very slowly.'

Again the Russian did as he was told and handed back the weapon. It was a SIG Sauer P226, similar to the one Standing was holding. It went into his other coat pocket.

'Fuck, I get it now,' said Frenchy. 'You're Dale. You're the one who's been looking for me. Now it all makes sense.'

'Just drive,' said Standing. 'Keep both your hands on the steering wheel and keep just below the speed limit.'

'I can't take you back to the farm. Sergei will kill you.'

'That's my problem, not yours.'

'What is it you want, Matt? What are you doing here?'

'Just drive.'

'Did someone send you to find me?'

Standing ignored the question.

'Is that what this is, a search and destroy mission, like we used to do in Syria? Did someone send you to kill me?'

'If I was here to kill you, wouldn't you be dead already?'

'Maybe you want to be the white knight who rescues the four girls they took.'

'They? Are you trying to shift the blame for what happened? Were you there?'

'Matt, I just follow orders. I'm a hired hand. Sergei's the boss.'

'And why are you working for the Russian mafia?'

'Why? Because these days there are limited employment options for someone like me, especially considering I left the SEALs under a cloud.'

Standing shrugged but didn't say anything. Frenchy was driving slowly now as the road twisted its way towards Fort Seward. A red pick-up truck came towards them and Standing lowered his gun.

'What about you, Matt? You still with the SAS? Did the SAS send you to Humboldt? That's unlikely, right? You guys always operate in four-man patrols and you're clearly flying solo on this.'

The red pick-up drove by them, a middle-aged woman in a hunter's cap at the wheel. 'Just drive, Frenchy. This isn't a social call. There's no need for chit-chat.'

'So not the SAS, then. What about The Pool? Are you here for The Pool?'

Standing frowned. How did Frenchy know about The Pool? He wanted to ask, but he didn't want to get into a conversation with the man.

'Matt, just tell me what it is you want and maybe I can help you,' said Frenchy. 'What's your objective here? What's your mission?'

'My mission right now is to get you to shut the fuck up,' said Standing. 'And if the only way I can achieve that is to put a bullet in your head, so be it. Just drive.'

'And what happens when we get to the farm?'

'I'll cross that bridge when I get to it.'

'You don't want to fuck with these guys, Matt.'

'Let me worry about that.'

'Were you told about the possible consequences of what they're asking you to do?'

'Frenchy, I'm not going to tell you again.'

'What, you'd shoot the driver of a car travelling at speed?'

Standing fastened his seatbelt. 'Yes,' he said. 'I would.'

Frenchy reached for his seatbelt but Standing tapped him on the side of the head with the barrel of his gun. 'No, leave that off,' he said.

Frenchy shrugged. 'I've got airbags.'

'Not sure they'll stop a bullet, but you can try.'

Frenchy drove in silence for the next few miles, but he was constantly checking Standing out in his rear-view mirror. Standing stared back impassively. The fact that the former SEAL knew that someone called Dale was looking for him meant that Frenchy had spoken to Brett. And if he had spoken to Brett, he was probably the man who killed him.

They drove through Fort Seward and across the bridge over Eel River.

'We were friends, right?' said Frenchy eventually. 'We got on well while you did your induction training at Coronado. And then when you were embedded with my unit in Syria, we bonded, didn't we?'

'That was a long time ago,' said Standing.

'Not that long, Matt. But you never had a problem with me, right? In fact you saved my butt a couple of times.'

'More than that,' said Standing.

'And I was your wingman on several ops. I never let you down.'

'Just drive.'

Frenchy's eyes narrowed in the rear-view mirror. 'The point I'm making is that this can't be personal. Somebody must have put you up to it.'

Standing said nothing.

'And I guess I'm wondering if that person might be Charlotte Button.' Standing was blindsided by the name and his eyes widened in surprise. Frenchy smiled. 'And there we have it,' he said quietly.

Standing fought to conceal his surprise but he knew he was too late and Frenchy was grinning in triumph.

'How do you know her?' asked Standing.

'That's a conversation we need to have in private,' said Frenchy. 'Just you and me.'

Standing stared out of the side window as the redwoods flashed by, his mind in a whirl. It was possible that Frenchy had learnt about The Pool. But Standing had only discovered who Charlotte Button was the evening she had appeared in his hotel room. This was a woman who clearly went to a lot of trouble to remain anonymous, so how did Frenchy know about her?

They turned off the main road and began driving along a track through the forest. The track wasn't quite wide enough for two vehicles to pass, but it was reasonably flat, presumably one of the original logging trails. There were no recognisable features to tell him whether or not it was the trail Brett had used when they had visited Dominic's farm. There were gates leading off the trail along with warning notices, and several abandoned vehicles rusting among the trees.

'We're about ten minutes away from our farm,' Frenchy said eventually. 'I don't know what your plan is, but if they start shooting I'm not going to be able to protect you.'

'Why would they start shooting?' said Standing. 'The windows are so tinted you can barely see anything outside. You went out with two passengers, you're coming back with two. Assuming that Russians can count.'

'We can count,' said Yuri sourly.

'Good to know,' said Standing. 'So when we get there you both smile and wave and no one is going to pay me any attention.'

'And then what?'

Standing shrugged. 'Then I'll play it by ear.'

'Sergei has more than a dozen men. Most are Spetsnaz but there are two Navy SEALs like me. They're all armed.'

'Oh, let's forget about it then, shall we? Drive me back to the diner and I'll pick up my truck.' He tapped the gun against Frenchy's seat. 'Just get me on to the farm, what happens then is up to me.'

Frenchy shook his head. 'What's wrong with you? Have you got a death wish?'

'You killed my friend,' said Standing quietly.

'Which friend?'

'Brett. Brett Mullican. The guy who told you about me. The guy who said Dale was looking for you.'

'I didn't know he was your friend,' said Frenchy. He sighed. 'It wasn't personal, Matt. I was just doing a job.'

'You killed a farmer. That's all he was. He just wanted a quiet life, he was no threat to anybody.'

'He killed three of Sergei's men. He would have killed me if he'd had the chance.'

'And if I'd been there when you guys had turned up, I would have, too,' snapped Standing.

'Your friend shot me,' said Yuri, rubbing his chest.

'You mean shot at you.'

'No. He hit me. Four times. But I was wearing a vest. He was a good shot.'

'Yeah, well I'm a good shot and if I pull the trigger I'll be aiming at your head. Now shut up.'

The SUV slowed and Frenchy turned along a narrower track that wound its way through towering redwoods. There was no gate and no warning signs, but the trail was clearly well used, with dozens of tyre tracks criss-crossing each other.

Standing could see several single-storey buildings through the trees. Off to the left was a wooden tower with a metal ladder leading up to a vantage point where a man stood cradling an assault rifle.

The farm was in a large clearing, a hundred metres or so across. To the left, at the treeline, was a row of large canvas tents, most of which had generators humming next to them. At the far end of the line of tents was a stack of fuel barrels and dozens of red plastic fuel cans.

The SUV bucked and rolled as it drove along the uneven track towards a line of vehicles including more black SUVs, pick-up trucks, two minivans and Brett's Jeep.

'Where will Sergei be?' asked Standing.

'Matt, you go anywhere near him and he'll kill you. He knows what you did to Mikhail.'

'Now how would he know that?'

'When Mikhail didn't turn up last night and didn't answer his radio, he sent a couple of guys over first thing this morning. They found his body in the woods. He's assuming that you did it.'

'Yeah, well he assumes right,' said Standing. He patted the barrel of the gun against Frenchy's head. 'Where will he be?'

'See the line of Portakabins to the right? There's five of them. He uses the one in the middle as his office.'

'What about the workers?'

Frenchy pointed to the left at the canvas tents. 'Those are for curing and drying . . .' he began, but as he spoke he threw his door open and rolled out of the vehicle. Standing was caught by surprise. He grabbed for his door handle and opened his door, but realised too late that he still had his seatbelt on. He undid the belt but before he could get out of the car Frenchy was already shouting 'armed intruder' at the top of his voice.

Standing went into overdrive. The SUV was slowing but still moving, so he threw himself out and went into a roll. Frenchy was still shouting and now he was pointing at Standing.

The man in the watchtower was turning around and raising his rifle. Standing got to his feet, went down on one knee and took aim, squeezing off two shots that went high and slammed into the watchtower's roof. He immediately compensated and the next two shots hit the man in the head.

Standing stood up. Frenchy whirled around and ran towards the Portakabins. The SUV had come to a stop and Yuri was easing his massive bulk out of the front passenger seat. Standing pulled out the other P226 with his left hand. Standing was right-handed, but like all members of the SAS he practised shooting with both hands so that he was almost ambidextrous in combat. Troopers had to be able to fire with both hands so that a hand or arm injury didn't put them out of action.

Standing wasn't a fan of firing one-handed but the technique would double his firepower and he was vastly out-gunned. He heard shouts off to the left. A big man with a shaved head carrying an AR-15 walked around the line of tents and raised his weapon when he saw Standing. Standing fired twice and both shots hit the man in the chest. He was about to go for a head shot but the man fell back, arms flailing, two red patches on his shirt. He wasn't wearing a vest and he slumped to the ground.

Standing heard more Russian shouts to his right. The gun in his right hand was already pointing in that direction so all he had to do was turn his head and he was on target. There were two men, casually dressed in T-shirts and fatigues. One had an AR-15, the other a handgun. Standing put one round in the chest of the man with the assault rifle, then two in the chest of the man with the handgun. Red flowers blossomed on their T-shirts. The man with the handgun slumped to the ground but the other man stayed on his feet, staring at Standing with a look of surprise on his face. Standing fired again, a head shot that sent him tumbling to the ground.

Standing started walking forward, his guns constantly moving. He heard a rapid footfall behind him and he twisted around. It was Yuri, running back down the track, zig-zagging to avoid any shots. Standing couldn't help but grin – the man was so big that all the zig-zagging in the world wouldn't make him any less of a target.

There was a rat-tat-tat of automatic fire behind Standing, the rounds passing so close to his head that he felt the wind. He went down in a crouch as he turned. A big bald man in a camouflage jacket and blue jeans had come out of the middle Portakabin with what looked like a Heckler & Koch G3 in his hands. Standing pointed both guns at the man and pulled the triggers. Both rounds hit him in the chest but they had no effect and the man fired again. Standing figured he wasn't familiar with the weapon because the shots went high. Standing fired again, this time two quick shots from the gun in his right hand, which both smacked into the big man's face. He fell back, arms wide, and the carbine hit the ground at the same time he did.

There were frantic screams coming from the farm employees in the tents off to his left. Standing hoped they'd stay put, because the last thing he needed was a pack of panicking civilians running around.

He was looking left and right again and his guns were constantly moving as he walked across the grass to the Portakabins.

He heard the thud of boots on grass and whirled around, his guns at the ready. Yuri had managed to get hold of what looked like an Uzi. Next to him was a man holding an AR-15. He was probably the same height as Standing but next to Yuri he looked tiny. Yuri fired first but he was at least fifty yards away and in the automatic mode the Uzi was notoriously difficult to control. The first couple of shots thudded into the grass by Standing's feet but then the weapon started to pull up and to the right and the remaining shots went high and wide. Standing aimed both guns at him and fired them at the same time. The round from his left gun hit Yuri in the face. The round from the right caught the other man in the neck and he fell backwards, clutching his rifle.

Most of Yuri's face had been blown away but somehow he stayed upright, holding on to the Uzi. Standing aimed both guns at Yuri's head but before he could pull the trigger, the Russian finally fell back and hit the ground with such a thud that Standing felt it through his feet.

The employees were still screaming in their tents. Standing kept both arms moving, covering as big an area as he could as he turned and began walking to the Portakabins. He hadn't seen where Frenchy had gone but he was fairly sure he had slipped into the middle Portakabin to join Sergei.

A large greenhouse came into view off to his right, bigger even than the one he'd seen on Dominic's farm. Through the plastic sheeting he could make out dozens of blurred figures, looking in his direction. He registered movement in his peripheral vision and when he turned his head he saw a big man in a black tracksuit heading out of the greenhouse. He was cradling a shotgun across his chest. He was about 200 feet away from Standing, so the weapon was useless at that range unless it was loaded with deer slug. But 200 feet was also too far for the P226, especially when used with one hand. On a range and using both hands, and if he regulated his breathing, Standing was capable of hitting a man-sized target at 500 feet. But on the run and one-handed, anything further away than a hundred feet involved a degree of luck.

The man stopped, put the shotgun to his shoulder and pulled the trigger. There was a loud bang but none of the shot reached Standing. He smiled to himself. At least he wasn't facing deer slugs.

Standing caught movement from his peripheral vision again, this time on his left side. It was Frenchy, coming out of the Portakabin. He was holding what looked like a Heckler & Koch 416. Was it Brett's gun? Frenchy stopped and aimed at Standing. Standing ducked and ran to the right just as Frenchy pulled the trigger. The first shot went wide but the second tugged at Standing's coat. Standing's run was taking him closer to the man with the shotgun. Standing fired at him with both guns but he missed. He fired again and the man with the shotgun ducked.

Two more shots whizzed by Standing's head. It was Frenchy. Standing whirled around and fired four shots – left, right, left, right. None of them hit the target but they were close enough to make Frenchy duck back into the Portakabin.

Standing heard another loud bang. The shotgun guy was up on one knee, the gun at his shoulder. As Standing watched, the man chambered another shell. Standing shoved one of the P226s into his belt, then dropped into a shooting stance, slightly side on, feet shoulder width apart. He brought up the gun and sighted on the man's face. The man fired the shotgun again and a few pellets peppered Standing's legs but did no damage. Standing took a breath, let half of it out, then gently eased back the trigger. It was a perfect shot and he knew immediately he was on target. Sure enough, the man's head exploded and he fell backwards.

Standing pulled out the second P226 and ran to the Portakabins. He reached the end one and moved along with his back to it until he got to the door. It was closed so he took a step back to kick it in. Just as he lifted his leg he sensed movement to his left and turned just as he heard the crack of an automatic weapon. The round whizzed by Standing's face and he fired with both guns. Frenchy had already ducked back inside. Standing turned to face the door again but before he could lash out with his foot, it opened. The man holding the door open had a shaved head and a tattoo of a cobweb across his neck. His mouth opened wide in surprise, but before he could say anything Standing kicked the door and the man staggered back into the Portakabin. Standing shot him twice in the face and he went down in a shower of blood and brains.

There was a man lying on a bed to Standing's left. He was trying to get up into a sitting position so that he could reach for the AR-15 at the foot of the bed. The man had an injured leg which hampered his movement so Standing had all the time in the world to put two rounds into his chest, one from each gun.

The screaming had stopped now and there was an eerie silence. Standing peered around the door then slowly stepped out, keeping both guns aimed at the door to Sergei's Portakabin. A shot rang out, far too loud to be the Heckler. It sounded like a Desert Eagle, Sergei's favourite handgun. No bullet emerged through the door so Standing figured that Sergei hadn't been able to handle the recoil and the round had buried itself in the roof. Either that or he had panicked and pulled the trigger by mistake.

Standing moved sideways, breathing slowly and evenly. There were at least two men inside – Sergei and Frenchy – and possibly more. It was a scenario that Standing had rehearsed hundreds of times in the Killing House in Hereford and he felt no fear, not even apprehension. In a perfect world he would have been able to throw in a thunder-flash or two or even a fragmentation grenade, but the world was far from perfect.

There was a window to the left of the door, two sliding panes in a frame. But to get to it he'd have to cross the open door. He'd have to do everything in one smooth motion and any delay would leave him exposed. He took a deep breath, exhaled, and started moving. He shuffled sideways, firing with both guns through the open doorway, until he reached the window. The bottom of the window was chest height so he had to raise his arms to shoot through it. Sergei was crouched in his chair behind a large wooden desk and resting his gun on it. His eyes widened when he saw Standing at the window and he began to move but the Desert Eagle was big and heavy and Standing was already squeezing his triggers. The round from the gun in his left hand shattered the glass and the second round hit Sergei in the neck. Sergei didn't drop the gun straight away, so Standing kept firing and put a bullet in his shoulder and another in his face. Sergei slid off his chair and on to the floor.

Before Sergei had hit the ground, Frenchy burst through the open door, the Heckler at his shoulder. But Standing had expected the manoeuvre and had taken two quick steps back, dropping down into a crouch. Standing fired first with both guns and hit Frenchy in the chest, left and right. Frenchy pulled the trigger but he was already staggering back and the rounds went up in the air. He fell back into the Portakabin and the Heckler clattered on to the floor. Standing followed him inside.

Frenchy dropped down on to a plastic sofa. His shirt was soaked in blood. He stared up at Standing, a look of confusion on his face. His chest was heaving as he breathed. The shots had gone through his lungs, puncturing them both, but missing his heart. It was a fatal wound, but it would be a minute or two before he died. Frenchy grabbed a cushion and pressed it against his wounds as he gasped for breath.

Standing looked over at Sergei. He was lying on the floor, his face a bloody pulp. Blood was pooling around his body. Behind Sergei's desk was a large safe, almost five feet tall. The door was ajar.

'You can't trust Charlotte Button,' gasped Frenchy.

'What do you mean?' asked Standing, turning to look at him.

'She sent you, right?'

Standing nodded. 'Yeah.'

'Did she say why?' He was taking short, quick breaths. His lungs were filling up with blood and his oxygen levels were dropping fast.

'She said you'd gone rogue. You'd killed a Russian mafia leader in New York, a Colombian drugs lord and a prospective congressman in Colorado.'

'Yeah, well I bet she didn't tell you that she gave me those contracts.' He gasped for air. 'Through The Pool.'

'What?'

Frenchy coughed and a bloody froth appeared between his lips. 'They were Pool contracts. I did twelve jobs for her. That wannabe congressman was the last one.' He coughed again. He took several shallow breaths before continuing. 'I found out afterwards that he was one of the good guys. Wife, kids, no criminal connections, no terrorist background, nothing. But he was involved in an investigation into the whole Jeffrey Epstein case. He was trying to get a list of names of Epstein associates who had been into the paedophile scene. Some very big names on that list. I realised that one of those big names had paid The Pool.' He ran out of breath and began panting.

'That's not possible.'

Frenchy smiled. 'I'd say that I was living proof, but, you know . . .' He coughed and blood trickled down his chin. 'I confronted Button on it and she denied it but I didn't believe her so I quit. A few weeks later I was in LA and two guys tried to kill me. It looked like a mugging but they were pros. I managed to get away but that's when I knew she wanted me dead.' He coughed and began to breathe in short, sharp, gulps. 'Looks . . . like . . . she . . . got . . . what . . . she . . .' He couldn't manage the last word. His eyes faded and the breath rattled in his throat, then his chin rested against his chest and he went still.

Standing stood looking down at the dead man, his mind racing. There was no reason for Frenchy to have lied. And it explained how he had known about Charlotte Button. And why Button had wanted Standing to track Frenchy down and kill him. The fact that Frenchy knew he was on Button's shit list explained why he had gone to ground on a cannabis farm in Humboldt County.

Standing was going to have to handle Charlotte Button with kid gloves, because if she turned against him he doubted that she would carry out her threat to expose him – it was far more likely that she would send a killer from The Pool to take care of business, as she had done with Frenchy.

He placed the two P226s on the sofa and used his phone to take two photographs of the dead man, figuring that Button wouldn't take his word that he'd killed the former SEAL. Then he used his shirt to clean his prints off one of the P226s and put it in Frenchy's hand. He wiped the second gun clean and put that in Sergei's hand. He cleaned the Desert Eagle and put it in one of the desk drawers.

He went over to the safe, pulled the door open and looked inside. There were stacks of US dollar bills and boxes of expensive watches, mainly Rolex, TAG Heuer and Patek Philippe. At the bottom of the safe was a black holdall. He pulled it out and unzipped it. Inside were bundles of dollar bills held together with thick elastic bands. They were all hundred-dollar bills and there looked to be a hundred notes in each bundle. He did a quick count – there were forty-five bundles so that made $450,000.

He zipped up the holdall and went outside. The workers

had come out of the tents and were looking around, stunned by the carnage. He spotted Amy and Angela and they came running over. He dropped the holdall and hugged them as they began to cry.

Then he saw Brianna and Olivia. Their eyes were red from crying and they came over and joined the hug. 'I'm going to take you to Dominic's farm,' he said.

'Who's Dominic?' asked Amy.

'He's a friend of Brett's.'

'Where is Brett?' asked Angela.

'I'm sorry, Brett's dead,' said Standing. All four girls began to cry.

Two male workers came over. They were in their early twenties, tall and gangly with their wrists and ankles barely covered by their overalls. 'Are you DEA?' asked one of the men. He rubbed his nose with the back of his hand. 'FBI?'

'Just a concerned citizen,' said Standing, bending down to pick up the holdall. 'I came to take these girls back. How many of you here are being kept against your will?'

'All of us,' said the man. 'None of us have been paid.'

'Anyone who complains just disappears,' said the other man. 'We think they're buried in the woods.'

More workers were gathering around them. They came from the tents and the greenhouse. Most of them were under thirty and didn't look as if they'd been eating well.

'How many of you are there?' Standing asked.

'Forty-five, maybe fifty,' said one of the female workers. She was in her twenties with dark curly hair cascading around her shoulders and a sweatshirt with a cartoon of a joint-smoking skeleton holding a scythe under the slogan 'DON'T FEAR THE REEFER'.

'Okay, this place is pretty much shut as of now,' said Standing. 'What do you guys want to do? Move to another farm, or go home?'

'We haven't been paid,' she said. 'I was banking on the money to pay for college.'

'Well the good news is that there's plenty of money in Sergei's office. Anyone here have any book-keeping or accountancy experience?'

A red-headed girl and a chubby guy with piercings in his nose, lips and ears raised their hands.

'Okay, there's cash in Sergei's safe, more than enough to go around,' Standing said, pointing at the middle Portakabin. 'Some very nice watches, too. It's a bit of a mess in there but I suggest you take the money and split it among everyone. Once you've done that, you should use the vehicles here to get as far away as you can. Either go home or go to Eureka and look for work there. I'll be taking the Jeep Wrangler, you guys can have the rest.'

'What about the cops?' asked the guy with the piercings.

'If anyone feels the urge to call the cops, go ahead,' said Standing. 'I doubt it'll achieve anything but no one will stand in your way.'

'Sergei's dead, right?' said the girl with the skeleton sweatshirt.

'They're all dead,' said Standing.

'So no one is going to come after us?'

'I don't know if Sergei has a boss,' said Standing. 'I'd recommend you all leave as quickly as possible.'

'What about the cannabis?' asked the guy with piercings. 'Do you think we can take it with us?'

'I think you can take whatever you want,' said Standing.

'I don't see that Sergei's in any position to complain. But there is one of his guys in Phillipsville who will probably be coming back here at some point, so I'd get a move on if I were you.'

The group started moving towards Sergei's Portakabin, talking and arguing among themselves.

'Right, you girls grab your things and put them in the Jeep,' said Standing.

'They wouldn't let us bring anything with us,' said Brianna. 'Our stuff is still at Brett's place.'

'You can collect it later,' said Standing. 'Let's get you to Dominic's farm first. He's not too far away.'

CHAPTER 32

Dominic came out of the house when he heard the Jeep, cradling his assault rifle, but he lowered the weapon when he saw Standing at the wheel. The girls piled out of the Jeep as Standing hurried over to Dominic. Tanya came out on to the porch. 'What's happening?' she asked.

'These girls were on the Russian farm,' said Standing. 'They need help. They were working on Brett's farm but the Russians took them.'

'Are they coming?' asked Dominic. 'The Russians?'

Standing shook his head. 'They won't be bothering you any more.' He smiled thinly. 'They won't be bothering anyone.'

Tanya called for the girls to go inside and they filed up on to the porch and into the house. Standing waved for Dominic to join him and they walked over to the SUV. 'Brett's dead,' said Standing. 'They killed him yesterday.'

'Oh sweet Jesus,' said Dominic.

'They're done now. Their boss, Sergei, is dead, and so are most of his men. If there are any of them still around, they'll clear out, they're only hired hands and now there's no one to pay their wages.'

He opened the rear door of the SUV and showed him the holdall of money. 'Take this. They owe it to you for all the trouble they caused. You can pay the girls what they're owed and keep the rest.' He handed the bag to Dominic and closed the door. 'I guess at some point the cops will find out what happened, but it won't be right away. If I were you I'd pay the girls off and send them home. If the cops do get involved, they'll check the ballistics and hopefully assume that the Russians were fighting among themselves. There's no reason for them to come looking at you.'

'What happened to Brett?'

'They turned up yesterday while I was away. He managed to get three of them and injured another but there were just too many. I buried him among his plants, I figured he'd want it that way.'

Dominic forced a smile. 'Yeah, that's what he would've wanted, for sure.'

'The girls' things are at Brett's farm. Can you take them to pick up their stuff at some point?'

'Sure. Of course. The girls can stay here if they want. There's plenty of work to be done.' He let his rifle hang from its sling and he unzipped the holdall. His eyes widened when he saw how much money there was. 'Are you kidding me? I can't take all this.'

'They threatened you and they threatened your family. Think of it as a fine.' Standing held out his hand. 'I'll be off. Say goodbye to your family for me. I hope it all works out for you.'

The two men shook hands. 'I'm sure it will,' said Dominic. 'I owe you. We owe you.'

'No,' said Standing. 'We're good. No one owes anybody anything.'

CHAPTER 33

Charlotte Button brought her white Mercedes to a stop in front of the garage and pressed the fob to open the door remotely. The red light on the fob blinked but the door stubbornly refused to move. She pointed it at the door and pressed the button again. Nothing. 'Seriously?' she muttered to herself. She sighed, grabbed her black Prada briefcase off the passenger seat and climbed out. She slammed the door and walked towards her house, reaching for her keys from her pocket. She stopped when the figure stepped out from behind the trunk of the oak tree at the edge of her front lawn. She recognised the man immediately. 'Hello, Matt, this is a nice surprise,' she said, and smiled brightly. He was dressed all in black and his hands were in the pockets of his pea coat. The collar was turned up.

'I'm sure it is,' he said. 'A surprise, anyway. Maybe not a nice one.'

She couldn't tell if he had anything in his hands. 'I do hope you haven't damaged my garage door,' she said. 'It costs an arm and a leg just to service it.'

'I really needed a chat with you, Charlotte, and I figured you probably wouldn't open the front door to me.'

'Oh that's ridiculous,' she said breezily. 'Come inside and I'll make you a cup of tea. Or something stronger. I've a really nice Pinot Grigio in the fridge.'

'I'm fine out here,' he said.

'There really is no reason for a face-to-face, Matt,' she said. She was still holding her briefcase. It was lined with bulletproof Kevlar and the man who had sold it to her had promised that there wasn't a handgun in the world that could penetrate it. 'I received the photographs you sent. Job well done.'

'I felt I needed to talk to you,' he said, his voice a low whisper. 'About the job.'

'Then let's go inside.' She heard her voice tremble and her cheeks reddened. She didn't want him to know how scared she was.

'No need,' he said. 'This won't take long, Charlotte. You neglected to tell me that Frenchy worked for The Pool.'

She shrugged. 'I gave you all the information you needed to get the job done.'

'You gave me the impression that he'd gone rogue. But that wasn't the case.'

Button frowned. 'It was very much the case,' said Button. 'He was let go from the SEALs and he was less than efficient when he worked for The Pool.'

'So you had him killed?'

Her heart was racing now. 'Why would you say that?'

'Because you sent me to kill him, Charlotte. Did you forget that?'

'You think the hit was my idea? Matt, you have absolutely no idea how my business operates.'

'I think I do. You threaten and blackmail people to carry out assassinations for you. I'm living proof of that. And Frenchy – well, he's non-living proof, isn't he?'

'I don't initiate contracts, that's not how it works.'

'How does it work, Charlotte?'

'I am instructed by various government departments, here and in other countries. The Pool exists to carry out the wishes of said governments when it's important that they have plausible deniability.'

'So the US government wanted the wannabe US congressman dead?'

'Yes they did.'

'Why?'

'That information is way above my pay grade.'

'And they also wanted Frenchy dead?'

'Yes.'

'Whose idea was it?'

'Do you mean who initiated the contract? I can't tell you that.'

'Can't or won't?'

'Both. But I can tell you that when it comes to the US, we tend to work for the White House, the DEA, the Office of the Director of National Intelligence, the National Security Agency, the Defense Intelligence Agency, the CIA . . .'

'I thought the CIA had its own people for wet work.'

'Not within the United States. The CIA is only authorised to carry out operations overseas.'

'So the CIA wanted Frenchy dead?'

'That's not what I'm saying. But I can tell you that he was talking to the wrong people and telling them too much. That much I do know.'

'He saw it differently.'

'Matt, Ryan French was a very disturbed individual. Not everyone handles the effects of combat as well as you. PTSD was only one of his problems.' She was holding the handle of the briefcase in both hands. If he pulled out a gun she could maybe block the first shot but that was probably as far as she could go.

Standing's right hand appeared. It was empty. He smiled when he saw Button tense. 'What do you think I'm going to do, Charlie?' he asked as he raised his hand and slipped it inside his pea coat.

'I guess that depends on what that hand brings out.'

'Are you scared?'

Her lower lip was trembling. 'Of course I am, damn you.'

His smile widened. He took out his hand and showed her the digital recorder he was holding. It was running, recording their conversation. 'Don't worry, Charlotte, I'm not here to kill you. Not that I don't think you deserve it. But I need to be sure that you won't do to me what you did to Frenchy.'

'Insurance,' she said.

'Exactly.'

'I can tell you from experience that you'll need to take very good care of any insurance you have.'

'I will, don't worry.'

'But there's no need for you to be scared that I'd do you any harm.'

'I'm not scared, Charlotte.' He put the recorder back into his inside pocket. 'I don't want to hear from you, ever again.'

'You won't. I promise.'

He looked at her for several seconds, then he nodded. 'Then we're good,' he said.

'I'm very pleased to hear that.'

'I'll let you go inside and enjoy your Pinot Grigio.' He turned and headed down the driveway to the road. He turned right and walked away without a backward look.

Her phone rang and she answered it. 'Yes, it's fine, thank

you,' she said. She looked across the road at the house opposite hers. She couldn't see the sniper, but she knew that he
was up on the roof. At the first sign of any attack, his instructions had been to put a bullet in Matt Standing's head. 'Yes,
you can stand down now, thank you. You have a good evening.'

She unlocked her front door and went in, heading for the
kitchen. She definitely needed that Pinot Grigio.

THRILLINGLY GOOD BOOKS FROM CRIMINALLY GOOD WRITERS

CRIME FILES BRINGS YOU THE LATEST RELEASES FROM TOP CRIME AND THRILLER AUTHORS.

SIGN UP ONLINE FOR OUR MONTHLY NEWSLETTER AND BE THE FIRST TO KNOW ABOUT OUR COMPETITIONS, NEW BOOKS AND MORE.